HAVEN'S
Knight

REGAN URE

Cover Design: © L.J. Anderson, Mayhem Cover Creations

Formatting by Mayhem Cover Creations

ISBN: 978-0-9932864-8-3

I dedicate this book to my father. You were taken before I was ready but you live on in my heart and memories.

TABLE OF CONTENTS

CHAPTER ONE

Haven

I touched my red, stinging cheek and stared up at Grant, my stepfather. At over six feet tall, he towered over my small frame. My face hurt so badly, but I knew there wouldn't be a bruise. He had learned early on that there was less chance of bruising if he hit me with an open hand.

He raised his hand again, so I prepared myself for another hit. However, this time he fisted his hand and punched me in the stomach. Winded, I dropped to the kitchen floor as pain exploded where his fist connected. I squeezed my eyes closed as a wave of pain gripped me. On any area of my body that was covered by clothing, he would hit hard enough to leave bruises.

I didn't try to defend myself against the kick that came next. It was pointless, because if I tried to stop him, he would hit me harder. Pain erupted in my stomach again when his foot connected with me. Satisfied with the punishment he had given me, he glared at me before taking a swig of his beer. He spun around on his heels and walked out of the kitchen.

Instantly, relief flooded through me. It was over, for the moment. I whimpered from the intense pain, but I didn't cry.

No matter how bad the beating was, I never cried. Even when he had broken my arm when I was twelve, I hadn't shed a tear. I never cried. It was my way to keep that part of me hidden. I hid it so deep inside so that no matter what happened to my body on the outside, I was still okay on the inside. If I was okay on the inside, I could carry on.

When they'd taken me to the hospital with a broken arm the doctors had asked Grant questions, and he'd realized there would be less scrutiny if I didn't make regular trips to the hospital. Since then, he never hit me hard enough to leave me with an injury that would entail such a trip.

I lay on the dirty tiles of the kitchen floor, trying to breathe through the pain. I waited until I could sit up without the pain flaring up. I didn't know what I'd done to set him off this time. Most of the time, just breathing was enough to offend him.

Some days, I felt like his personal walking-and-talking punching bag. I was an object he could hit without any repercussions to ease his anger and frustration. I was never good enough or quiet enough to suit him.

Up until the age of ten, I remembered being a happy and carefree child. My mom and dad had loved me, and I'd felt safe. That had all changed drastically the day my dad died. He had died suddenly from an aneurysm, and that was the moment that changed my life forever.

My mother had disintegrated under the weight of her grief. Alcohol became her coping mechanism, and a way for her to numb the pain. From that moment on, I was just a reminder of what she had lost, and who she'd have to live without. All the love she had for me had evaporated, and all that remained was indifference. In a way, I had lost both my parents that day.

It shouldn't have been that way. A mother was supposed to love her child unconditionally, but mine hadn't. I could have coped with her indifference, but then she'd met Grant only months after my father's death. At first, I had hoped that he would help heal my broken family, but that hope had disappeared the first time he'd hit me. Over time, the hits had gradually gotten worse with every incident, and now I expected it.

Finally, I took a deep breath and slowly tried to stand up. I wanted to stay where I was on the floor until the pain eased —I couldn't risk the chance that Grant would come back. My legs wobbled, but held when I stood upright. I kept my arms firmly wrapped around my aching stomach while I walked slowly out of the kitchen.

Hesitantly, I did a quick scan of the tiny living room for Grant. The only thing there was the cigarette-burned, alcohol-stained two-seater couch that faced a bare wall. The room was empty of all other furnishings, because we couldn't even afford a TV. I bit down on my lip as the pain in my stomach shot through my body. Even the walls were an off-white color that looked dirty.

By the time I made it to my small bedroom I was in agony. I closed my bedroom door and leaned against it, sighing with relief. Grant rarely invaded the sanctuary of my bedroom to punish me. It terrified me that one day he might move on to other ways to punish me. Physically hurting me was one thing, but if he tried to do something worse, it would break me.

I'd survived seven years of this, and I just had one year left in high school. After I graduated, I would have my high-school diploma, and then I could escape. I held onto the hope that soon I would be free.

I shuffled to my bed, which was just a single mattress on the floor that was pushed up against the wall. The sheet that covered the mattress was a dull-gray color, though it had once been white. I lay down on the lumpy mattress, a groan escaping my lips from the pain. I reached down and pulled the medium-sized blanket, which had been folded at the foot of my bed, over me. I didn't have much, but I made do.

The light-blue walls of my room did nothing to lighten the heaviness inside of me. I watched as my old, tattered curtains moved with the slight whisper of wind through my window.

There was no way I could tell anyone what was happening to me. Grant told me many times that he would kill me if I ever told anyone what was going on. There was no doubt in my mind that he meant what he'd said, so I kept my mouth shut.

We had just moved to a new town a couple of weeks ago. Some of the teachers at the previous school I had attended had become suspicious about what was happening to me at home. It would only have been a matter of time before their suspicions were confirmed. Then social services would have been called in.

Tomorrow, I was starting my senior year at a new school. It was not like anyone from my old school was going to miss me anyway. I never made any friends because I kept to myself. It was just easier that way. I didn't have to hide anything if I didn't make friends.

It was dark, and I wasn't sure what time it was, but I was tired. I had spent most of the weekend trying to clean the tiny two-bedroom flat. My mom had no ambition, and her sole purpose in life was the ease her pain with bottles of cheap alcohol, so she didn't work. She spent most of her time at home, drunk. Grant was the only provider, and he didn't make much working as a mechanic. When he wasn't working, he was with my mom, drinking. The only place we were able to afford had been in the seedy part of town. The apartment was small, but at least it was a roof over our heads.

Despite the pain throbbing in my stomach, I pulled the

blanket up to my chin. I closed my eyes and quickly drifted off to sleep. I didn't have an alarm clock or a phone to set an alarm on, but somehow my body had an internal alarm, so I was wide awake by six the next morning.

The pain in my stomach was still aching when I woke. My tummy rumbled. I decided to grab something to eat on my way out.

I didn't waste any time getting ready for school. Quickly, I pulled a brush through my shoulder-length dark hair. My eyes were the same shade of brown. My wardrobe was limited, but I found a clean pair of faded blue jeans and a shirt. I pushed my feet into my shoes. Everything I wore was secondhand and looked well-worn, but I tried not to let it bug me.

With my high-school bag clutched tightly in my hand, I opened my bedroom door. Quietly, I tiptoed past Grant and my mom's bedroom door. I didn't want to run the risk of waking him, because he'd punish me. On the rare occasion I actually did something wrong, he would hit me harder.

I made a quick stop in the bathroom to brush my teeth. Then I went to the kitchen. There was not much food in the cupboards, so I grabbed two slices of bread. I stuffed the bread into my school bag while I darted toward the front door.

I kept my eyes focused on the path ahead of me while I walked toward the bus stop. I ate the sliced bread as I walked. I was skinny. It was not a vanity thing for me; it was the fact that I never ate properly and often skipped meals to avoid Grant. The less he saw of me, the fewer opportunities he had to hit me.

Consequently, the years of abuse had stripped away any confidence I had. I always kept my face down and rarely looked anyone in the eyes. I used my hair as a curtain to shield me from prying eyes. It was my only protection to help hide me from the world. There were times when I wished I were invisible. It would make things so much easier for me. The less interaction I had with other people the better, and it had worked for many years—I hadn't formed any friendships. I had the body language down to a fine art; it said, "Leave me alone."

I didn't have to wait long for the school bus. As it neared the stop I hitched my school bag back up on my shoulder. I climbed into the bus and kept my eyes fixed downward. The first open seat I came to was a window seat, so I sat and gazed out, looking at the scenery, but not really seeing it. I was too lost in my own thoughts. The nervous knots in my stomach worsened the closer I got to my new school. The bus pulled to a stop outside a modern-looking school building with a brick exterior. I filtered out of the bus with the rest of the students, all the time keeping my eyes down, not making any contact with anyone.

I walked through the entrance of the school. I held the strap of my school bag nervously as I searched for the reception area to get my schedule and paperwork. I prayed that I would be able to find it on my own without having to stop and ask someone to point me in the right direction. Thankfully, I found it and walked through the door into a spacious office. Once in the reception area I waited patiently for someone to help me. An older lady with wire-rimmed glasses peered at me over her lenses.

"How can I help you?" she asked kindly.

"I'm new," I said, nervously tucking a stray strand of hair behind my ear. Luckily I was early, so the reception wasn't busy.

"What's your name?" she asked when she glanced down at some paperwork in front of her.

"Haven Williams," I said while I anxiously clasped my hands together on the counter between us. She gave me a smile, probably to try to help me feel less nervous. It didn't work.

"You have a beautiful name," she said before she looked down and selected a few pieces of paper and handed them to me.

"Thank you," I replied.

"Here's your schedule," she said while handing me another piece of paper. "Your locker number is written in the right-hand corner," she informed me as she pointed at the numbers with a pen. Then, with another friendly smile, she said, "I hope you have a good first day."

"Thank you," I mumbled before I exited the reception area with the necessary papers in hand. I didn't return her smile. Frankly, there was nothing in my life to smile about. The only thing I was thankful for was the fact that I was still alive. There had been a few times when Grant had lost control, and I'd been terrified that he'd kill me. Every day that I survived was a day that got me just a little closer to freedom.

The hallway began to fill up with rowdy students as I tried to figure out where my locker was. The problem was that the gray rows of lockers on each side of all of the hallways made them all look exactly the same. Finally, after about fifteen minutes I was convinced that I had gone around in a complete circle. I was now at the school's entrance once again. I let out a frustrated sigh and turned directly into something hard and solid. I lost my balance, but hands shot out and steadied me. I suppressed a groan at the dull pain that came when the hands gripped old bruises on my arms that were covered by my sleeves.

"Careful," an annoyed voice said to me. My eyes widened when I took in the sight of the owner of the voice. He was tall. He had the most hypnotic eyes that I had ever seen. His midnight-black hair was long enough to cover his dark, sapphire-blue eyes. My mouth dropped slightly open in shock. The pale-blue shirt he was wearing was molded to his athletic body, and he was wearing a pair of faded jeans that hung low on his hips. I'd seen good-looking guys before, but I kept well clear of all boys. Yet, one look into these deep blue eyes and I was losing myself. I felt a flutter in my stomach and my throat started to close up. My heartbeat sped up.

"Watch where you're going," he spat gruffly and let me go, abruptly causing me to stumble a few steps back. The gruffness in his voice and the abruptness of his actions stung me. Was I so disgusting that he had to act like that? I stepped back and clutched my school bag defensively in front of me. I was using it like a barrier against what I was feeling at the very sight of him.

I had to pull myself together. My gaze fell to the floor and I closed my mouth. I dug my fingers into the strap of my bag even tighter.

"I'm sorry," I whispered when I walked away from him. I hurried down the hallway. I felt the red tinge of embarrassment on my cheeks and I dashed into the nearest bathroom. Thankfully, it was empty. I splashed some water on my face and tried to pull myself together. I had no idea what time it was, but I didn't want to be late for my first class.

I walked out of the bathroom and decided to walk to the left in search of my locker. Finally, after another five minutes, I found my locker and I put some of my books in it. I still had to find the classroom for my first class before the bell rang. After studying the map for a minute, I realized that I needed to head in the opposite direction that I'd previously gone. Luckily, this time I managed to find the classroom, and I made it to the room just as the bell rang.

The class was nearly full, so there were only a couple of seats empty. I walked directly to the nearest empty seat and sat down. I dropped my bag next my chair and waited for the lesson to begin. The hum of conversation surrounded me, but I didn't look up until the teacher started the lesson.

My first class seemed to end almost as quickly as it had begun. When the bell rang I quickly put my books back into my bag and walked out of the room, making sure not to make eye contact with anyone. I found the next classroom easier than the first one, and I walked in and found an empty seat, sitting my bag down to get my books out. I kept my face hidden behind the curtain of my hair. Ignoring the students talking and walking past me, I just kept my gaze on the writing pad in front of me.

Suddenly, I felt someone brush past the back of my chair and I heard the distinctive scrape of a chair being pulled out from the desk next to me. I heard a schoolbag drop to the floor next to the desk and I heard someone sit down beside me. I glanced at my neighbor out of the corner of my eye. Instantly, I felt the flutter in my stomach again, and my heart instantly began to speed up. Sitting beside me, watching me, was the guy I'd walked into earlier.

CHAPTER TWO

Haven

I quickly averted my gaze, and for the entire lesson I refused to allow my eyes to drift in his direction. It was hard to concentrate on what the teacher was droning on about when I could feel him staring at me.

You can do this! I told myself.

I didn't have time for pointless crushes. I had enough on my plate. I was in survival mode, and that didn't include complicated things like boys. There was no way I could form any kind of relationship with anyone, because if I did they would notice things like my skittish behavior and the bruises. I couldn't risk that, not now—I was so close to being free.

After what felt like an eternity, the bell finally rang, signaling the end of the class. I gathered my stuff and shoved it into my schoolbag before I made a quick exit. I hoped that he was not in any of my other classes. The less I saw of him the better.

The rest of the morning went by quickly. I kept my gaze down and never made eye contact with anyone. I even managed to keep the friendliest and wanting-to-make-a-friend type students at bay with my clear body language that told them to stay away.

At lunchtime, I stayed clear of the cafeteria. I decided to go outside and sit by the athletic field. It was fairly quiet, and there were only a few students sitting on the grass eating their lunch. I found a spot far from the others and lay down on the grass and looked up into the sky. It was quiet outside except for the low murmur of voices around me.

I gazed up and started to watch the clouds pass me by. I loved to watch the clouds, and decide what shapes they made. It gave me the escape I desperately needed, even if it was just for a few minutes. The first cloud I spotted reminded me of a castle from the fairy tales my father used to tell me when I was a little girl. He would tell me about the knight in shining armor who would save the beautiful princess from evil, and then they would live happily ever after. When I was a little girl I'd believed in those fairy tales, but now I knew better. There were no happy endings, there was only survival.

I was looking at an unusually puffy cloud, trying to decide if it had a face or not, when I blinked. When I looked up I saw the face of a boy. He had straight, dark-blond hair that reached past his ears, and expressive green eyes.

"Hi," he greeted with an infectious smile. "I've been looking all over for you."

Startled, I sat up and backed away. I stood up and reached for my schoolbag. I was about to turn and walk away when he grabbed my wrist to stop me. He was tall, like Grant, but he was smaller in build. I immediately cowered away from him. He let go of my wrist immediately and raised his hands in surrender and said, "I'm not going to hurt you."

I stood rooted to the spot with my big eyes fixed on the stranger in front of me. He looked at me with a confused expression at my reaction.

"I know you're new and you just really look like you need a friend," he said in a gentle tone. His expression softened and he gave me a tentative smile. I continued to stare at him silently. I didn't return his smile while I clutched my schoolbag strap tighter, contemplating whether I should just make a run for it.

He sat down on the grass next to me. "You don't have to talk. I can talk enough for the both of us," he said as he looked at me expectantly. I'd had lots of people try to befriend me over the years, but no one had ever been this direct. His bright and friendly eyes watched me as I wrestled with the decision to sit with him, or turn my back and walk away.

"I'm going to get a pain in my neck if you stand while I talk," he said while he rubbed the back of his neck to emphasize his point. Normally, I would have bolted by now, but this boy made me do something that stunned even me. I let my bag drop to the ground, and I sat down.

"My name is Chris," he introduced himself. I gave him a brief nod.

"I know your name is Haven," he revealed. He settled his packet of lunch between us.

I didn't respond to him. I wasn't ready to interact with him, but just sitting in his company felt like warm sunshine in the middle of a cold rainstorm. He offered me half of his sandwich. My stomach grumbled at the sight, reminding me that I was hungry. I'd only had two slices of bread today, and there was no guarantee that I would get supper tonight, so I accepted his offer and began to nibble at it.

"Are you really going to make me hold this entire conversation?" he said, as he tilted his head to the side to study me.

He received no response from me while I held his gaze.

"All right," he conceded. "My mom didn't name me Chatterbox Chris for nothing."

I couldn't help but smile. In the space of five minutes of

meeting him, he'd made me smile. I couldn't remember the last time I'd smiled before this. It had always been easier to just be a loner. However, Chris' attitude was so infectious that I couldn't seem to help myself. For the time being, he happily chatted away about nothing and everything. It made me smile.

Soon, I finished the food he had given to me. The grumbling from my stomach finally stopped. He gave me a rundown of who was who in my new school while we watched people walk past. It didn't matter to me. I didn't care who they were. I wasn't interested in getting to know anyone. I wasn't even sure I was going to continue whatever this was that I was doing with Chris. Surviving to graduation was my only goal.

"Ah, here comes the pretty boy," Chris said.

I turned in the direction he was looking and looked straight into the blue eyes belonging to the boy I'd bumped into early that morning. The very boy I was trying to avoid. My stomach did a flip while his gaze held mine. He was surrounded by a couple of girls.

Suddenly, Chris' voice was in my ear again, "How do you know Damien Knight?"

It pulled me out of the connection with the pretty boy, and I quickly dropped my gaze back to the ground. I turned to look at Chris and gave him a shrug. I didn't know Damien Knight, so there was nothing to talk about. If I had my way, I would not be getting to know him either.

Immediately, Chris' eyes moved to something over my shoulder.

"He's still staring," he revealed when his eyes moved back to mine.

"As pretty as he is, he really isn't someone you want to get involved with," he warned me. The infectious smile was gone and there was a serious tone to his voice. "There are players, and then there's Damien Knight. He has a flavor of the week. He doesn't do dates or anything like that. I don't think he even knows how to spell commitment. For him it's just a fuck for the week and nothing else. Sometimes they don't even last a week. He holds the record for closing the deal the quickest: the rumor is that it took him less than five minutes!"

I just shrugged my shoulders. He didn't need to warn me, because it was never going to happen. I had enough to deal with, and I didn't have time for trivial stuff.

"There's a fragileness about you. Stay away from him, otherwise he'll break you," he warned. He didn't know that Damien couldn't break me, because I was already broken.

Fortunately, I had nothing to say about Damien Knight. I just shrugged my shoulders again. Thankfully, Chris took the hint and dropped the subject.

He spent the rest of lunch babbling on about nothing. I had never met anyone that could talk so much about nothing significant. Most people would have found it annoying, but I enjoyed it. He held the entire conversation and I never felt obligated to give any input at all.

The main reason I never spoke was because I was shy, and I didn't want to build any type of friendship with him. I decided that I would let him talk, and I would enjoy the conversation, even if it was one-sided, but when lunch ended I wouldn't let this to happen again.

The bell rang. We both got to our feet and began dusting the grass off of our clothes. I pulled my schedule out of my bag to see which class I had next. While looking at the paper, Chris broke into my thoughts. "Where is your next class?" he asked, peering over my shoulder while I was trying to find it on the map. I pointed to a box on the map that read 'room 19A.'

"Come on, I'll walk you to class," Chris said and

wrapped an arm around my shoulders. I stiffened when I felt the dull pain radiate through my back. His touch had pressed into the bruises on my upper back.

"Sorry," he muttered and let his arm drop away from me. "You don't like to be touched, do you?"

He waited for me to answer his question, but I ignored him and started to walk back into the school building. He caught up with me and showed me to my next class. I walked into the class and I didn't look back to see if he'd left or not. I never had friends because I was good at keeping people at bay. I could tell from the little time I had spent with Chris that he was not going to give up that easily; but I had more to lose, and there was no way I was going to let him in.

I sat down in the seat nearest to the windows and gazed out at the scenery below. The sun shone brightly down on the trees surrounding the class. The teacher appeared in the front of the class to begin the lesson. For the rest of the day I kept to myself and tried to blend into the background. It worked well, because no one tried to talk to me or look at me. I didn't see Chris or Damien again either. I walked out of the school and to the bus stop. I stood, gazing at the ground until the bus appeared, which did not take long.

The nervous knots in my stomach grew larger the closer I got to home. I wondered if Grant had gone to work today, because if he hadn't, he'd be home when I got there. That never ended well for me.

I held my breath as I quietly opened the front door. Peeking inside, I could see that the living room was empty. I slipped through the door and turned and closed it. There was a faint click as the door closed.

The house was quiet. I walked quickly to my room. Once I got to the safety of my room, I closed my door. I walked over to my bed and dropped my school bag next to it. I needed to have a quick shower. I always made sure I showered when I got home because if things got out of hand later I didn't have to worry about going to school feeling dirty.

I collected my pajamas and snuck quietly into the bathroom situated across from my bedroom. Inside the bathroom, I didn't waste any time. I switched the shower on and stripped naked. In five minutes I was done. I rinsed the soap from my body and switched the shower off. I dried myself quickly and put my pajamas on. After dressing, I slipped out of the bathroom and back into my bedroom. The house was still quiet.

My next task was to get my homework done. An hour later I was finished and I began to relax a little. I lay down on my bed and thought about my dad. I thought about him every single day. Not only did I miss him, but he was a reminder of happier times, of when I'd been loved. Sometimes, I dreamed of when I was little, before Grant had come into my life. A time when I felt safe and I didn't live in constant fear.

I realized it was time to start supper. I hated leaving the sanctuary of my room, but I had to cook, because if I didn't have supper ready by the time Grant got home in the evenings I was guaranteed a beating.

I got up and left the safety of my room to go to the kitchen to start cooking. I searched the cupboards for something I could make, but there weren't a lot of options. I settled on some pasta with meat sauce. I glanced up at the old clock fixed on the kitchen wall. Grant would be home in thirty minutes. I was extremely glad that the pasta wouldn't take that long to make.

Unfortunately, the only thing we never ran out of in this house was alcohol. My mom's drinking problem had worsened over the years. She was drunk almost ninety percent of the time. I didn't see her often because she spent all of her time in her room drinking herself into a stupor. The only time I would see her was when I went into her room to change her bed linen. I did all the chores in the house. I cleaned the house and did the laundry. Luckily, we had a washing machine, so I didn't have to wash everything by hand.

Ten minutes after I had finished making supper, I was busy dishing up the food, and I heard the front door open. I couldn't help the nervous twist inside my stomach at the sound of Grant entering into the flat. I stood still. My breath instantly hitched in my throat when Grant walked through the kitchen doorway. His brown hair looked greasy and in need of a wash. He glared at me and his dark-brown eyes pierced mine. I waited for the inevitable. Then his gaze swung to his plate of food on the kitchen counter.

He walked to his plate of food and picked it up. He made a stop at the fridge to get a beer and then he threw me a glare before he disappeared out of the kitchen. I immediately grabbed my plate of food and went straight to my room. I ate my food quickly until my stomach was full. It was not often that I ate three meals in one day. Most days I was lucky to get one.

I switched off my bedroom light and lay down on my mattress. I couldn't help but think about Chris. I had never met anyone like him before. I couldn't allow us to be friends. However, if my situation were different, he was the type of person I would want to be friends with. In the short time I had known him, he had shown me more kindness than anyone else in recent memory ever had.

CHAPTER THREE

Haven

The next morning, I woke with a start. I was drenched in sweat and breathing hard. The brightness of the sun that streamed through the curtains lifted the dark memories. Nightmares had caused me to toss and turn for most of the night. I'd been dreaming about Grant. I tried to take a deep breath to calm my erratic breathing. My heart was still pounding in my chest. I sat up and rubbed my hands over my face, trying to shake off the remainder of the nightmare. I buried the memories of my nightmare deep inside.

That night, I'd dreamed of the first time Grant had hit me. I was ten at the time, and it was a couple of months after he had moved in with us. It was not the severity of beating that had made me suppress the memory. It was the fact that it had been the first time he had ever hit me, and the first time I'd seen the evil inside him. It had happened over something trivial. I'd knocked over a glass of juice onto the carpet. He'd stood over me while I'd tried to clean it up. When I'd looked up at him, his jaw had twitched as he'd fisted both of his hands. I hadn't seen it coming. He had hit my face. I'd looked up at him in stunned shock, holding on to my aching cheek when I saw the face of evil for the very first time.

During that time, I'd been trying to deal with the loss of my father and being ignored by my mother while she dealt with her grief. I'd held so much hope that Grant would be able to make everything right. Up until that point I'd trusted him, and I'd thought he'd be able to fix my broken family. I realized that day that he had every intention of breaking me. And over the years, he had. I was broken. Even if I did escape from his brutality, the physical pain would stop, but the emotional pain would live with me forever.

I drew in another ragged breath to calm down my pounding heart, and I reached under my mattress. I pulled out an old photo. The emotions that flooded through me every time I looked at the photo were overwhelming. It was a photo of my father and me. It had been taken a few months before he had died. In the photo, I was so happy as my father had held me lovingly in his arms. We were both smiling as we looked into the camera. I still missed him, and what he'd symbolized. He was last person who'd loved me, and when I looked at the photo I could remember what it felt like. When I was tempted to give up, I would look at the photo and remember that feeling. It would give me the strength to get through another day. Someday I would find someone to love me again, and for that reason I couldn't give up.

After I calmed down, I leaned over to return the photo to its hiding place under my bed. I got up and got dressed. I stopped abruptly when I heard a noise in the apartment. With my ear against my bedroom door, I listened, but it was quiet. A feeling of dread began to build up inside of me. My mom rarely came out of her room, so that meant that Grant was the one downstairs making the noise I was hearing. I would have to go past him to get out of the house.

I prayed that he was not in a foul mood today so that I wouldn't have a couple of fists flying my way. I wanted to stay hidden safely in my room, but I couldn't miss my second day of school. A nervous knot joined the dread inside me when I left my bedroom and headed to the bathroom. I hastily brushed my hair and my teeth before I walked into the living room.

Immediately, I knew that the noises were coming from the kitchen. I anxiously clutched the strap of my school bag tighter as I entered the living room. I held my breath when I got closer to the kitchen.

Suddenly, the noise stopped. I took a tentative step and peered through the kitchen doorway. My eyes settled on the source of the noise, and it was my mom searching through the cupboards. I sighed with relief when I walked into the kitchen. My mom didn't notice that I was in the kitchen while she continued her search through the cupboards.

"What are you looking for?" I asked her. I knew her well enough to know that she was looking for alcohol or cigarettes, her two vices.

"Wine," she muttered as she continued to search.

I walked to the cupboard where the wine was and got a bottle out. I handed it to her. She was probably drunk already, and that was why she couldn't find what she needed. As she turned to take the bottle from me I got a strong whiff of alcohol. No matter how many times I saw her in this state, it still shocked me. My beautiful, loving mother had disintegrated into the complete stranger standing in front of me.

Once, she'd been beautiful. Her dark-blond hair had once been smooth and silky, but was now greasy and messy. Her once flawless skin was hollow and wrinkled. Her toffee-colored eyes had once sparkled with promise; now they were a dull brown color, and glazed over with the effects of the alcohol. She looked ten years older than she actually was. The alcohol was literally sucking the life right out of her. She didn't look at me or say anything. She just left the kitchen with the bottle of wine tightly clutched in her hand. Her indifference hurt me more than the physical abuse. I gulped down the emotion it pulled from me and grabbed some bread and shoved it into my bag.

The bus ride to school was uneventful. When I got to school, I walked inside. I made a quick stop at my locker to get the books I needed. There was still time for me to eat my breakfast before school started, so I looked for a quiet place where I could eat my bread without prying eyes.

I found a quiet spot in between two school buildings. I sat down and ate the bread I'd shoved in my bag earlier. One thing I had promised myself was that when I finally escaped the clutches of evil I would never eat plain bread again. I tried to disappear into the background, but I got some curious looks from some of the students when I made my way to my first class of the day. I had nearly made it to my classroom when I spotted Damien out of the corner of my eye.

He had some cheerleader pushed up against the locker and their hands were all over each other. I couldn't take my eyes off of the two of them. I'd never seen two people go at it like that out in the open for everyone to see. I thought about what Chris had told me. From the physical evidence in front of me, I knew what Chris had told me about Damien Knight was true.

Not that it really mattered. I didn't know Damien Knight and I didn't want to know him. I pulled my gaze from him and the cheerleader, and continued to my class while I ignored everyone around me. During class, I concentrated on the teacher in front of me. But when I was in my second class of the day I felt the heat of a gaze. Glancing out the corner of my eye, I saw Damien a couple of tables away from me. He was openly staring at me. I had no idea why, but I wished he'd stop.

I breathed a sigh of relief when the lesson finally came to an end. Quickly, I gathered my stuff and shoved it into my bag, walking past Damien and out of the classroom. I felt his gaze follow me.

Later, I began to notice the looks I was getting from some of the girls. Some looked at me curiously, while others openly glared at me. I kept my eyes down and tried using my hair as a curtain to hide behind. I wanted to blend into the background, but I was getting attention, and it was the last thing I needed.

By lunchtime, I was a nervous wreck. I was ready to hide out in the bathroom to get away from all of the unwanted attention. I was washing my hands in the sink when three girls entered the room and cornered me. I recognized one of the girls from earlier this morning. She was the girl who Damien had been playing tonsil hockey with.

Up close, she was gorgeous. Her skin looked like white porcelain, and she had beautiful, sea-blue eyes, and shiny, long blond hair. The red mini skirt and white blouse she was wearing fit her perfectly. She looked like a real-life Barbie doll. The other two girls were rather plain looking, both with brown hair.

Her two friends stood on either side of me, cornering me against the basin. Barbie stood directly in front of me while she glared at me. I had no idea what I'd done for them to act this way. I tried to take a step back to get away from her, but the sink dug into my back.

"I just wanted to clear something up," Barbie said with a flick of her hair, looking at me like I was a piece of dirt that had been found under her shoe. I noticed that even her nails were perfectly painted with red nail polish.

"Damien," she began. This whole situation made absolutely no sense to me. I gave her a blank look. Why on earth would she want to talk to me about Damien?

"He is *mine!*" she said. "I give him everything he needs."

This was way too much information. I had images of the two of them doing the dirty deed. Besides, why would I care who he belonged to, and why would did she have the need to tell me?

"I don't want you to get ideas," she sneered, while her friends glared at me. I was beginning to think that they had all gone crazy.

"I don't know what you're talking about," I said quietly as I fiddled with my hands in front of me. When that didn't help my nervousness, I grabbed onto the strap of my bag and clenched it tightly in my hands.

"You might think that because he has shown you a little interest that you have a chance with him, but you don't," she continued while she looked at me with disgust. "Look at you, look at your clothes, you're ugly!"

I flinched at her words and her friends laughed at my reaction to the insults. I had no idea what she meant when she said Damien had shown a little interest in me. I had bumped into him once, and he had been rude. Other than that, I hadn't had any interaction with him at all.

Suddenly, Barbie gave me one last dirty look and paraded out of the bathroom with her little followers right behind her. Once they were out and the door was closed behind them, I began to shake uncontrollably. I hadn't done anything to anyone, yet somehow I'd made an enemy. It took a few minutes for me to compose myself before I could leave to find another place to have lunch. I couldn't go back to the field because I was pretty sure that would be the first place that Chris would look for me.

After walking around the school for a little while, I found another quiet spot. I sat down on the grass beside one of the smaller school buildings. Although it was quiet, there was a steady stream of students walking past. I heard movement behind me, and I didn't need to turn around to know who it was. Chris had found me. I was sitting with my arms wrapped around my legs with my chin resting on my knees when he sat down in front of me.

"Where were you? You weren't in our usual spot," he said to me with a friendly smile. His hair fell across his face, and he brushed it out of his eyes. He knew full well that I'd been avoiding him. He couldn't have a one-sided friendship if he couldn't find me.

Though, at the moment, I had bigger issues than dodging the guy who stalked me and who also wanted to be my friend. Just then, Barbie and her minions walked past us and threw me a dirty look. I immediately dropped my gaze to the grass in front of me. I hoped Chris hadn't seen the interaction between us, but he had. He looked from Barbie and her followers to me, then back to Barbie again.

"What was *that* about?" he asked, turning back to me a second time with a curious look on his face. He asked the question like I was actually going to open my mouth and answer him. Instead, I just shrugged my shoulders and dropped my gaze back down to the ground once more.

By talking to him I would be agreeing to the friendship he was offering, and I couldn't do that. Besides, even if I told him what had happened with Barbie earlier, there was nothing he could do about it. I had a feeling that she was going to make my life very difficult at my new school. I still had no idea why she would think that I wanted Damien. I didn't want anyone. I kept to myself and I hadn't interacted with anyone. How on earth had I landed up in this mess?

Eventually, Chris realized I was not going to tell him what he wanted to know. I noticed that he held two bag lunches in his hands instead of one. He set one bag down in front of himself and dropped the other bag in front of me. I wanted to ignore him and his thoughtful lunch, but my stomach growled at the thought of food. I tentatively opened the bag and peeked inside. The bag held a wrapped sandwich, an apple, and a soda. I couldn't stop the emotions that his thoughtfulness provoked from me. He didn't make a fuss about it, but to me it was a big deal. I glanced up at him and gave him a weak smile.

I took out the sandwich and unwrapped it. It was ham and cheese, and it tasted great. I ate slowly so I could savor the taste. While I ate, Chris began to talk about some TV show that he enjoyed, but I had no clue what he was talking about. We hadn't owned a TV since Grant had come into our lives. He talked about the latest movies that were playing at the cinemas.

Even though I didn't make eye contact or act like I was interested in his conversation, he continued to talk. The truth was that I loved listening to his voice, and to his opinions. I knew that I shouldn't like it, but I did. My stomach was full after I ate the apple. I hadn't opened the soda, so I stuffed it into my school bag. Out of the corner of my eye I saw Chris secretly smile while he watched me.

When the bell finally rang, I got to my feet and Chris followed me to my next class. Like the previous day, I ignored him completely while we walked. When I got to my class I went in and sat down at my desk without a backward glance.

For two days in a row, he had held the conversation alone at lunch and shared his food with me. He wasn't going to give up trying to be my friend, but I needed to be strong, and keep him at arm's length. If I let him get close, he would notice things I didn't want to have to explain.

CHAPTER FOUR

Haven

Luckily, the rest of the day went by quickly. The couple of times I had spotted Barbie and her followers in the hallways, she, along with her two sidekicks, had glared at me. I tried to ignore them but I couldn't help feeling nervous that she'd singled me out. My life was difficult enough and I didn't have the time or energy to deal with a jealous bimbo, especially when she had no reason to be jealous.

I hoped that if I just ignored her she would eventually leave me alone, but somehow I knew she was one of those people that would just keep at it. From what Chris had told me about Damien Knight, I didn't have a very high opinion of him. The fact that he was interested in someone like Barbie, the superficial type, made me think even less of him.

I walked to my locker after the school bell rang, signaling the end of school. At my locker I sorted through my books quickly so I would still make it to the bus stop on time. If I missed the bus it would take at least thirty minutes, if not longer, to walk home. Once I was done, I closed my locker and hitched my schoolbag over my shoulder. I walked quickly down the hall toward the front of the school. Just as I was about to walk out of the school, I heard someone call my name.

I didn't turn around to see who it was, but someone grabbed my wrist and spun me around. Automatically, without even registering the owner of the hand around my wrist, I cowered away. It was a reflex that had developed with years of abuse. My skittish gaze locked with the blue eyes of Damien Knight.

What the hell did he want?

"Sorry," he mumbled. Seeing my reaction to his touch, he released my wrist. "I called out to you but you obviously didn't hear me."

From where I stood by the entrance to the school I could see the school bus was at the bus stop and students were starting to filter into it. I began to panic because I didn't have long to make it to the bus stop before the bus left without me.

"I just wanted to talk to you," he informed me, a little out of breath. He ran his hand through his hair.

My eyes scanned the nearby vicinity for any sign of Barbie or any of her sidekicks. If any of them saw me standing there with Damien, they wouldn't be happy. I didn't give Damien a chance to say whatever he was going to say because I turned and walked quickly toward the bus stop. He didn't try to stop me and I made it onto the bus.

I sat down in the first open seat I could find; it happened to be a window seat, and as much as I tried to not look, my eyes found Damien still standing where I'd left him. His eyes met mine and he looked a little annoyed. I turned and concentrated on the floor of the bus in front of me, ignoring him.

Most girls would probably kill for any type of attention from him, but there was nothing he could say to me that I would be interested in hearing. I couldn't understand that despite all my efforts to keep everyone at a distance somehow Chris still sought me out at lunchtime. He was determined to be my friend even though I'd made it perfectly clear I wasn't interested. Now I had Damien trying to talk to me as well. I wished everyone would just leave me alone.

I pushed thoughts of Chris and Damien from my mind when I entered my house. The nervous knot began to tighten in my stomach. The house was quiet. There were empty beer bottles littered around the sofa. The stale smell of smoke hung in the hair. The ashtrays overflowed with cigarette butts that added to the horrible stale smell in the air. I hated the smell.

With a sigh, I dropped my schoolbag by the front door. First, I began to pick up the discarded beer bottles, and then I emptied the ashtrays. Once I was done cleaning up I went into my room. I got my pajamas and went for a quick shower. Then in my room I got my books out and I finished my homework. When my homework was done I went into the kitchen to start making supper.

There wasn't much in the cupboards. It was my responsibility to buy the groceries. My mom would give me a certain amount of money to buy what I needed for the week. It wasn't much, but somehow I managed to get enough groceries out of it to last the week. We lived on mostly pasta and sauce or canned food.

My mouth watered at the memory of the apple Chris had given me for lunch today. I couldn't stop the warm feeling from blooming inside me when I thought of how kind he'd been, making an extra lunch for me. He never asked why I never had lunch, he just packed me one. I shook my head to shake the thoughts from my mind. I couldn't let him get under my skin.

I made some packaged spaghetti with cheese sauce. Pasta dishes were always quick and easy to make.

Dread began to build up inside of me while I waited for

Grant to get home from work. He hadn't hit me yesterday, so chances were I wouldn't be so lucky tonight. Some weeks were worse than others, but he would hit me at least three times a week. If it was a bad week, he'd hit me every day. Sometimes he'd only punch me once or twice and other days he'd hit me more than that; it all depended on his mood.

Most people would run or fight back, but it only made things worse, so I just let him hit me. It was easier. If I didn't put up a fight, it would end quickly. I'd learned from an early age to let him hit me without fighting back, because once I'd fought back and he'd beaten me black and blue. I hadn't been able to go to school for a week.

My breath hitched in my throat when I heard the front door creak open. I stood by the fridge, waiting for Grant to enter the kitchen. A few seconds later, he stepped through the doorway. He looked tired and annoyed. It wasn't a good sign. His clothes were dirty from working on cars. He stepped closer. He smelled of car oil and cigarettes. His cold eyes remained on me as he took another step closer. His expression was hard to read. It took such restraint to just stand there when I knew what was coming. Instinct cried for me to run, but I ignored it and held my body still in front of him.

I didn't look directly at him; instead, my eyes kept watch on his hands. They were dirty from working on the cars. He stopped right in front of me. That was the first sign. The second sign was him fisting his hands. My eyes flickered to his and I could see the evil glint in his brown eyes. I closed my eyes and waited. It took all my self-control not to run and hide. I knew what was coming and there was no escaping it.

He didn't make a sound when his fist connected with my stomach. Pain exploded where he'd hit me, but I bit down on my lip to stop from crying out. Somehow I remained upright on my feet, but I was leaning against the fridge for support. A grunt was the only sound he made when his fist connected with my right ribcage. I groaned while I clutched the spot he'd just hit. I knew he hadn't broken anything, but it hurt so much. I tried to take a breath and a sharp pain shot through my side.

Two more hits to my other side and I collapsed onto the kitchen floor. As I lay on my side he gave me one more kick to the stomach, and then it was over. He turned and sauntered over to his food, took his plate, and without looking back at me walked out of the kitchen.

I closed my eyes and tried to breathe through the pain. If I lay on the kitchen floor without moving, and breathed in short and shallow breaths, the pain wasn't too bad; but when I tried to move, the pain intensified. I wanted to stay on the floor, but there was always a chance he would come back and hit me again. I couldn't let that happen. I needed to get to my room.

I held my breath as I pulled myself up into a sitting position. It hurt but I leaned with my back against the door of the fridge and took another breath and pulled myself up by the handle of the fridge. I took a moment for the wave of pain to ease before I started shuffling slowly toward the kitchen doorway. The back of Grant's head was visible on the sofa while I continued to shuffle down the hallway to my room.

It felt like forever before I reached the safety of my room. In the darkness, I breathed a sigh of relief when I finally lay down on my bed. I reached for a bottle of painkillers I kept next to my mattress and swallowed a couple of the tablets without water. They wouldn't help that much, but I would do anything to try and ease the pain.

Under my mattress I reached for the photo of my father and me. I held it in my hands while I lay in pain. Physically, I battled the pain, while emotionally I clung to the memories of happiness. No matter what, I had to hold onto the hope that one day I would be free and happy.

I drifted off to sleep only to be woken up with a sharp pain in my side. My hand soothed the injury under my shirt. I bit my lip when I pushed down slightly. It was definitely bruised. I didn't sleep well. I managed to fall asleep again, but every time I moved in my sleep the pain would wake me up. Eventually, it was time to get up.

My rib was still sore, but the rest of my injuries weren't as painful anymore. I held my side when I stood up.

Everything took longer to do because of the pain every little movement caused. It took twice as long to get dressed and I was running late. I had to hurry because I didn't want to miss my bus to school. If I missed my bus, I would be forced to stay home.

By the time I made it onto the bus, I slumped down in the seat and suppressed a groan when I adjusted my aching body. It had been the hit to the rib that was going to take a few days to heal. I was so used to this and my threshold for pain was higher because of it. For most people these injuries would be too severe for them to function, but I could still walk and move around as long as I didn't overdo things.

I promised myself I'd rest for a bit when I got home after school. My forehead leaned against the cool window while I watched the scenery outside.

When I got to school, my stomach grumbled. I hadn't eaten last night and I'd forgotten to eat breakfast, but the grumbling in my tummy was nothing compared to the pain caused by the bruised rib. On my way to my first class a couple of the students bumped into me, and I had to bite down on my lip to stop from crying out in pain.

Even though I had a lot on my mind, and I was in pain, I kept an eye out for Barbie and her sidekicks. I saw them once after my second lesson and they all giggled and laughed while pointing their fingers at me. I put my head down and tried to ignore them but I couldn't help the flush of red caused by embarrassment that crept into my cheeks.

It wasn't like I'd never been bullied at school before. I was the quiet and weird girl who didn't have friends or talk to anyone, so I was singled out to be bullied by the popular kids. Usually it wouldn't last too long before they moved onto their next victim and forgot about me.

This was the first time I was being picked on because of a guy. A guy I didn't want anything to do with. Barbie definitely had issues if she was jealous of me.

It was finally lunchtime. My hunger pains were getting worse because it had been nearly twenty-four hours since the last time I'd eaten, and my bruised rib was still sore and aching. I decided there was no point in trying to avoid Chris because he would find me anyway, so I started walking toward the field.

"Hey," someone called from behind me.

I kept my eyes down and I continued to walk.

"Hey." The person called out louder.

The person was definitely trying to get my attention, but I wasn't interested. A hand grabbed my arm to halt my escape. The unexpected jolt caused a pain to shoot through me. I bit my lip as I turned to see who'd grabbed my wrist and my eyes clashed with the blue eyes of Damien Knight.

I shrunk away from him. It didn't matter that he wasn't Grant. The only time I was touched is when Grant hit me, so anytime someone touched me, my body reacted instinctively, even though I knew not everyone was like Grant. I tried to pull my wrist free but he held on firmly. His eyes narrowed at my reaction to him.

"I'll let go if you promise not to run away again," he told me.

I glanced from his face to where he held me at my wrist and gave him a brief nod. He released me. He hadn't hurt me, but instinctively I rubbed the spot on my wrist where he'd held it. I dropped my arms to my side while I glared at him.

"I just want to talk to you," he said.

I crossed my arms over my chest and waited. I knew there was no point in trying to get away; he would grab my wrist again, and I didn't like to be touched.

"Why did you run away from me yesterday?" he asked. I continued to stare at him, but I remained silent.

CHAPTER FIVE
Haven

"Look," he said, running a hand through his hair. "I just wanted to say I was sorry about Angela." His tone had softened and his wide, expressive blue eyes conveyed the apology sincerely.

Who was Angela?

"The blonde that was giving you shit yesterday," he explained, when he saw my confusion. My eyes widened in surprise.

So Barbie has a name, I thought. The name Barbie suited her better: pretty and plastic. How did he know about Barbie giving me shit yesterday, anyway? I frowned at him.

"Your friend, Chris, told me what happened and gave me a piece of his mind," he explained. "His exact words were, 'keep your whores away from her.' "

Chris. Even though I didn't want him to get involved in my life, I couldn't help the warm feeling inside me, there because of what he'd done for me.

"She had no right to do that," he began to explain. I shrugged. I didn't care.

I'd come to the realization that it was mainly his fault. If he hadn't stared at me in a few of our classes then Barbie wouldn't have gotten jealous.

"She isn't my girlfriend or anything like that," he continued with his eyes on me. I still didn't care if they were dating or not. It didn't matter to me and I didn't know why he felt the need to explain it to me. I had no designs on him and I wished they would leave me alone.

"Angie can be a bitch sometimes," he explained further as he stuffed his hands in the pockets in the front of his jeans.

Only sometimes? I thought.

It didn't say much for him. Why would he associate with someone he knew wasn't a nice person? Then I remembered what Chris had told me about him. He had only one thing on his mind when it came to girls, and it had nothing to do with conversation or their personality. He wasn't that different from most boys his age. Most of them had one thing on their mind and nothing else, but he seemed to take it to the extreme.

"I told her to stay away from you," he assured me. My eyes widened in alarm. I honestly didn't think that she was going to listen to him and I was sure the fact that I'd told someone what happened was probably not going to end well for me. Barbie and her followers were probably going to make my life even worse.

"Trust me, she won't be a problem anymore," he told me when he saw my reaction.

Trust him? Was he kidding? I didn't trust anyone. I didn't even trust my own parents. My father had died—it hadn't been his fault, but he'd still left me. My mother had stopped loving me and it had literally happened overnight. Everyone I'd ever trusted had let me down. If I couldn't trust my own parents, how on earth was I supposed to trust strangers?

"I got something on her, something she wouldn't want

everyone to find out," he whispered to me with a smirk. He was blackmailing her into doing what he wanted. I didn't want to know what he had on her, but if it was enough to keep her in line and off my back, I was happy.

"If she comes near you again, you let me know," he held my gaze. He knew as well as I did that if Blondie did try to bully me again, I wouldn't tell him.

"You don't talk much," he murmured as he brushed his hair out of his face. He watched me with fascination.

I'd done my part, I'd listened to what he'd had to say, but I wasn't interested in making pointless conversation. If he could keep Blondie away from me that would be great, but other than that I didn't want anything to do with him. He didn't need to know anything about me and I didn't want to know anything about him.

While he waited for me to respond to his comment, I picked up my school bag and hitched it over my shoulder. Pain shot through my side and I winced. I'd forgotten about my rib.

"Are you okay?" he asked with concern when he reached for my arm. I pulled my arm out of his reach and I took a step backward. This was one of the reasons I preferred to keep my distance from people, because if I slipped up I didn't want anyone to witness it and ask questions.

"I'm fine," I assured him softly. His eyes widened in shock at the fact that I'd finally spoken. "Please leave me alone."

I'd said what I had needed to, so I turned and walked away from him, leaving him standing slightly open-mouthed while he watched me disappear. I was mad with myself for talking to him. I don't know what had made me speak to him.

No Damien and no Barbie was what I wanted. Then I thought about Chris, and as much as I knew it wasn't a good idea, I didn't want there to be no Chris.

By the time Chris dropped down next to me at our usual spot by the field I was fuming. I crossed my arms and glared at him—I wanted him to know I was angry with him. Like the day before, he set a brown paper bag in front of me and one in front of him. He seemed oblivious to my anger. When I didn't open the lunch he'd brought for me he looked at me and saw my expression.

"I take it you found out about my little talk with Damien," he said.

My glare intensified as I pressed my lips together.

"I'm not sorry I said something. Someone had to do something about that blonde bimbo," he insisted. I smiled at the nickname he'd given her—Bimbo. It almost suited her better than Barbie.

I eased my glare but kept my arms crossed.

"Ah, come on, you can't stay cross with me," he insisted playfully. Then he flashed that wide smile at me and I felt my resolve begin to crumble. "I couldn't do nothing and let her bully you."

Even though I hadn't wanted anyone to know about it, I understood why he'd done what he had.

"I knew she wouldn't listen to me, but I knew she *would* listen to Damien," he added, before he took a bite out of his sandwich. At the sight of food, my stomach grumbled in response. I was so hungry.

My anger vanished and I dropped my arms and opened the packed lunch Chris had given to me. I nearly hugged Chris right there and then. He'd packed a cheese sandwich, a pear, a chocolate bar and a soda.

I'd learned to keep a tight control over my emotions, it was how I survived the hell that was my life, but I struggled with the emotion that his kindness pulled from me. I felt the emotional lump in my throat and I swallowed hard.

He hadn't been offended when I'd tried to hide away from him. Instead he had brushed it aside. He'd never asked me why I never had lunch—instead, he brought lunch for me every day. I never talked to him but it didn't seem to matter to him. He would talk enough for the both of us and I could just sit there and listen to him. Even when he found out Barbie was bullying me, he'd done something about it. I couldn't control the tenderness I felt toward this boy who in a couple of days had done more for me than anyone else had in the last seven years.

I unwrapped the sandwich and ate while Chris talked. One of things I loved was listening to him ramble on about trivial things like what he watched on TV or the latest gossip from the school. The sound of his voice was relaxing and for those few minutes I could relax.

My stomach was stuffed by the time I finished all the food. I opened the soda and took a sip. I loved the fizzy bubbles.

"Thank you," I said softly, when I glanced in his direction. His eyes met mine and they widened in surprise. Then he smiled. It was a big smile that showed his perfectly white teeth.

I didn't want to form any type of friendship with him but he was slowly starting to break the walls I'd built up around myself. I'd tried to fight it, but he was so damn persistent.

"You're welcome," he said. "Do you have any requests for lunch tomorrow?"

I shook my head. Just the fact that he was thoughtful enough to bring me lunch was enough for me, so I wasn't going to get fussy. There was no way Chris would have any idea what was happening to me at home and, if he did, he'd realize how much I appreciated the lunches he packed for me and the company he gave me during lunch.

I'd led a very lonely existence for the past seven years and for once it was nice to have someone to keep me company. I'd actually started to look forward to spending my lunches with Chris. I would just have to make sure that I was careful and that he didn't find out anything about what was happening to me. If he did become suspicious, then I'd have to move again, and I didn't want to. I'd just started to settle down into my new life.

"Did you hear the big news?" he asked, before he took a sip of his soda. I looked at him curiously because I never kept up with the gossip. I only vaguely remembered what he would babble on about at lunchtime.

"Damien dumped Angela," he revealed, watching my reaction. I gave him a shrug. "Not that they were dating, they were just doing each other. So technically they are not doing each other anymore."

I remembered Damien pushing her up against the lockers. They'd definitely been doing each other. I don't know why he thought I'd be interested in that news. Who Damien 'did' had nothing to do with me. In the back of my mind I couldn't help but wonder if Damien had dumped Angela because of the little incident between me and her. Why would Damien care about what happened to me? It was a ridiculous thought.

He probably didn't like the fact that Angela was insinuating to people that they were dating when technically they weren't. From what I saw and what Chris had told me, he was the type of guy that kept things casual. He probably got nervous when Angela starting talking about a more permanent arrangement.

I shook my head. I needed to get rid of thoughts of Damien. It shouldn't matter to me what was happening in his life. As long as he left me alone I was happy.

"Apparently he wasn't happy about her telling people

that they were dating when they weren't," he explained with a smirk. I'd hit the nail on the head.

He dropped the subject of Damien and started talking about something else while I drank my soda.

When lunch ended he walked me to my next class and, when we got to my class, instead of ignoring him like I had previously, I gave him a weak smile before he turned and left. Baby steps.

The rest of the day passed quickly. The couple of times I saw Barbie she just glared at me; time would tell if she actually listened to Damien and left me alone. In my last class of the day I got held up. The teacher had wanted to ask me how I was settling in. So even though I ran as fast as I could, sore rib and all, I didn't make it to the bus stop in time. The bus was long gone.

Frustrated, I looked up to the sky. Dark clouds were beginning to form the in the sky above me. It looked like it was going to rain and I was going to have to walk home in it.

I clutched my tender side while I struggled to catch my breath. I felt so annoyed that I'd been held up in class. When the pain in my side eased, I began to walk. I kicked a loose stone while I walked down the sidewalk and hitched my school bag higher over my shoulder. The sound of rumbling clouds didn't ease the anxiousness that had settled inside me. I was lost in my thoughts, so I didn't notice a sleek, dark-gray SUV slow down beside me. I only noticed it when it stopped beside me.

The window of the SUV opened.

"Can I give you a lift home?" Damien asked from inside the car.

I glanced from him to the path in front of me. It would make my life a lot easier if I got a lift home with him, but letting Damien get involved in my life wouldn't be a good idea.

"Come on, it's not safe for you to walk home," he argued. He was right, but to be in a confined space with him for any amount of time wouldn't be safe for me, either. "And it looks like it's going to rain."

With another few moments of deliberation I finally relented and gave in. If I got home too late I wouldn't have dinner ready by the time Grant got home, and he wouldn't be happy. I reached for the handle on the passenger side and opened the door. Once I climbed into the car and closed the door I was overwhelmed by a smell that was distinctly Damien. It was a blend of spice and musk, and I had to admit I liked it. It was kind of comforting.

"Where do you live?" he asked me when he pulled the car away from the sidewalk.

I was ashamed to give him my address. If his car was anything to go by, he probably lived in a nice neighborhood. I, on the other hand, lived in an unsavory part of town, in a crappy apartment. I mumbled my address under my breath, embarrassed about him finding out where I lived. He didn't say anything as he started the drive to my home.

"So you talk," he said, shooting a quick look in my direction. Water droplets spattered against the windscreen as it began to rain lightly.

All I wanted to do was get home—I didn't want to be dragged into a conversation with Damien. The less he knew about me the better.

"Is there a reason you don't talk a lot?" he prodded further. He glanced in my direction, and then brought his attention back to the road as the wipers swept the water from the windscreen.

I shrugged and stared out of the window through the light rain spattering against the glass, trying to ignore his attempts to start a conversation with me.

"Has Angela given you any more trouble?" he asked. I

looked at him and shook my head. So far so good.

Then I did something that surprised me.

"Why did you break up with Angela?" I asked quietly.

He gave me a surprised look and then he turned his attention back to the road.

"Whatever was going on between us had run its course," he answered. His answer was short and to the point. "It was never going to be a permanent arrangement and she knew that up front. But she kept pushing me for more than I was prepared to give."

I wasn't surprised by his answer. I'd pretty much guessed that already.

I didn't like the way I felt when I was around Damien, and being in a confined space with him was just amplifying it. I kept sneaking glances at him. He was really good looking. He also had that confident air about him that made the girls flock to him. As hard I could, I tried to ignore him. By the time he pulled up in front of my house, I was relieved. It had started to rain more heavily.

"Thank you," I said when I climbed out of his car. I didn't wait for him to say anything. By the time I walked to my apartment and opened the door I was wet from the rain. When I glanced back, Damien was still sitting in his SUV, watching me.

I closed the door and leaned against it. Only then did I hear the sound of his car pulling away.

CHAPTER SIX

Haven

As the next few weeks eased past, I settled into a routine. The warm summer weather cooled into autumn. The leaves of the trees turned brown.

I kept to myself. The only person I didn't shy away from was Chris. He still sat with me every lunch break and he still brought me a packed lunch each day. Slowly but surely, with his perseverance, I'd begun to open up to him. He was now my friend, not just my stalker. All the little things he did for me helped me build trust in people again. I trusted him. He hadn't gained my trust overnight; it had taken time.

Grant still hit me regularly but he didn't seem to hit me as hard. I had less bruises which I had to cover up for the outside world. I barely saw my mom, and when I did it was still shocking to see the evidence of her descent into self-destruction. Sometimes I wondered how long it would be before her body finally gave in. It could only take so much punishment.

I wondered how I would feel if my mom died. To be honest, I wouldn't miss the person she was today. I'd miss the distant memory of the mother who had loved me.

Whatever Damien had on Barbie must have been really good, because she'd left me alone. She'd still glare at me every time she saw me, but she didn't try to corner me again. I saw her groping some other football player the other day. Clearly, she'd moved on from Damien.

Damien.

Since the afternoon he'd given me a lift home I hadn't seen much of him. Every now and then I would see him in the hallways, but he never tried to talk to me again.

In the classes I had with him he would still stare at me. I couldn't help but wonder why he seemed so fascinated with me. I didn't see him with any other girl. I knew it shouldn't matter, but it did. My eyes had a mind of their own as they swept the hallways looking for a glimpse of him. I couldn't stop the fluttering feeling inside my stomach at the sight of him when I spotted him out of the corner of my eye.

I tried hard to fight it, but I wasn't winning. I knew I needed to put a stop to whatever I was starting to feel for this boy, because it wasn't going to end well. Chris had noticed my interest in Damien and even the regular speeches from him about what a player Damien was and how he'd break me fell on deaf ears.

It was difficult enough trying to keep the truth of what was happening to me at home from Chris. That was the problem with letting people in—if they were observant, it wouldn't take them long to figure it out and confront me with it.

Then one afternoon, after school, I was walking toward the bus stop when someone stepped into my path.

I looked up to see Damien standing in front of me.

"Can I give you a lift home?" he asked, his hands in the pockets of his jeans. I glanced past his shoulder to the bus stop, where the bus was waiting.

"I haven't missed the bus," I told him, not understanding

why he was offering me a lift.

"I know, I wanted to give you a lift home," he said, his eyes watching mine.

It only took me seconds to make my decision, and although I knew I'd probably regret it, I nodded my head. He reached for my schoolbag and slung it over his shoulder while he walked me to his car. I ignored the curious glances we got from some of the students lingering in the parking lot.

Thoughts of why he wanted to give me a lift home swirled through my mind and I couldn't come up with a valid reason why. It made absolutely no sense. He opened the passenger door for me and I nervously got in. I tucked a stray piece of hair behind my ear while I waited for him to get into the car.

I couldn't help but fidget nervously with my hands when he got into the car. Like before, his car smelled like him, and I liked it. Silence settled between us as he started the drive to my house. I flickered my gaze from the scene outside the window to sidelong glances of Damien. He seemed to be deep in thought while he drove. I wasn't good with people, because I kept to myself. I had no idea how to start a conversation with him, so I kept my mouth shut.

"Have you had any more run-ins with Angela?" he asked softly. His eyes glanced in my direction and then settled back to the road in front of us.

I shook my head, unable to talk. I was always nervous, and when I was around him he made me even more nervous than normal.

"Is anyone else giving you any trouble?". I pulled my gaze away from him and kept my eyes on the scenery in front of me. I shook my head again.

It took me until the end of the ride to gather up enough courage to ask him the question I wanted to know the answer to. He'd just pulled up outside my apartment block, switched his car off and turned his attention to me.

It's now or never, I thought before I licked my dry lips.

"Why do you care?" I asked, keeping my head down, unable to make eye contact with him.

He was silent for a few moments.

"Because you look like you could use a friend," he whispered. At his soft answer, my eyes rose to meet his.

Normally his eyes were guarded, and for the first time since I'd met him I saw a vulnerability in him that I'd never seen before. He didn't realize that my lack of friends was how I protected my secret. The less people I had around me to see the bruises, or the limps, or to ask questions, the better.

"The first time you bumped into me, I saw it in your eyes," he whispered, his eyes piercing mine. It was almost like he was trying to see deep inside of me. His finger touched my cheek as his eyes held mine. "Do you know that saying 'the eyes are a mirror to the soul'? The first time I looked into your eyes, I saw your soul. It's broken, just like mine."

I couldn't deny it.

"We're both broken," he explained.

I knew what had broken me, but I was curious about what had happened to him. Mine had been years of abuse and the result of being unloved. What had happened to him? I gulped down the emotion his words caused me while his eyes held mine. Now I could see the sadness evident in his dark-blue eyes. Seconds ticked by into a minute as his eyes held mine. I wanted to ask him what had happened to him; but if he shared his story with me, then I would need to share my story with him, and I wasn't prepared to do that.

"If you ever need anything, just let me know," he said. I watched as the sadness in his eyes disappeared before they left mine.

I was too emotional to speak, so I just nodded my head.

"Give me your phone so I can give you my number," he

instructed quietly.

"I don't have one," I whispered hoarsely. He looked at me like I was an alien from another planet. Most people our age had their own phones, so I knew it was rare that I didn't have one.

"Okay, I'll sort something out for you," he murmured. I didn't know what exactly he meant by that, so I shrugged my shoulders.

"Thank you for the lift," I said to him. He gave me a brief nod as he watched me pick up my bag and get out of his car. I gave him a weak smile, and then I closed the passenger door and turned to walk to my apartment. He waited until I was safely in my apartment before he drove away.

Little did he know the evil that he was trying to keep me safe from lived in the apartment with me.

Now I knew why he watched me so closely: I intrigued him because he saw something in me that he understood. I remembered the sadness I saw in his eyes—is that what people saw when they looked into my eyes?

I was so wrapped up in my thoughts that I paid no attention to the noises coming from the kitchen. Still clutching my schoolbag, I didn't even realize what was happening until it was too late. Grant stepped out of the kitchen and straight into my path. His fist connected with my stomach.

"Who the fuck was that?" he shouted at me as I dropped to my knees. Pain exploded in my stomach and my breath hitched in my throat. I didn't get a chance to move before he reached down, grabbed my hair and pulled my face to his.

"I asked you a fucking question!" he yelled. He was so close I could smell the alcohol on his breath.

"A boy from school," I answered through my haze of pain.

"What the fuck are you doing with a boy from school?"

he screamed in my face. I closed my eyes and gulped down my pain.

"Nothing, he just gave me a lift home," I whispered.

"Are you fucking him like the whore you are?" he hissed at me.

"No, I'm not," I whispered, but I knew I could deny it all I wanted, it wouldn't make a difference to Grant. He slapped me hard across the face.

"Don't lie to me," he scolded. I closed my eyes to try and block out what was happening to me. I'd never seen Grant this angry before and I could feel the cold fear rise up inside me. I had no idea what he was going to do to me.

"You need to be punished." He stated it with such venom in his voice that my eyes shot open. He looked at me with disgust and I tried to plead with him. He lifted me to my feet by my hair. I grimaced with pain.

"Take off your shirt," he instructed me when he released me. He'd never asked me to do that before. My hands began to shake as I followed his order and pulled my shirt over my head. I dropped it to the floor.

A new wave of fear hit me.

"Face the wall," he sneered at me as he began to undo his belt. Our eyes met for a brief moment and I knew I was looking into the eyes of someone who had pure evil running in his veins.

I closed my eyes and tried to keep the tears from overflowing. I'd never cried before but I knew this was going to be bad. I wanted to run and hide but he would find me and he would make me pay for disobeying him. Silently, with the sting of tears on my eyes, I turned to face the wall.

His belt hit against the bare skin of my back. The next hit made me gasp out in pain. I bit down on my lip to keep from screaming as my back burned from the hit. I lost count of how many times his belt ripped across the soft skin of my back. With my hands against the wall, I tried to breathe through the pain.

"If I ever see that boy with you again, I'll kill him," he warned me before I heard the retreat of his footsteps.

I had no doubt he meant every word he'd just said to me.

I clung my body to the wall but my legs gave in and I sunk to the floor. My back burned from the pain. The pain was so bad that it took me a while before I could get up, wincing with pain at every little movement, which made the pain shoot through me. In one hand I held my discarded shirt, my other hand wrapped around the strap of my school bag as I walked to my room.

I held onto my bedroom door when I finally made it up into my room. I whimpered as pain sliced across my back at every slight movement. I still needed to shower and I knew it was going to be agony.

I got my pajamas and went to the bathroom. There was no way I could see what my back looked like, but I knew it was bad. I started the shower and then I got undressed. My back throbbed; it felt like he'd hit every inch of my back with his belt. My back stung while I stood under the running water and I clamped my hand over my mouth to keep from crying out.

My back was throbbing with pain as I climbed out of the shower and switched the water off. I quickly brushed my teeth. I pulled my pajama pants and held my pajama top against my chest as I walked back to my room. There was no way I was going to be able to wear a shirt over the welts on my back.

It took me a few minutes to ease myself onto my mattress on my stomach. The pain eased slightly because I was lying still. I reached for the bottle of painkillers and swallowed two tablets. I hoped it would help with the pain. I pulled the picture of my dad out from under my mattress. I closed my eyes and imagined what it felt like to be ten again, when I was a happy little girl.

I tried to imagine what my family would have been like if my dad hadn't died. My mom wouldn't be the uncaring drunk she was now. She would still love me. I would have a father that loved me, too. We would live in a nice house with a white-picket fence with a yard big enough for a dog.

With those happy thoughts, I drifted off to sleep.

But even in my dreams, I wasn't safe from Grant.

He screamed and he shouted while he punched me again and again. He didn't stop hitting me until I couldn't move and all I could do was lay on the ground on my back, whimpering. Blood seeped from the wounds on my face as Grant leaned over me.

"You are worthless," he stated with an evil smile on his lips.

I felt a tear slid down my face at his words.

CHAPTER SEVEN

Haven

My dreams were filled with nightmares about Grant. By the time morning came around, I was tired from a restless night's sleep. My back was in agony. I didn't want to stay at home but I wasn't sure if I could handle going to school considering the pain that I was in.

What if Damien decided to stop by after school to check up on me if I didn't go? The fear of Grant seeing him again made me decide to go school. I also had to find a way to keep Damien at a distance. Ignoring him wasn't working.

It took me twice as long as usual to get ready for school. I bit down on my lip as I slowly pulled a shirt over my head. The slightest touch of the fabric on the welts on my back was so painful that I would bite harder on my lip, drawing blood. I felt a drop of perspiration on my forehead. My stomach growled with hunger as I walked slowly to the bathroom. I brushed my teeth and my hair. I went back to my room and swallowed two painkillers.

I grabbed some bread from the kitchen before I closed the front door and walked to the bus stop. I carried my schoolbag in my hand because there was no way I was putting the strap over my shoulder. My back hurt too much. Every jolt of the bus on the way to school made the pain shoot through my back, and I had to bite down on my lip to keep from crying out.

When I got to school I was seriously wondering if I'd made the right decision to go, but seeing Damien by his locker reminded me of why I was doing this. I had to make sure he kept his distance from me or else Grant would do something about it. Grant meant every word he'd said. He would kill him if he saw me with Damien again.

As if sensing my stare, Damien turned and his eyes met mine. He smiled. It was enough for the flutter in my stomach to take me by surprise. I didn't smile back; instead, I pulled my eyes away from him, and made my way to my locker.

It was hard trying to keep him at a distance, especially when he was trying to befriend me. I had no idea how I was going to keep him safely away from me. I didn't want to drag him into my messed-up life. From the haunted look on his face yesterday, I knew he had his own stuff to deal with without adding my problems to it.

"Hey." I heard his voice behind me while I packed a couple of my books into my locker. I didn't greet him back.

"Are you okay?" he asked when I ignored him. I closed my locker and turned to face him. His blue eyes were dark with concern.

"I'm fine," I assured him when I began to walk away from him. His hand wrapped around my wrist and I stopped. I took a deep breath and turned to face him again.

"I got you this," he said as he reached in his pocket and produced a phone. He held it out for to me, but I refused to take it from him.

"I can't," I said, shaking my head.

"Please just take it. I need to know that you can call me

if you need to," he explained. His eyes held mine.

I wanted to stand firm and say no, but the look in his eyes broke through to me and I took the phone from him. I wasn't even sure how to work it, but I would take it so that he would feel better. Maybe he would back off a little now.

"I set it up so my number is on speed dial for you," he revealed as he showed me how to dial his number if I needed to. A faint ringing came from the phone, and then he ended the call and handed me the phone.

"Thank you," I said. There weren't a lot of people in this world that would go to the lengths that Damien or Chris did for me, and for that I was grateful. But as much as they wanted to help, there was nothing they could do to help me.

"Promise me that if you ever need anything you'll call me," he insisted. I gave him a brief nod even though there was no way I could call him. I feared what Grant would do to him.

I walked away from Damien without looking back. I don't know how I made it through the day without letting on to the pain I was struggling with. Every time the fabric of my shirt touched the wounds on my back, a sting of pain seared through me. In the bathroom, I splashed some water on my face and dried it off. I took a couple of deep breaths before I picked up my school bag in my hand and walked out to the field to meet Chris for lunch. He was waiting patiently for me. As usual, the extra bag of lunch was there waiting for me. Somehow I sat down next to him without grimacing.

"Thank you," I said.

"As always, you're welcome," he said softly. I could feel his eyes on me as I opened the packed sandwich. The hunger pains in my stomach reminded me how hungry I was. I began to eat the sandwich he'd brought me.

Chris began to chatter away. I just listened to him babble on. It helped take my mind off the throbbing reminder of what Grant had done to me. It was getting worse. For the past seven years Grant had beaten me, but he'd never hit me with his belt before. My fear of him was growing. The abuse was escalating and I feared that he was capable of taking it too far. I could barely cope before, and if it continued to worsen, I had no idea how I was going to handle it.

A couple of concerned looks from Chris told me he'd noticed that something was up with me but he didn't ask any questions, and when break ended he walked me to my next class like he did every day.

"See you tomorrow," he said, before he left me in the doorway of my next class.

"See you tomorrow," I whispered back to him as I walked into my class and sat down. I leaned my head into my hands just for a moment to pull myself together.

By the end of the day I was exhausted and all I wanted to do was get home and lie down on my bed. My back still hurt and I knew it would be a couple of days before the welts on my back began to heal. My back throbbed for the entire bus journey, and then I got off the bus and began my five-minute walk home. As I turned the corner, I stopped.

Outside my apartment block a few cop cars were parked. I took a tentative step forward as my eyes flickered to my apartment. The door was open and a body in a black bag was being wheeled out. My world stopped as I held my breath, and then I watched Grant walk out behind the body. He was upset and a cop walked beside him. My heart stopped.

I don't know how long I stood there, watching the scene in front of me. It was as if I were in a dreamlike state. Voices echoed around me while I watched the body bag being lifted into a police van. Grant stood a few steps away, watching the body bag with tears in his eyes.

I'd never seen him show any emotion other than anger and disdain, which was normally directed at me. I didn't see much of my mom and didn't see them interact that much, but I knew he had cared for her in his own fucked-up way.

My mom was gone. Instead of feeling the same gut-wrenching grief I had felt when my dad died, I felt nothing.

For me, my mom had died the day my dad had stopped breathing. The person I'd been living with for the past seven years had been a shell of that person, hell-bent on doing everything she could to join my father in death. At least she was at peace, because she wouldn't have to deal with the grief anymore. I should feel upset, but I wasn't. She hadn't been my mother for these last seven years and, even though she'd lived with me, I'd never felt more alone.

The thought of living alone with Grant made me shiver with fear.

Grant's eyes caught mine and my heart plummeted into my stomach at the look he gave me. I walked over to our apartment block and Grant stepped forward and pulled me into a hug. My arms hung by my side and I fisted my hands as the pain in my back pierced right through me. I knew better than to think that the hug was anything but for show for everyone watching. In front of everyone Grant spoke quietly to me and showed me affection that he'd never shown me before. Once everyone had gone and we were alone, we walked back into our apartment. His usual look of disdain and contempt crept over his face when he looked at me.

Fear took hold of me while I waited to see what he would do. I had a feeling that now that my mom wasn't around to distract him, things were going to get much worse for me. He gave me a glare before he walked past me to the bedroom and slammed the door closed.

I sighed with relief.

Once I'd closed my bedroom door I sat down and allowed myself to think about my mom. The last time I'd seen her had been a couple of days ago. She'd been looking for alcohol again. The police had explained to me that they suspected my mother had died from a mixture of alcohol and pills. I hadn't even been aware that she'd been taking pills. They would only be able to confirm it once the toxicology results were completed.

Grant had explained that my mom had been prescribed pills for depression. Even though she wasn't supposed to take the tablets with alcohol, she had.

The depression, which had started when my dad had died unexpectedly, had clawed at her and pulled her into a spiral that had ended with her dying alone in her bedroom, surrounded by empty bottles of wine and empty pill containers. I wanted to be able to cry and mourn the loss of my mom, but I didn't feel anything. The only feeling I felt was fear at what would happen now that I was alone with Grant.

He'd left me alone for the moment, but it wouldn't last.

I didn't sleep much that night. Every time I closed my eyes I would think about my mom. I felt guilty because I knew I should feel some grief, or shed a tear.

The next day I decided to go to school because the only alternative was to stay home with Grant. He'd be busy organizing funeral arrangements for my mom. My mom had lost both her parents at a young age. She been an only child. There was no family to mourn her.

I had no idea where my father's family was. After my father's death my mother had pulled away from them and within a few months we'd lost touch totally with them. I wasn't sure why. I always thought perhaps it was that it hurt too much to be reminded daily of what she'd lost that had made her cut them out of our lives.

When I got to school, I was still in a daze. The numbness that had crept over me the day before when I'd found out my mom had died had settled into my body. I walked into school, my eyes on the floor as I walked to my locker. Voices continued to echo around me. It was like I were in my own bubble, and I wasn't paying attention to anything going on around me.

"Haven," I heard a voice behind me through the echo.

I didn't stop. I kept walking. I felt someone reach for my wrist and I turned to see Damien looking at me with concern.

"Are you okay?" he asked. His eyes scanned my face.

I nodded my head at him and then pulled my arm out of his hand. He let me go but I could see from his expression that he didn't believe me.

"You seem out of it," he said as he lifted my chin with his finger and took a closer look at me. I pulled away from him.

"I'm fine," I said, this time with more conviction, before I walked away from him while he stood watching me.

The guilt I'd been wrestling with grew with every passing moment. How was I supposed to tell someone my life-changing news and explain why I wasn't upset? I tried to carry on as usual and pretend nothing was wrong, but by lunchtime I was exhausted. My back still hurt.

Chris gave me the same concerned look Damien had given me this morning when I sat down next to him on the grass. He put a bag of lunch down in front of me. Even the sight of what he'd packed me for lunch wasn't enough to make me smile like it usually did. He waited patiently, watching me as I opened the sandwich he'd packed for me. Today he didn't talk or babble on like he normally did. I ignored him and ate the sandwich. I opened the soda and sipped it quietly.

Once I'd finished eating he looked at me and asked, "Are you going to talk about it?"

He could tell that something had happened. I just looked

at him and his eyes softened.

"I don't want to talk about it," I whispered. I was scared that if I told him what had happened and I didn't react the way I was supposed to, it would raise more questions that I couldn't answer. What kind of girl didn't cry for her dead mother? I knew why I didn't feel anything, but I couldn't explain that to Chris or Damien without revealing my secret.

"If you change your mind, you let me know," he said softly to me. I looked at him and nodded my head. There was no way I was going to change my mind.

I still had to keep my secret otherwise Grant would make sure I wouldn't live to see another day. Some days I wanted to give up, it would just be easier, but the tiny bit of hope that one day I would be free kept me going.

The rest of the school day passed and I kept to myself. I breathed a sigh of relief when the bell rang for the end of day. At least I wouldn't have people watching me and trying to pretend everything was all right when it wasn't. I just wanted to be on my own away from everyone.

Damien stepped into my path as I walked toward the bus stop.

"Are you okay?" he asked, when I stopped in front of him. Couldn't he just leave me alone?

"I'm fine," I said, trying not to make eye contact with him.

I was scared he would see the truth in my eyes. He would see that I was lying. I felt the heat of his gaze on me.

"I've got to go," I insisted when I saw the bus arrive at the bus stop.

"I'll give you a lift home," he offered as he stuffed his hands into the front pockets of his jeans.

There was no way I could let that happen. Grant had warned me that he would kill Damien if he saw him with me again.

"I can't," I answered as I tried to walk around him, but he grabbed my wrist. I stopped but I kept my eyes glued to the ground, unable to look him in the eye.

"I know what happened," he whispered.

CHAPTER EIGHT

Haven

My eyes shot to his.

What did he mean, he knew what happened? There was no way he could know that my mom had died, I hadn't told anyone.

I stood silently in front of him with my eyes wide, waiting for him to tell me what he knew. He still held my wrist gently in his hand—maybe he thought I was still going to try and make a run for it. I felt my heart race with the fear that he would discover what an unfeeling monster I was.

"I heard the ladies in reception talking about it," he said softly. He watched me closely for a reaction. The school would have been notified. Damn the gossiping ladies in the office.

It was like lifting the lid to the bottle of my secrets. If there weren't a lid to keep my secrets firmly bottled up, they would escape one by one before they would all come out. To stay alive, I had to keep my secret.

"I don't want to talk about it," I whispered to him as I pulled my wrist from his hand.

"You can't keep it bottled up," he said, stuffing his hands

into the pockets of his jeans. "If you don't find a way to deal with it it'll fester inside and tear you apart."

His eyes looked haunted.

Why did it sound like he was talking from experience? He didn't know my history or why I felt no grief for my mother dying. He would never understand why there was no grief to deal with.

"I'm not going to talk about it," I told him, with a determined look.

"I'm sorry, I didn't mean to push. I'm just trying to help," he said with a shrug. His gaze dropped to the floor.

I felt bad that I was pushing him away but it was for the best. He looked over his shoulder and toward the bus stop. My eyes followed his. The bus had left already. I could feel the anxiety clenching at my stomach. I'd have to walk home because I couldn't let Grant see me with Damien again.

"Can I at least give you a lift home?" he asked when he turned back to me.

"No," I said as I walked around him. I had to fight the urge to look back over my shoulder at him.

It was one thing for Grant to hurt me, I'd been handling it for years, but I couldn't stomach the thought of Grant hurting Damien. I'd only gotten a few minutes away from the school before I heard a car pull up next to me. I didn't have to look to know it was Damien.

"Get in the car," he ordered through the window of his car. I ignored him and continued to walk.

I had to keep him away from me but he was making it nearly impossible. Why did he have to be so stubborn? I heard a car door slam and I turned to see him walk around the front of his car.

"Don't make me put you in the car," he warned with a steely edge in his voice. Why was he making it so hard? I knew from the determined look on his face that he would put me in the car if I didn't get in on my own.

I held his gaze for a minute and then his features softened.

"Please, it's my fault you missed the bus," he pleaded. He was just trying to help, but he was making things worse.

Why couldn't he just leave me alone? He took a step toward me and I held my hands up.

"Okay." I finally gave in, knowing I had no choice. I walked to the passenger side as he opened the door for me. Once I was inside he walked around the front of the car and got in.

I didn't look at him as he started up the car. I felt like I was watching an accident happen in slow motion and there was nothing I could do to stop it. He had no way of knowing that by trying to help me he was putting us both in danger.

"Please, could you just drop me off at the bus stop instead of my apartment?" I suggested nervously. If he dropped me off at the bus stop around the corner from my house, he would be safe in case Grant was at home.

He glanced in my direction and noted my nervousness. He looked at me thoughtfully for a moment as if he was trying to figure out why I suddenly didn't want him to drop me off at my apartment.

"Okay," he relented, looking back at the road.

I began to relax a little.

It wasn't long before he pulled up by the bus stop and he switched the car off. Even though we were around the corner from my apartment block, I still looked around nervously, hoping not to spot Grant.

"Thanks," I muttered. I reached for my bag and opened the passenger door, but before I could get out he reached for my wrist to keep me from leaving the car.

"I don't want what happened to me to happen to you," he revealed softly. His eyes had that haunted look again.

He was definitely talking from experience. I couldn't help but wonder who he'd lost. Was it a close family member or a friend?

"I know," I said. I still couldn't stop the nervous fear that somehow Grant would see us somehow.

"If you need anything, just call me," he murmured, and he released my wrist. He gave me one last look before he started his car. I got out and shut the door.

No matter how hard I'd tried to keep away from people, Damien and Chris had gotten too close. Now everything around me felt like it was starting to unravel.

I hurried home. While I walked around the corner and then up the stairs toward the apartment, I started to think of something I could tell Damien to keep him away from me.

He'd seen that I was damaged like he was and that was why he'd made it his mission to watch out for me. Somehow I had to come up with a way to keep him away. The abuse had escalated and I knew without a doubt that Grant was capable of murder. I hesitated for a while outside the apartment door. I couldn't help the nervous fear that settled over me as I reached for the door handle.

Now that my mom wasn't around anymore I knew the abuse would get even worse, and I just needed that moment to build up enough courage to open the door and step inside.

I stepped inside the apartment and I closed the door behind me. I took a few steps toward the living room and I was about to peer into the kitchen to see if Grant was there when he stepped through the doorway. He glared at me and I took a step backward. I wasn't sure what had set him off but he was going to give me a beating. There was no doubt about that. I could see it in his eyes.

He took a step closer to me and then I watched in horror as his right hand curled into a fist. I felt the pain explode in my head when his fist hit the side of my face. I dropped my schoolbag and it landed with a thud on the floor. It was such a vicious hit that I put my arms up to stop him.

Everything slowed down while the pain throbbed in my head. I opened and closed my eyes as my eyesight blurred.

"I fucking told you!" he yelled at me and I flinched. I watched as he pulled his fist back and he hit me again. This time my left arm took the brunt of the hit while I cowered away from him. I felt the snap before I felt the pain. He'd broken my arm. I cried out in pain.

It was excruciating. It was worse than when he'd broken my arm when I was twelve. I cradled my broken arm close to my chest while I closed my eyes to try and block out the pain.

He wasn't finished with me yet.

"I told you to stay away from him. You think you're so clever, getting him to drop you off at the bus stop," he sneered at me. "I fucking saw you!"

How on earth had Grant seen Damien drop me off at the bus stop? It made no sense. The apartment was around the corner.

"I went to the shop and I saw the two of you when I walked out," he revealed when he saw my confusion. His eyes darkened with anger. He'd seen us and then he'd come back to the apartment to ambush me.

My worst fears were becoming a reality. Terror gripped me when I realized I'd be lucky if I made it through this beating alive.

The next fist hit my eye and my head flew back. Pain exploded in my head. I was in agony now. I wanted to touch my eye but I couldn't stop cradling my injured arm.

I lay on the floor in a haze of pain as he knelt down next to me. A cold, evil smile spread across his face. He looked like he was enjoying every moment of this.

The adrenalin pumping through my veins staved off the pain from my wounds. I felt his fist connect with my shoulder. Pain swept through me and I screamed. I couldn't take much more, I felt like every inch of my body was screaming out in agony.

"Shut up," he snarled at me. He stood up and he kicked me in the stomach. I cried for him to stop but he just kept going. Kick after kick, I lost count of how many I endured.

I struggled to breathe, my chest hurt. My one eye had swollen completely shut and I could barely see out of my other eye.

"Please, no more," I whispered, while I hung on desperately to hold onto consciousness, trying to fight the urge to let my body down and give into the darkness. He looked down at me and laughed. I groaned and tried to take a breath, but my lungs wouldn't work. I could only breathe short and shallow breaths.

"You're going to join your mom," he told me as I watched him turn and disappear into the kitchen. My eye was already starting to swell.

What did he mean, I was going to join my mom? It took a few seconds for the meaning of what he'd just said to sink in. *He's going to kill me.*

I couldn't help the sob that welled up inside of me. I felt the sting of tears as I realized I was going to die. I'd always hoped that I would make it out of this alive but that hope had evaporated. He was going to kill me. The sob broke free from my lips as I felt the wet tears begin to slide down my battered face. I struggled to breathe because of the pain and the emotion breaking free from me.

All through the seven years that this had been happening to me I'd never cried. It was how I'd kept it all together. I'd always feared that if I broke down and cried I would fall apart and I'd just give up. For the first time in seven years, I let the tears free, and a heartbreaking sob racked my broken body as I waited for him to finish me off.

I heard his footsteps as he re-entered the lounge and knelt down next to me again. I watched in horror as I saw him holding a knife in his hand.

Oh. My. God.

He was going to stab me. For a brief moment my eyes connected with his and I saw the evil that lived within him.

Fear locked the air in my lungs and I lay there unable to get away or fight him off. Another sob tore through me as I realized that these were going to be my final moments.

"Please," I whispered as the tears ran down my face. I was pleading for my life.

He said nothing as he pushed the knife into my stomach. I screamed. The pain was worse than anything I'd ever felt. It felt like a hot, molten lance slicing into my body.

My body began to shut down as the pain became unbearable. I lay as still as I could to try and ease the pain. I closed my eyes.

I heard him walk into the kitchen and I heard water running. Then I heard his footsteps closer to me. I held my breath, trying not to move. If he thought I was dead, he might leave me alone.

A minute passed and then I heard some shuffling and the sound of a door opening and slamming shut. Slowly, I opened my eye and looked around. He'd left the apartment.

I had no idea how long he would be gone for. I felt the blood oozing onto my hand that held the knife still embedded in my stomach. He probably left hoping that by the time he returned I would have bled out.

My school bag was within reach. Then I remembered the phone that Damien had given me.

I bit down on my lip as I tried to reach for the bag with my broken arm. Every slight movement closer to the bag was absolute agony but I couldn't give up. No matter how bad the pain was I was still conscious, and this was my only chance.

If he came back before I could get help, I was dead. The pain from my stomach reminded me that even if I got help, I might bleed out before they arrived.

I gasped as I reached my schoolbag and pulled it closer. A wave of pain hit me and I bit down on my lip to keep from screaming.

When my hand found the phone, I pulled it out of the bag. I wasn't even sure how to work it. I tried to think back to how Damien had shown me how to dial his number. I pushed the speed dial for Damien and then I put the phone against my ear. The pain was so intense that I bit down on my lip again as I listened to the phone ring.

First ring, second ring, third ring. With every ring I felt myself lose hope.

Then he answered.

"Hey," he said.

"Damien—" I gasped against the phone as the pain tore through me again. I groaned. A wave of pain washed over me and left me gasping.

"What's wrong?" he asked. I could hear the nervous edge in his voice.

"I—"

But I couldn't finish my sentence. Everything began to blur as I released the phone and I slipped into the darkness, where there was no more pain.

CHAPTER NINE

Haven

I heard his voice. It was desperate.

"Haven, open your eyes," he pleaded. I was fighting through the darkness toward his voice. The pain seeped back and I began to whimper. Everything hurt. I could feel the pain radiating from my stomach.

"Help is on the way," he soothed hoarsely. I recognized the voice: it was Damien. He'd come to help me.

"Hurry up," I heard him yell. He was talking to someone else. I tried to open my eyes but the one was swollen shut. I couldn't see well through the other eye because everything was blurry.

"Damien," I said as I tried to breathe, but my chest hurt too much. I felt the tears slide down the side of my face.

I was still alive but I was in bad shape. Grant had managed to damage me on the outside as much as he'd damaged me on the inside.

"I'm here. Just hold on, they're nearly here," he reassured me. I heard the hitch in his voice. He was scared. And so was I.

"Please stay with me," he pleaded when I whimpered

again. "Keep your eyes open and stay with me."

I wanted to do as he asked but I felt cold. I think I might have lost too much blood. I heard additional voices.

Voices rattled off vitals and medical jargon. The paramedics were here. I felt a prick in my arm. I couldn't hold on anymore. I felt the numbness spread through my body and the pain begin to subside. I could feel the touch of the hands of the paramedics as they examined my arm and the knife in my stomach.

Through my haze I heard the paramedic say, "We need to get her to a hospital now!"

"Please don't let her die," I heard Damien whisper to them before I passed out.

Beep. Beep.

I felt disoriented and my mouth was dry. The incessant beeping continued. My eyes wouldn't open—they felt like they'd been glued closed. I tried to move, but my body felt too heavy. Memories of what happened flooded back, and my heart rate increased. The beeping began to speed up.

"It's okay," I heard Damien say. "You're safe."

Those words broke something inside of me, and I felt the tears escape and slide down my face. And my vision blurred. I hadn't felt safe in seven years, and I'd nearly died. I didn't know if I would ever feel safe again.

"Shh, it's okay. I'm here, I won't let anything happen to you," he assured me. I felt his hand wrap around mine. My hand hurt a little and it felt like a drip had been put into my hand.

Then I remembered being stabbed and I moved my free hand, which I could feel was in some sort of cast, to the place in my stomach where Grant had stabbed me. The knife was gone.

More tears slid down my face at the reality of what had happened and how close I'd come to dying.

"I won't let anyone hurt you ever again," Damien promised me as I felt him tighten his hold on my hand.

A fresh wave of tears slid down my face at the fear that Grant would find me and finish me off. The fact that I was lying in the hospital with every part of my body battered attested to the fact that Grant had meant every word when he'd told me he would kill me.

"You need to rest," he told me. "You're safe. I promise I won't leave you."

Memories of what had happened flitted through my mind and I felt my heart begin to pound against my chest as the fear took over. The beeping from the monitor began to speed up again. The air locked in my lungs and I couldn't breathe. Panic began to rise inside of me.

"Nurse," I heard Damien yell when the heart monitor began to sound an alarm.

Nurses rushed into the room.

"You need to leave the room," one nurse said to Damien.

I went into full panic mode and I struggled to draw a breath in, and just when I thought my heart would explode because it felt like it was pounding against my chest, I felt my body begin to relax.

"It's okay, you're just having a panic attack," I heard a female voice say to me. "I've given something to calm you down so that you can rest."

Whatever they'd given me began to ease the panic inside me, and I felt like I was floating in a bubble. My heartbeat returned to normal as I began to breathe easier and I drifted off to sleep.

The next time I woke up I could feel more pain and my body ached. The beeping was still coming from a monitor beside me. I felt someone holding my hand and turned to see Damien sleeping with his head next to my hand.

He looked exhausted and there were dark circles under his eyes. I wanted to reach out and touch his face, but I didn't want to wake him up. His midnight-black hair fell across his forehead.

It was dark and a soft light illuminated the hospital room. I wondered how long I'd been out of it for.

I looked down to see a drip in my hand that lay beside Damien. A cast encased my other arm from my elbow to my wrist. I remembered how I'd panicked before and I didn't want that to happen again, so I took a deep breath and tried to calm myself down.

Thoughts began to race through my mind and I couldn't help but fear what would happen to me. Did they know that Grant had done this to me? But there was no way they could know that, could they?

The only thought that gave me some sort of comfort was the fact that I hadn't seen Grant since I'd been in the hospital, which meant he wasn't trying to pretend everything was okay. That either meant that he'd taken off or that the police had him in custody.

With my mother gone and the fact that I still had four months to go before I turned eighteen, I couldn't help but fear what would happen to me now. I had no other family, so would they put me into foster care? My heart rate began to speed up and I could hear the beeps from the monitor speeding up as well.

I took a breath and released it to calm down.

"You're awake," Damien whispered as I felt his hand stroke mine.

I'd been so engrossed in my thoughts that I hadn't

realized he'd woken up. His eyes softened as he gazed at me with a weak smile.

"How are you feeling?" he asked as he shifted closer to me with the chair.

For the first time since the abuse had started, it was out in the open for someone to see, and I felt vulnerable. I'd tried so hard to keep my secret and the fact that it wasn't a secret anymore was difficult for me to process. The sympathy in his eyes was too much and I felt a pressure build up inside. I swallowed the emotion down, trying to keep from crying, but then I saw the concerned look and it undid me.

"Shh, it's okay," he soothed as a tear slipped down my face. I felt his fingers brush the tear from my face gently.

I closed my eyes to try and shut out what I wasn't ready to face. I wasn't ready for someone to see the reality of what my life had been like for the last seven years. I took a breath and released it.

"If I keep upsetting you, they're going to kick me out of your room," he teased softly. I knew he was trying to lighten the mood but the fear that he would be forced to leave me alone scared me and I tightened my hold on his hand.

"Don't leave," I managed to whisper hoarsely.

He shifted the chair closer to me as he held my hand gently in his.

"I'm not going anywhere," he assured me as his gaze held mine. Believing him, I loosened my hold on his hand.

"How are you feeling?" he asked. I felt his thumb stroke the outside of my hand as he watched me.

"Thirsty," I croaked. He offered me some water from a cup with a straw. He helped me lift my head and I managed to take a couple of sips from the straw. The cool water soothed my dry throat.

"Thank you," I murmured.

Silence settled between as for a few minutes as he waited

patiently for me to take everything in. I gazed down at my broken arm in the cast. My fingers gently touched my swollen eye and I winced from the pain. Dark blue and black bruises covered most of my visible skin. I knew the bruises hidden by the hospital gown would be worse.

"How long have I been here?" I whispered. I'd been in and out of consciousness a couple of times but I had no idea how long I'd been here for.

"A few days," he answered.

Days!

"What day is it?" I asked incredulously.

"Sunday."

I couldn't believe that I'd been out for nearly four days.

"Are you in any pain?" he asked with concerned eyes. It reminded me of what had happened. My hand reached down to my stomach and I touched my stomach gently.

I was afraid of what came next and I was unable to talk because I could feel the emotion clogging my throat.

"I don't want to upset you," he started, his eyes shifting nervously to mine as he ran his free hand through his hair, "but I need to know what happened."

My eyes held his and I remained silent. I'd been keeping silent for so long it was hard to tell the truth. He released a heavy sigh when he realized I wasn't going to talk.

"Haven. I found you with a knife in your stomach and you'd been beaten black and blue," he explained as he winced at the memory.

I watched him with wide eyes and as he relayed what happened. Bits and pieces of what had happened flitted through my mind.

"You'd lost a lot of blood and the paramedics tried to stabilize you so they could get you to the hospital in time," he informed me. His eyes showed his emotion and he swallowed hard.

I closed my eyes for a moment, taking it all in.

Grant's voice echoed in my head. *You're going to see your mom,* he'd said to me just before he'd stabbed me.

"Haven, the doctors found older injuries." With that one sentence I knew that he knew about the abuse. When I opened my eyes, I averted my gaze, unable to look at him. Years and years of lying were over. Whether I wanted it or not, my secret was out in the open for all to see.

I felt his fingers gently touch my chin and lift my eyes to his.

"I'm so sorry," he whispered to me. His eyes glistened. I felt the sting of tears, but I refused to cry.

What was he sorry for?

"I had no idea," he said. I'd spent years keeping the secret from everyone around me and I'd been good at it. It wasn't until I'd moved here that it had become more and more difficult to keep people at bay.

"I'm sorry I never realized what was happening. If I had, I could have stopped it," he whispered to me. His eyes were haunted. I squeezed his hand.

"You couldn't have stopped it," I whispered hoarsely. My throat was dry and a little sore.

"The cops are going to want to know what happened," he told me softly watching for my reaction. "They've been able to piece most of it together, but they still have some questions for you."

What had the police managed to piece together? Did they know it had been Grant who'd tried to kill me?

"They are looking for your stepfather, Grant."

"I don't want to talk to them," I said, shaking my head and trying to sit up. I needed to leave. Pain sliced through my stomach and I slumped back, gasping.

"You need to take it easy. You've had surgery and your body is still healing," he said with concern as he leaned closer with my hand still in his.

"I don't want to talk about what happened," I reinforced in a whisper, my eyes begging him to understand. Panic began to build up in me.

"I know you're scared but you have to tell them what happened so they can put him away," he said fiercely. He didn't understand that I was scared of Grant. My fear for him had reached a new level when he'd tried to kill me. I knew the only way I would be safe is if Grant was no longer breathing.

I shook my head fiercely. The beeping on the heart monitor began to beep quicker as my heart rate increased.

"You can't let him get away with this," he said. I felt the panic began to build up more. "I'm sorry, I didn't mean to upset you."

I tried not to think about Grant so that I could calm myself down.

"I won't let him hurt you ever again," he whispered softly, his eyes darkening with emotion. I closed my eyes tightly, wanting to believe him, but the reality was that I would probably be put into foster care and I would never see Damien again. I would be on my own.

I felt so tired. Maybe it was the emotional roller coaster or the fear that had suddenly drained me of all my energy. I let out a sigh. My eyelids began to droop and as much as I tried to stay awake I couldn't keep my eyes open.

"Sleep, I promise I'll watch over you," Damien whispered next to my ear.

I'd never trusted anyone before other than Chris, but I knew I could trust Damien. I drifted to sleep as I felt a feathered kiss to my forehead.

My sleep was restless, I dreamed of the attack. It replayed in my nightmares exactly how it had played out in reality. I thrashed against the inevitable of the knife pushing into my stomach as I screamed from the pain.

I heard a voice say, "Shh, it's going to be okay, Haven."

It was Damien. My subconscious believed his words, because my nightmares vanished and I fell into a peaceful sleep.

CHAPTER TEN

Haven

I wasn't sure how long I'd slept for, but it had to have been a while, because the sun was shining brightly into the hospital room.

True to his word, Damien was sitting beside the bed when I woke up.

"Hi," he greeted as he watched me closely.

"Hi," I greeted back hoarsely. My throat still hurt. I gave him a weak smile. My body ached and the wound on my stomach was still tender. I glanced around the room. The heart monitor was gone.

Thank goodness. That beeping had started to get on my nerves a bit. It was probably a good sign that it was gone. Maybe I would be out of here soon. Then the reality of my situation set in. I had nowhere to go. I managed to sit up with Damien's help. The door opened and someone stepped inside.

"The coffee machine is broken—" the stranger muttered, and then stopped when he saw me and he smiled. He was dressed in a smart, dark-gray suit.

I glanced from Damien to the stranger—there was no

doubt about it, the resemblance was astonishing. They shared the same midnight-black hair, the same dark-blue eyes and the same dark-olive skin. The stranger looked like an older version of Damien. It was his father.

I couldn't help the fear that gripped me when Damien's father took a step closer. I tightened my hold on Damien's hand as my eyes flickered anxiously to him.

"It's okay, he's not going to hurt you," he soothed. It was ridiculous that I was scared of someone I'd never met before, especially since I knew he was Damien's father. His father gave me a tentative smile.

"He's my dad," Damien explained. I didn't need the explanation; I'd already figured that out. It still didn't ease my fear.

"Haven, Dad—Dad, Haven," he introduced, watching my reaction. His father gave me a slight nod as I stared at him.

"How are you feeling?" he asked gently, keeping his distance, maybe trying to ease my fear.

"I'm okay," I mumbled. I forced myself to relax, but I still held Damien's hand tightly in mine. Not every man was like Grant, I had to remember that.

An awkward silence followed. I didn't know why his father was here.

"My father would like to talk to you, if that's okay?" Damien asked softly. My eyes flickered from him to his dad as he waited patiently for me to answer.

"Only if you stay," I murmured, feeling nervous all of a sudden. Damien's father smiled at me and I could see a warmth in him that Grant had never had. I could see that he wouldn't hurt me, but I still felt safer with Damien around.

"Sure," he said and then released my hand and stood up. He moved past his dad as his dad sat down next to me. I clasped my hands together. Damien stood at the foot of the bed.

"I'd like you to call me Steven," he told me. I nodded my head, even though I wasn't sure I'd ever really see him again.

"I know you've had a lot happen to you in the last week and I know you're scared." He paused for a moment. He had no idea how scared I'd been for the last seven years.

"Damien told me about you and what happened. He also told me about the fact that your mom just died as well," he continued.

I had no idea what any of this had to do with him. My eyes fell on Damien, who was watching me silently with his hands in his pocket. It also made me wonder exactly what Damien had told him.

"Do you have any family?" he asked softly.

I swallowed hard and shook my head. I had no one.

"We would like to help you," he said with a sympathetic smile. I frowned. I wasn't sure exactly how he could help me.

On top of everything that had happened to me the thought of that happening scared me.

"My wife and I have discussed it and we would like you to come and stay with us."

My jaw dropped open and my eyes widened in surprise. I hadn't seen that coming. I looked to Damien, who was watching me anxiously. Had he known about this? I glanced back to his father, who gave me an encouraging smile.

"I don't understand," I whispered. How would it be okay just to go and stay with them? Surely there was more to it than that.

"I'm a lawyer and if it's okay with you I could get started on the paperwork to get temporary custody of you until you turn eighteen," he explained. "But that doesn't mean that you need to move out when you turn eighteen. What I'm trying to say is that we would like to take you in and give you a home, not just a place to live."

I blinked and felt the sting of tears. I hated feeling so vulnerable.

"I don't want to push you to make a decision, so think about it and let me know," he said with a friendly smile as he stood to leave. He glanced to his son and then nodded his head.

When he left, Damien returned to the seat next to me. I was still trying to process what his father had asked me. My eyes lifted to his when he reached for my hand again.

"Why would your parents care about what happens to me?" I asked. Their actions didn't make sense to me. The people that should have loved me hadn't and strangers that had no reason to care for me were offering me a home.

"It's a long story," he answered vaguely with a touch of sadness in his features. Whatever the long story was about wasn't something Damien was comfortable talking about. "They want to help you. My father is a lawyer and my mom's a doctor. They'll be able to provide you with everything you need. When I told them what had happened to you, my mom cried. They want to be able to give you a stable and loving home."

I knew there was more to it than that, but I wasn't going to push him. The truth was that I was petrified of being placed into a foster home. I'd have to live with complete strangers and then I would be all on my own again. At least if I agreed to being placed with the Knights, I would stay here where I had Damien and Chris. And possibly, with time, I would be able to trust his parents as well. When I thought about it, there wasn't much of a choice. Staying with the Knights would be better than going into foster care; but, once, I had trusted Grant, and look where that had gotten me.

"How do you feel about it?" I asked softly.

This would impact him as well, and I wanted to know if

he was okay with it.

"I think it's a great idea," he answered, his eyes wide with excitement. "After everything that has happened you need a little light in your life and my family would be able to give it to you. My mom always wanted a girl, so she is going to spoil you rotten. Besides, I want to be able to keep you safe and I can't do that if you're not with me."

I wasn't interested in material things. What meant more to me than anything wasn't something you could put a price to. For a few minutes there was silence and he watched me expectantly.

"I need to think about it," I told him. He looked a little disappointed but he tried to mask it with a weak smile.

"You have to understand that almost everyone I've ever trusted before, including my own mother, who was supposed to love me unconditionally, betrayed that trust in the worst way possible." I paused for a moment to collect myself. It was hard to voice that.

My mother hadn't cared when Grant had hit me, she hadn't even flinched when he'd broken my arm the first time. She'd been annoyed with me about it. I'd trusted my mom to keep me safe and she'd failed. Instead of stopping the abuse and kicking Grant out, she'd ignored what was going on, leaving me vulnerable to Grant's abuse.

"But I trust you," I whispered. His hand tightened around mine. "And I trust Chris."

They were the only ones I trusted at the moment. Maybe with time, I would be able to trust others.

"When you didn't show up for the school the day after the attack, Chris began to freak out a little. I haven't been to school since the attack either, so he thought I might know something. He tracked a couple of my friends and threatened them with some choice words before they relented and gave him my number," he told me. I felt bad that Chris had been worried.

"He has been calling a couple of times a day to get updates. He has been to the hospital a couple of times but they wouldn't let him in to see you and they wouldn't give him any details about you. The only reason I've been allowed in is because I was the one that found you, and when they asked who I was I told them I was your boyfriend."

Boyfriend. I looked at him, a little shocked that he'd lied.

"I would have told them I was the pope to get in to see you," he admitted seriously. My heart tightened at his admission.

"What did you tell him?" I asked, not sure if I wanted everyone to know all the details of what had happened. I knew Chris well enough to know he was persistent.

"Honestly, I wasn't sure if you wanted any more people to know what really happened. I didn't know how much he knew before, but I didn't want to take a chance at telling him something he didn't know," he explained with a worried look. He was right—I wanted to limit the number of people that would find out the true details of the events that had landed me in hospital. "I told him you'd been in an accident. I wanted to be able to give you the choice on whether you told him the truth or not, if he didn't already know the truth about what was happening to you. It wasn't my secret to tell."

This boy sitting in front of me was so thoughtful that I felt my throat constrict. When my heart fluttered as I looked at him I reminded myself that he didn't care for me in that way, that he only cared for me as a friend. What he'd told Chris hadn't even been a partial truth, it had been a complete lie. Nothing that happened to me had been an accident.

"Did he know what was happening?" he asked me with a tight jaw and his eyes reserved. I looked him, confused at his obvious attempt to keep his temper under control.

I shook my head and he began to relax. The tightening in

his jaw eased and his eyes softened.

"I don't know what I would have done if he had known and he'd done nothing about it," he said. His reaction surprised me, and I had no doubt he would have hurt Chris if he hadn't been oblivious to what was happening to me.

"He knew nothing," I assured him. I doubted that Chris would have done nothing if he'd found out, and that was why I'd tried so hard to keep my secret from him.

I wanted to see Chris, but I was worried about what he would say when he discovered what I'd been hiding. It wasn't my fault, but I couldn't help feeling ashamed. It was hard having it out in the open for everyone to see.

I wondered what my face looked like. I touched my fingers to my face—it still hurt. Suddenly, I had a desperate need to see my face. I'd seen my arms, they were covered in bruises, and my face probably looked the same. I tried to sit up and move off the bed, which was a little difficult with the drip in one hand and the cast on my other arm.

"You can't get up, you need to take it easy," he reminded me sternly as he held my shoulders to try and keep my in the hospital bed. A need I couldn't control made me shrug out of his hold and I winced at the slight pain in my stomach.

"I need to see my face," I told him, determined to make it to the small ensuite bathroom. Understanding dawned on his features.

"I'll find a mirror, you stay put," he ordered while he helped me back into the bed and I slumped back.

He wasn't gone for long before he reappeared with a small compact mirror and handed it to me.

At my questioning glance he said, "I asked the nurses in reception if any of them had a mirror."

I held the compact in my hand for a moment; I hesitated, trying build my courage. It wasn't going to look good, and I knew that. Knowing was one thing, but seeing it was completely different. I took a deep breath and opened the compact and looked at my reflection. Nothing could have prepared me for the image I saw.

I gasped at my reflection, which was barely recognizable. Both of my eyes were circled in dark bruises and my one eye was red. Dark bruises covered nearly my entire face. I bit down on my lip to keep my emotions from escaping. Tears welled up in my eyes. I touched my cheek as a tear slid down. The skin under my fingertips felt tender. I felt a sob well up inside of me as another tear slid down my face.

Years and years of abuse had led to this. Grant had tried to kill me with his bare hands and when he'd failed he'd gone to get a knife. The sob I'd tried to keep from welling up inside of me broke free and tears began to stream down my face.

Without a word Damien stood up and pulled me gently into his arms as he took the compact from me and shoved it into his jeans. I cried and cried until there were no more tears. I felt numb inside. Damien eased me back gently and brushed the tears from my face.

"You're beautiful," he reassured me, holding my face gently in his hands, careful not to hurt me. I didn't explain to him that I hadn't cried because of what I looked like.

When I'd seen my reflection I'd realized how close I'd come to dying and it had hit me hard. No matter how hard I tried, the tears I'd been keeping at bay for years had overwhelmed me. I felt emotionally raw and tired.

"I'd like to see Chris," I told Damien as he released my face. His eyes still watched my closely.

"I'll call him," he said softly. "Try and get some sleep, I'll wake you up when he gets here."

"Thank you," I said as I closed my eyes.

CHAPTER ELEVEN

Haven

I felt a gentle nudge.

"Haven," I heard a voice whisper.

I was sleeping so nicely and I didn't want to wake up. Keeping my eyes closed, I tried to ignore the voice. A soft touch of a hand on my arm shook me gently.

"Haven." The voice was more insistent this time.

Finally, resigned to the fact that the voice wasn't going to go away, I opened my eyes. The familiar face of Damien smiled as he leaned over me.

"I'm sorry to wake you up, but Chris is here," he informed me.

He helped me sit up and I glanced behind him to see Chris looking at me, horrified. It reminded me how bad my injuries were. He masked his horror and gave me one of his signature wide grins even though it never reached his eyes.

Damien stepped away and Chris took his place. I smiled weakly. I was happy to see him, but nervous about everything else. I was finally going to tell him the truth.

"Hi," he greeted.

"Hey," I greeted back nervously.

"You had me so worried," Chris whispered as he leaned forward to hug me, trying not to hurt me as he gave me a gentle squeeze. I hugged him back and my eyes connected with Damien watching us from the foot of the bed. My throat thickened with emotion.

"I'll be outside if you need me," Damien informed me when he left, closing the door quietly behind him.

Chris pulled back and he scanned my face. He was trying his best to keep calm in front of me but I could see that he was upset.

"What happened?" he whispered to me. I swallowed hard, trying to gather the courage to tell him the truth.

He sat down in the chair vacated by Damien and he waited patiently for me to answer his question.

"My home life hasn't been very good." It was the understatement of the year.

"Who did this to you?" He had gasped at the mention of the word home.

"My stepfather," I answered hoarsely, trying to keep myself together.

I saw the flash of anger in his eyes and his lips tightened together.

"Why would he do this to you?" he asked. His eyes flickered over my injuries.

"I don't know," I whispered as my lip trembled a little. I'd been asking myself that same question for the last seven years. I didn't know why.

"Has this happened before?" he asked as he reached for my hand and took it into his own.

I swallowed hard as I held his gaze and gave him a nod. He closed his eyes and watched him deal with my revelation. When he opened his eyes he was clearly upset as he took a deep breath.

"I don't understand... where's your mom?" he asked,

trying to figure how this had been allowed to happen to me.

"She died this week," I said softly.

"I'm so sorry," he said, trying to comfort me. Then the penny dropped.

"Your mom allowed this to happen to you?" he asked.

I felt a sharp pain in my chest at being reminded that my mom hadn't loved me enough to protect me from him, and that she'd been responsible for bringing him into our home.

"I can't talk about it yet," I told him, shaking my head. I wasn't ready to tell him everything yet. I needed time to work through things before I could tell him everything he wanted to know.

"I'm sorry," he whispered.

"There was nothing you could have done," I assured him softly as I gave his hand a reassuring squeeze from mine.

He couldn't blame himself for what happened to me. The only person to blame for what had happened to me was the monster that had tried to take my life from me.

"If I'd known what was happening to you I would have tried to help you," he assured me softly. His eyes were still fixed on the bruises on my face.

"I know," I whispered.

"Are you in any pain?" he asked, his eyes taking in the cast on my left arm.

"Not really. They're giving me pain medication, so the pain isn't that bad," I explained while I touched my stomach. At least Chris didn't know I'd been stabbed as well.

He looked visibly upset as it was, there was no need to upset him more. There weren't many people in the world that I cared about, but Chris was special to me, and I wanted to protect him from the all the ugly details of my attack.

"I was so worried about you when you skipped school," he began to explain. "It was only when both you and Damien weren't there that I thought he might know something," he said. I listened patiently to him. "I didn't have any way to contact you to find out if you were okay so I went and got Damien's number from his friends. It wasn't easy getting his number, it was like trying to draw blood from stone. But I used my charm and they handed it over."

I couldn't help the smile that touched my lips as I imagined Chris stomping over to Damien's group of friends, who were the most popular kids in the school, and demanding his number. That was something I loved about Chris—his outgoing, take-no-crap personality. It was also the reason why we were friends in the first place.

"All he told me was that you'd been in an accident and that you were in the hospital," he explained. "I tried to come and visit you but they wouldn't let me in. They explained that only your immediate family and your boyfriend were allowed in to visit you."

At the mention of the word boyfriend he wiggled his eyebrows at me. I rolled my eyes.

"So is Damien your boyfriend?" he asked with a smile.

"No," I assured him. "He lied to the nurses so they'd let him in to see me."

"That may be the case, but I can see the way he looks at you," he revealed. "He cares about you."

I knew that Damien cared about me.

"How did Damien even know about the attack?" he asked after a moment.

"I called him after it happened," I answered softly. I hated remembering what happened and I wished my memories from the attack would disappear. It would be easier. "He'd given me a phone in case I needed anything. He called the ambulance."

I could see understanding in his features as the pieces of the puzzle began to fit together.

"He didn't give me any details about what had happened

other than it being an accident."

"He was trying to protect me. He didn't know how much you knew and he said it wasn't his secret to tell," I explained. I wanted Chris to understand.

"I didn't like being kept in the dark but I get why he did it," he told me. "In the future, my number is also going to be programmed into your phone."

It was so like Chris.

"Is there a pen around here?" he asked, scanning the side table next to the hospital bed.

"Why are you looking for a pen?" I asked, confused as to why he suddenly needed one. He was already opening the drawer of the side table as he continued to search.

"Jackpot," he said when he closed the drawer, clutching a black pen.

With a devious smile he got up and walked around to the other side of the bed. It was only when he uncapped the pen and began to write on the cast on my arm that I realized why he'd been looking for a pen.

"As your best friend I get to write on your cast first," he said, absentmindedly scribbling a message.

"There, I'm done," he said as he began to chuckle.

I couldn't help but smile at his infectious laugh. It was only when I saw what he'd written that my laughter stopped and I glared at him playfully.

He laughed even harder as he doubled over, clutching his stomach.

His message on my cast read, *I love Damien Knight and I want to have his babies.*

I continued to glare at him as he tried to control his laughter. That was the thing about him: he had a way of easing a heavy emotional atmosphere with a small action that had him doubled over in laughter, and before I knew it I was smiling.

He was convinced that Damien's feelings for me went way beyond friendship, but I knew better. Damien had felt connected with me because he'd seen something in me that he recognized.

When Chris managed to get his laughter under control again he sat down in the seat next to my bed. He still had a wide grin plastered to his face as his green eyes sparkled with mischief.

"Thanks, now I'm going to have to walk around school with that message." I tried to frown and act like I was mad. The message wasn't big and it would be difficult to read unless you got a closer look, so I doubted anyone would see it.

"Ah, come on, it made you smile, didn't it?" he asked, still trying to get his laughter under control.

I couldn't help the smile that spread across my face. He was right—it had made me smile, and it had lifted me up from the heavy emotional rollercoaster I'd been on the last few days.

"I'll forgive you this time," I teased him.

The door opened and Damien stepped inside. He looked a little surprised to see us smiling.

"Visiting hours are over," he informed Chris. "The nurses will be coming around soon to clear the visitors out."

Chris stood up and leaned over to give me a hug.

"Any time you need to smile, just read the message," he suggested before he gave me a brief kiss on the cheek and then pulled away. "I'll be back again tomorrow."

He walked to the door and gave me one last smile.

"See you tomorrow," I said and then he left, closing the door behind him leaving me alone with Damien.

"He really does have a way with you, doesn't he?" said Damien softly, watching me closely. I was still smiling.

"Yeah…I guess so," I replied, feeling a little shy under his watchful gaze.

From the first time I'd met him, his bubbly and outgoing personality had steamrolled right into my heart, and I cared about him. I loved the way that he hadn't pushed me too much in the beginning. I loved the way that he noticed that I never brought lunch with me and had started to pack an additional one for me.

It was one of the sweetest things anyone had ever done for me.

"It's nice to see you smile," he said as he came to a stand beside me. He had his hands stuffed into the front pockets of his jeans.

"I haven't had a lot to smile about," I replied. My gaze dropped and I began to fidget with my hands. My smile began to wane as the memories of the attack began to filter back. For a while, I'd managed to forget, and the heaviness inside me had lightened.

"We'll change that," he whispered, taking my hand into his. I looked up at him and I saw a tenderness there that I'd never seen before.

I'd never been so affected by a boy before. When he was around I felt more aware of everything going on around me. I had no control over it. I shook my head to try and dislodge the thought. There was more important stuff to deal with than a crush on a boy. I'd nearly been murdered.

A decision still had to be made on whether I'd go to live with the Knights or go into foster care. I felt like my life was spiraling out of control and I was struggling to hold on. I took a deep breath and felt Damien rub my hand with his fingers.

The door opened. I couldn't help my hand tightening on Damien's when a doctor stepped into the room.

"Hi, Haven," he greeted with a smile as he walked to the bottom of my bed. "I'm Doctor Johnson."

He was tall and lean with short brown hair and brown eyes. He didn't look older than thirty.

"Hi," I mumbled softly. I couldn't help my immediate reaction. I struggled to relax around new people I didn't know, especially men.

He reached for a clipboard that I assumed had my patient file and had a look in it. I held my breath as I waited for him to speak.

"Relax," Damien whispered beside me. I released the breath I'd been holding as Damien gave my hand a reassuring squeeze.

"How are you feeling?" Dr. Johnson asked, putting the clipboard back at the bottom of my bed and coming to stand on the other side of the bed from Damien.

"Okay," I murmured, trying to keep my anxiety at bay. I knew what I was feeling was ridiculous because Damien was with me, and I knew that the doctor was here to help me and not hurt me. But years of abuse had unfortunately painted most men with the same brush as Grant. I couldn't stop the fear I felt.

"You're a very lucky girl," he commented. I knew he meant I was lucky I'd survived the attack, but the fact that I'd been abused for several long years didn't make me feel lucky at all.

"How is the pain?" he asked, with a concerned look.

"It's manageable," I replied. He looked at me with a little disbelief.

"I have you on a low dose of painkillers, so if you're in any pain I can give you more," he offered, his eyes still a bit wide with surprise.

"No, thank you."

I understood his surprised look. With the years and years of abuse, I'd built up a high pain tolerance.

"I just need to have a look at the wound to make sure it's

healing," he informed me. He waited for me to nod my head.

"Do you want me to step out?" Damien asked.

I shook my head. I needed him with me.

The doctor examined the wound on my stomach. He could tell from my body language that I was nervous. The doctor lifted the gauze and studied it for a moment. It was still red and the cut was a couple of inches long, with five stitches holding the wound together. I still had to come to terms with the fact that I'd have the scar for life—it would be something to remind me of what I'd endured and what I'd survived.

"It looks like it's healing well," he told me as he covered the wound with the gauze.

"You still need to take it easy, but if everything goes well you should be out of here in a couple of days," the doctor said, giving me his verdict.

I only had a couple of days to decide what I was going to do.

"I'll see you at the same time tomorrow," Dr. Johnson informed me as he left the room with a smile.

"That's good news," Damien said.

"Yeah…"

I couldn't help the slight panic at the thought that everything was happening faster than I could deal with.

"What's wrong?" he asked when he saw my panicked expression.

"It's just everything seems to be happening so fast and I haven't had time to think about your parents' offer," I babbled, and as I said the words my panic began to grow.

Damien leaned over so that our eyes were at the same level.

"Everything will be fine," he assured me.

CHAPTER TWELVE

Haven

Damien popped out a couple of hours later for a few minutes when the nurse came in to change the dressing on my wound. I was surprised when he walked back in the room with a girly, pink and flowery vanity bag. It was early evening already.

"My mom went and got you some stuff," he said as he handed me the bag. "She wasn't sure what you preferred so she bought you two of everything she thought you'd need."

I opened the bag. He wasn't kidding. I couldn't help but stare at the shampoos, conditioners and other toiletries. One body wash and body cream was vanilla fragranced, and the other set was rose fragranced. I felt the sting of tears as my bottom lip began to tremble slightly. I bit down hard on it to try and stop the emotional outburst that was about to take place. My eyes were still on the contents of the bag while I took a deep breath.

"Did she forget something?" he asked when he noticed I was still staring at the stuff in the bag.

"No," I croaked before swallowing my emotion back down.

"What's the matter?" he asked gently. His eyes were filled with concern.

"Nothing," I managed to whisper hoarsely.

"I can see something is wrong," he said softly, looking a little confused.

"It's just… I'm not used to people doing such generous things," I explained with a shrug.

"It's how parents are supposed to be," he explained. "They're supposed to do thoughtful things like this because they love you."

Only in my distant memories had my mom been the mother that had loved and cared for me. He stood in front of me for a minute in silence.

"Sorry," I mumbled when I felt the sting of tears.

"After everything you have been through, you're allowed to be emotional. It doesn't make you weak, it makes you human. Never think that you are weak. You've dealt with some seriously tough stuff and you never gave up. You're the strongest person I know," he expressed. I felt a flutter in my heart.

I was speechless.

"Cry if you need to," he whispered, his face only inches from mine. He was so close that I felt his breath tickle my face.

My eyes flickered to his lips for a moment and then my eyes darted back to his. He leaned in a little closer as his eyes remained fixed on my lips. I felt the butterflies in my stomach start to flutter at the anticipation of his lips touching mine.

The door opened and the night nurse walked in. He pulled away and I averted my gaze. Our first near kiss evaporated into thin air.

"I'm going to get a soda," he told me, unable to look at me directly as he shifted nervously beside me. "Do you want one?"

"No," I mumbled, glad he was going to give me a few minutes to collect myself.

"I won't be long," he assured me before he walked out the door.

The night nurse walked over to me and checked my drip.

"How are you feeling?" she asked while she adjusted the drip, giving me a friendly smile.

"I'm okay," I murmured. I still felt very nervous around strangers, but women didn't instill the same fear that men did.

"How is the pain?" she asked.

"It's fine," I answered, fidgeting with my hands to contain my nervousness.

"Would you like something to help you sleep tonight?" she asked. They'd asked me the same question the previous evening and I'd declined.

I was about to decline again, but then I decided it might help me get a decent night's sleep and keep the nightmares about Grant away.

"Yes, please," I replied.

"I'll be back in a few minutes," she said before she left the room.

Another nurse brought in a tray of food and I began to eat.

Thoughts of Damien began to monopolize my thoughts. My fingers touched my lips when I thought about what had nearly happened a few minutes before.

There was no doubt about how I felt about Damien—I'd wanted him to kiss me. There was enough to deal with without trying to complicate my life further with a boy, but I couldn't help the way I felt when I was around him. I wasn't sure if I'd begun to have feelings for him only because he'd been my pillar of strength while everything else around me was falling apart. If it hadn't been for him giving me the phone, I would have died. He'd saved my life.

I suppressed a laugh when I thought about his surname. Knight. And just like a knight, he'd swooped in and saved the day. But I didn't believe in fairy tales anymore. Besides, Damien wasn't exactly the love-professing and commitment type who was going to give me the happy ending that I'd read about in fairy tales.

I knew his reputation with girls. Chris had warned me about him before, although I hadn't seen him with a girl since he'd broken it off with Angela.

But what really baffled me was that I couldn't understand why he'd nearly kissed me. Was I just a girl he wanted to use, and then move onto the next one? That thought hurt. Over the past few days I'd depended on him so much, and I wouldn't know what I'd have done without him to lean on. I couldn't lose him.

So I made up my mind. I'd ignore the brief temptation to kiss him and I'd keep him at arm's length.

No girl wanted to be used and then discarded when they'd outgrown their use. But I could see why Damien had a line of girls waiting for the chance to have their go with him. Not only was he extremely good looking, he had a confidence about him that was attractive and hard to turn down.

That settled, my next decision to make was a major one. It was whether I should go stay with the Knights. It would be easy to just say yes to the Knights' offer, but I was scared. I trusted Damien, but I'd only met his dad once and I'd never met his mom. I was scared to take that leap of faith and trust again.

The thought of foster care did scare me. I'd heard a few horror stories. What if they were worse than Grant? I shuddered. It was hard to contemplate an evil worse than him.

At least I knew Damien and trusted him. I'd met his

father, and he seemed nice and friendly. I couldn't help but wonder what his mom was like.

Damien walked back into my room with a soda. His eyes avoided mine when he sat down in the chair next to my bed. He seemed to feel like I did: slightly uncomfortable.

When the nurse walked back in with a cup of water and my sleeping pill, I wasted no time in swallowing it. She picked up the tray of food and left.

Sleep would give me a reprieve from having to deal with Damien and thinking about all the stuff I needed to do, and decisions I needed to make. And hopefully I would get a good night's sleep as well. I'd never taken a sleeping pill before. I must have had a low tolerance for it, because minutes later I could feel my body relax. My eyelids grew heavier, and I drifted into a deep sleep.

When I woke up, Damien was sleeping. He was seated in the chair next to the bed and his head lay next to my hand as I watched him sleep. He'd pretty much spent all of his time with me. He was missing school but I couldn't help but feel grateful that he was with me. He made me feel safe, and after everything that had happened I needed that.

I wondered if the police had caught Grant. If Grant was in police custody, I wouldn't be so dependent on Damien. It wasn't fair to him that I needed him so much. He barely had a life outside of me at the moment.

Besides, I wasn't sure how much more school his parents would allow him to miss to be with me.

The only time he would disappear for an hour or so was when he went home to shower and change and that usually coincided with the morning visit from the doctor. I was still nervous around my doctor, so I would request one of the nurses to stay with me while the doctor did what he needed to.

Dr Johnson didn't get offended; he seemed to understand my nervousness around him.

With my hand so close to Damien I had to resist the urge to touch his hair. After our near-kiss yesterday, I couldn't deny that what I felt for him was more than feelings of friendship.

When the nurse brought my food in a little later, Damien finally woke up. Even though he'd gotten some sleep, it was uncomfortable trying to sleep in a chair, and I was sure he wasn't getting enough of it. He looked tired.

"I need to go home and shower and change," he said as he stood up and ran a hand through his hair. Even first thing in the morning with his unruly hair he was gorgeous.

"Sure," I said, and nodded my head.

His phoned dinged with a message. He reached for his phone and read the message.

"My mom wants to come and visit you this morning during visiting hours," he told me, tucking his phone into the front pocket of his jeans.

I nodded my head. I'd met Steven, Damien's father, already, so it seemed to be a good idea to meet his mom as well.

His mom had been so thoughtful to send me the vanity bag full of toiletries. I wasn't too nervous about meeting her because from her actions I could tell she was a very thoughtful person. I was actually looking forward to meeting her.

Damien left while I eyed the tray of food the nurse had brought in for me.

It was scrambled eggs and toast, with yogurt and some orange juice. When asked whether I wanted coffee or tea, I settled on tea.

Most people would turn their noses up at the thought of hospital food, but when you'd gone hungry more times than you could count, you appreciated everything you got. It wasn't long after I'd finished breakfast when the doctor came in for his morning visit. The day nurse looking after me for the morning followed in behind him. I gave the doctor a small smile.

"How are you feeling this morning?" he asked as he surveyed my file.

"Good," I replied. I was feeling better, although I probably still looked terrible. Since the first time I'd looked at myself in the mirror and fallen apart, I hadn't been brave enough to do it again.

"We can take out the drip today," he instructed the nurse. I felt relieved that I would finally be able to walk around without having to drag the drip with me. It also meant that I would be able to bathe myself.

"Everything is looking good, Haven," he informed me as he closed my patient file and handed it to the nurse. "You should be able to go home tomorrow."

I should have been happy that I was getting out of hospital tomorrow, but I still hadn't made up my mind on where I was going to go. The information the doctor had just given me would push me to make a decision today. I couldn't procrastinate over it any longer.

He left with a smile as the nurse started to take my drip out. There was a bruise where the needle had pierced the skin on my wrist. It was only a small bruise compared to the other bruises still decorating the rest of my body.

When the door open about twenty minutes later, I expected to see Damien, but instead an older lady stepped into my room, giving me a tentative smile.

"Hi," she said softly as she stepped closer. In her hand she held a bag.

"Hi," I greeted her back. I was almost always nervous around new people, but I felt completely relaxed around her.

"I'm Amy, Damien's mom," she introduced herself. I already knew who she was. Although Damien looked just like his father in many ways, there were a few physical traits he'd inherited from his mom, like the shape of his eyes and his mouth.

She was beautiful, with shoulder-length blond hair and vibrant turquoise eyes. She was slender and looked to be slightly taller than me. She was dressed in a suit with matching pants. I remember Damien telling me she was a doctor. She walked to the bed and sat down in the chair beside me. I could see her studying the bruises on my face and I saw her lip tremble for a moment before she regained her composure.

"How are you feeling?" she asked, her voice steady.

"I'm better," I answered softly. Physically, I was recovering, but mentally I wasn't sure if I would ever recover.

"I didn't come to see you to pressure you into a decision," she told me as she placed the bag on the floor next to the chair. "I wanted to meet you. I know you probably think it's weird for strangers to offer to take you in, but I want you to know that we have your wellbeing at heart and the best of intentions," she explained nervously.

I wanted to reach out and place my hand over hers so that she wouldn't be nervous.

"When Damien first told me what had happened to you, I was so upset," she said. "Children are meant to be loved and cherished, not mentally and physically abused, no matter what the circumstances are. I want you to know that you deserve a safe and loving environment to grow up in. My husband and I would like to give you that. There are no strings attached."

My bottom lip began to tremble at the impact of her words on me and a tear slid down my face.

"Oh, honey, I didn't mean to make you cry," she said

softly as she reached for me and pulled me into a gentle hug. I didn't like to be touched and I was usually fussy over who I felt comfortable touching me, but it seemed to be different with Amy.

I felt totally relaxed with her, and when she touched me I didn't feel a need to pull away. For the first time in a while I felt what it should be like to be hugged by a mother.

My tears began to flow as I hugged her back.

My decision was made.

CHAPTER THIRTEEN

Haven

I pulled back from the hug with Amy and I looked up at her.

"I'd like to come and stay with you," I whispered, my face soaked with tears. I knew it was the right choice.

"I'll get Steven to start on the paperwork," she whispered hoarsely to me. I think they needed me as much as I needed them.

"I'd like to start decorating your room. Do you have a favorite color?" she asked.

I didn't really have a favorite.

"Anything is fine," I replied. She didn't understand that I would be happy with just a safe home and a bed to sleep in. What they were offering was more than I thought I would ever have, and it was enough for me.

"Are you sure?" she asked as she tilted her to the side, watching me with her big, expressive eyes.

"Yes, you can make it whatever color you want," I answered.

"I will make sure it's beautiful," she assured me. "I brought you some stuff, I hope the sizes are right."

She placed a bag on the bed and I leaned closer as she opened it up. I was curious.

"I wasn't sure what you needed, so I got some of everything," she informed me as she began take some clothes out of the bag.

She'd bought me clothes.

"Thank you," I whispered hoarsely. I couldn't believe she'd been so kind to offer me a place to stay. She'd bought me toiletries and a vanity bag, and now here she was with a bag full of clothes.

It was something I hadn't even thought about because I'd been wearing hospital gowns. I swallowed hard to keep my emotions in check. If I cried again she would probably think I was losing it, or that I was a crybaby. I never cried and now I was so emotional because of her kindness.

"I brought you a couple of pajama outfits as well as a couple of tracksuits and some T-shirts, and I also got you some underwear and bras. Once you get out we will be able to go shopping for more stuff," she said as she took the clothes out the bag and set them down in front of me.

"I just hope they fit," she murmured, while she watched me lift up a pajama top and hold it up against my chest. The clothes were beautiful.

"Thank you," I whispered.

"You're welcome, Haven," she told me gently. "Visiting hours are nearly finished and I need to get back to work."

She stood up and gave me a quick hug.

"Whatever doesn't fit, send it home with Damien and I'll get it changed," she offered as she turned to leave.

When she got to the door she turned and said, "I'm so happy you're coming to stay with us."

I gave her a weak smile because I feared if I tried to talk I'd end up crying again.

I looked at the clothes for a while, still trying to wrap my mind around the thought that someone could be so kind. Most of the clothes I owned had been secondhand; I couldn't remember getting new clothes.

She'd bought me two simple T-shirt pajamas with matching pants—one was a baby blue and the other was pink. There was a light gray and a light blue tracksuit. The underwear she bought was plain cotton with matching bras and she'd brought me a couple of white T-shirts.

I'd been dying to shower but I hadn't been able to with the cast and the drip, so the nurses had been giving me wipe downs in the bed and I'd hated it. Now that the drip was out and I had some clean clothes, I wanted to have a shower or a bath. I wasn't sure which one would work better with the cast on my arm, because I couldn't get it wet.

Still unsure of how exactly I was going to get this right, I slowly shifted to the side of the bed and slid down until my feet touched the floor. My stomach was sore and my whole body ached. I remembered the nurse saying that the dressing over my wound was waterproof, so it didn't need to be kept dry. It hurt too much to stand up straight so I crouched over a little and it eased the pull on my stomach muscles. I shuffled slowly to the ensuite bathroom with the new blue pajamas Amy had bought me in my hand. Damien had put the vanity bag full of toiletries into the bathroom yesterday.

As I reached for the hand of the bathroom door I heard Damien say, "What the hell are you doing?"

Moments later his hands were on either side of me, helping me.

"I want to shower," I murmured to him, trying to concentrate on putting my next foot forward, intent on getting to my goal.

"Why didn't you wait for me?" he asked, sounding slightly exasperated with me.

"You can't exactly help me shower," I retorted as I

frowned at him.

"I could help you get there and back in one piece," he informed me. He decided that walking wasn't a good option and he picked me up gently, like I weighed nothing, and carried me into the bathroom. He set me down on the toilet seat.

"I could have done it," I assured him. There was no way I was going to admit I was having difficulty accomplishing my goal and that he'd made it easier for me.

"What if you'd fallen?" he questioned with frustration as he frowned at me. He knelt in front of me and tucked a piece of hair that had fallen in my face back behind my ear.

"You can't be there all the time, I need to learn to do things on my own," I insisted. As much as I wanted to rely on him for a lot of things, I needed to start taking control of my life.

"I just want to make sure you don't hurt yourself in the process," he told me softly, and then he stood up as he surveyed the small white bathroom.

"It might be easier for you to bathe than shower," he said. He started to run a bath for me.

"A bath sounds good, thanks," I said, nervously holding my new pajamas.

"Are you sure you're not going to need some help?" he asked, turning to look at me.

"I think I can manage," I replied, feeling a blush taint my cheeks at the thought that he might be offering to help me.

He smirked.

"I wasn't offering to help," he explained. "I'd get one of the nurses to help you."

I blushed harder.

"I don't need help," I muttered, watching him turn to test the temperature of the water with his hand. He adjusted the water accordingly and when the bath was half full he turned the taps off.

"If you need anything just shout and I'll get a nurse, okay?" he said.

"Sure," I confirmed as he left the bathroom and closed the door. I sighed with relief.

Being so close to him made me feel things I'd never felt before, and it was hard trying to figure out what I was feeling and hide it from him at the same time.

I began to undress. The hospital gown was easy to get off and I stood in front of the sink, naked.

It was the first time I'd seen my body naked since the attack. I knew the attack was bad—I remembered every hit—but to be faced with the physical proof of what had happened was hard.

After all the tears I'd cried, I honestly didn't feel that there were any left, but I was so wrong. Tears gathered in my eyes and then slid down my face as my fingers touched the bruises all over my stomach. Even my thighs were marked with bruises. I turned to look at my face in the mirror. It wasn't the first time I was seeing my face after the attack, but it was still a shock. My one eye was still badly bruised and there were still dark bruises covering most of my face. I looked hideous. To think that someone could hate me enough to do this to me was hard to cope with.

I sobbed into my hands, trying to cry quietly so that Damien wouldn't hear.

"It's okay, Haven," I heard Damien say from the other side of the closed bathroom door. "You're still beautiful."

I tried to stop crying, feeling guilty that he'd heard me. His words had been so sweet but he didn't understand that my crying had nothing to do with the superficial state of my body. It had more to do with the fact that Grant had done this to me. Furiously, I brushed my tears from my face. I needed to pull myself together. I'd been through so much and

I'd held on. I wasn't going to fall apart now.

Trying to ignore the fact that Damien was probably still on the other side of the bathroom door I got the toiletries I needed out of the vanity bag. I decided on the vanilla body wash and I found a small tube of face wash. Amy had really thought of everything.

Slowly, I climbed into the warm bath. My aching body reveled in the warmth and I couldn't help but sigh as I sank into the bath.

I was careful with my cast arm, as I didn't want to get it wet. Once I was seated in the bath I leaned back and took a deep breath as the heat from the water eased my aching body. Trying to wash myself with only one working arm was a lot more difficult than I'd first imagined, but after a while I got the hang of it. I washed my entire body, then rinsed off and got out of the bath. It took longer to dry off with one hand as well. I opened the vanilla body cream and rubbed it light across my body. I couldn't help but take a deep breath of the calming smell. I smelled good enough to eat.

"Are you still okay in there?" Damien asked, sounding nervous through the bathroom door. I wasn't surprised, as I'd been in here for a while already.

"I'm almost done," I assured him as I picked up the new underwear Amy had bought me. I slipped into the underwear, and it fit perfectly.

It was only after I put the blue pajama bottoms on and I took the bra in my hand that I realized I wouldn't be able to put the bra on myself.

"I'm going to need a little help," I told Damien through the door, feeling a little nervous.

I slipped the bra on and held it against my chest. All I needed was for him to join the clasp at the back for me.

I opened the door and Damien stepped inside the small bathroom. I didn't miss the quick look as he took the sight of me nearly half naked in front of him. Suddenly, I wasn't sure this was my best idea.

"I need you to do up the back for me," I instructed as I turned my back to him.

After a moment he stepped closer. He remained silent as I felt his fingers graze my skin as he began to work the clasp together. I felt a tingle on my skin where his hands touched my skin. I held my breath, trying to calm my breathing down at the excitement of having his hands touch me. I mentally wanted to kick myself. This had been a bad idea.

His fingers worked the clasp for a few more moments before I felt the strap tighten around my chest.

"Done," he murmured, but his fingers were still touching my back. He bent down closer to me, and I could feel his breath on my neck.

"Thank you," I said breathlessly. I pulled away, unable to deal with the effects he had on me.

He was out of my league. With just the slight brush of his fingers against my skin he had sent my dormant hormones into overdrive. He should come with a warning: *Do not touch!* I didn't have the experience necessary to know how to handle him.

"Do you need more help?" he asked while he watched me pick up the pajama shirt.

I wanted to say no, but I knew it would be nearly impossible getting into the shirt with my arm in a cast without some help.

As much as I wanted to say no, I said, "Yes."

Luckily the shirt was made from a stretchy material, so with Damien's help I was able to get my cast arm through the short sleeve and then over my head. Then I slipped my other arm into the other sleeve.

I smoothed the shirt down over my exposed stomach, and when I looked up I stared straight into his dark-blue eyes.

I would have sworn that they'd darkened slightly. I bit down on my lip, unable to pull my gaze from his.

"Do you want to wash your hair?" he asked, before he averted his gaze, breaking the spell between us.

My hair felt so grubby and I wasn't sure how easy it would be to do with only one hand. I knew I was probably playing with fire, but I nodded.

"Sit down by the bath and lean over," he instructed as he picked up the shampoo and conditioner from the vanity bag.

I kneeled down by the side of the bath and tried to lean over as much as I could. The water began to run into the bath and then he adjusted the taps. I heard the water spray through the pull-out showerhead. His fingers glided through my hair as the water began to run over my head and down my hair. I held my breath the entire time he shampooed my hair. He delicately kneaded my head with his fingers. He rinsed my hair and then he conditioned it. By the time he began to rinse the conditioner I was straining against the effect his hands had on me. He was helping me wash my hair for crying out loud, and yet my whole body was concentrated on every small touch as his fingers moved through my hair.

"All done, but we need to dry it," he told me as he stood up and reached for a small towel. While I remained bent in the bath, he wrapped the small towel over my head and began dry my hair with the towel.

Once he was happy he'd dried most of the water out, he helped me stand. My body ached from being bent over in the bath for so long and I felt a little wobbly on my feet as I tried to stand.

"Sit down," he instructed to me. He took me by the arms and guided me over to the toilet seat and pushed me down to sit.

He turned around and opened the cupboard door to look for a hairdryer. He found a small one. I sat still and watched him quietly—he seemed to know exactly what he was doing. Once he plugged the hairdryer in, he began to dry my hair. I couldn't believe I was here unable to do a lot of things for myself and Damien Knight, the school heartthrob, was helping me wash and dry my hair. The noise stopped when he switched off the hairdryer and looked into the vanity bag for something. He pulled out a brush and began to brush my hair. I fidgeted with my hands, trying to concentrate on anything but him.

"You seem to be really good at this," I murmured, wanting to break the awkward silence.

"Yeah, my mom hurt her wrist once and I had to help her wash and dry her hair for a couple of weeks," he murmured while he brushed my hair. It felt so good to have nice and clean hair again.

He switched on the hairdryer again and began to dry my hair properly. It didn't take long before he switched the hairdryer off and unplugged it. He turned and stuffed it back into its place in the cupboard. Gently, he brushed my hair once more before he put the brush down beside the sink. I stood up and touched my hair and smiled at him.

"Thank you."

"You're welcome," he whispered while his eyes held mine. I felt captivated and unable to pull my gaze from his.

He stepped closer. His hand touched my hair and he slid his hand into my hair and threaded it through his fingers as he pulled me closer. Unable to fight what I wanted anymore, I moved closer. My hands settled on his chest and I could feel the warmth from his body through his shirt. His eyes flickered from my eyes to my lips. He leaned closer and I held my breath. I felt a flutter in my stomach at the anticipation of my first kiss.

CHAPTER FOURTEEN

Haven

Nothing could have prepared me for what happened to me when his lips finally touched mine. His lips were so soft as they pressed against me. Instinctively, I closed my eyes and savored the feeling of being kissed for the first time. The butterflies fluttered wildly in my stomach and my whole body tingled all over. I bunched his shirt under my hand to keep him in place. I'd never felt like this before.

His lips moved against mine, more demanding, and I followed his lead and pressed my lips harder against his. I breathed him in. He smelled of musk and spice. I felt his tongue sweep into my mouth and I opened my lips to accommodate him. My knees weakened at the first touch of his tongue against mine. His one hand remained threaded through my hair as he angled my head back slightly to get better access to my mouth.

His other arm wrapped around my waist, keeping me firmly where he wanted me, pressed up against his hard body. All thoughts evaporated and all that mattered was this boy kissing me for the first time. I didn't want to overanalyze it, I just wanted to feel, just this once. His tongue stroked mine as he gripped me tighter. I loved the taste of him. He tasted like fresh mint and apples. I groaned as the kiss became heated and I wanted more, so much more.

Then he was gone. I opened my eyes to see him standing a foot away from me, looking at me, horrified.

"I'm sorry," he gasped, running a hand through his hair. He backed up to the door, then turned and left.

I touched my bruised lips, trying to figure out what had happened to make him stop kissing me. Had I done something wrong? I replayed the kiss in my mind trying to figure out what had happened, but I couldn't figure out what had gone wrong. How could he be sorry about something that had made me feel so much? I was so shaken, I sat back down to try and get myself together. Why had he kissed me? My lip trembled slightly at the memory of his face when he'd pulled away from me.

I wished I could have stayed in the bathroom instead of going back into my room, but I couldn't stay here forever. I tried to get myself together and process my thoughts as I finished up what I needed to. I stalled for another fifteen minutes after I'd finished brushing my teeth before I reached for the handle of the bathroom door.

He was waiting outside the door.

"I wanted to make sure you were okay," he murmured awkwardly, his hands shoved into the front pockets of his jeans.

His eyes were glued to the floor in front of him. He couldn't even look at me. There was nothing like telling a girl you were sorry after you'd kissed her.

"You were in there for a while."

He wanted to make sure that I was okay? I wasn't okay. I averted my gaze from him and shuffled past him to the hospital bed.

"I'm fine," I whispered.

I was exhausted. I wasn't sure if it was because of the physical exertion or the emotional drain that had depleted my energy. I struggled to get back into bed. He sighed and then he lifted me, bridal style, onto the bed. Although I was upset with him, I was relieved to be back in the bed.

"Thanks," I muttered. I pulled the blanket over my body. My body ached and I could feel every bruise.

He hovered next to me.

"Are you okay?" he asked, with concerned eyes.

"I'm just tired," I murmured. It wasn't the whole truth. I was tired, but I also was sore, and my body was aching. Maybe I'd overdone it. And my heart was a little raw, too. I wasn't vulnerable to many people, but I was vulnerable to Damien. He had the power to hurt me emotionally.

"You look a little pale, are you in any pain?" he asked, stepping closer to study me.

"A little," I mumbled before I closed my eyes to try and manage the pain.

"I'll tell the nurse," he told me before I heard him leave the room.

A few moments later, he returned with a nurse who held a cup of water and a couple of tablets.

"Drink this," Nurse informed me.

I tried to sit up but suddenly I was just too weak.

Damien helped me sit up as the nurse handed me the tablets and water.

"Thank you," I said.

I swallowed the tablets and then sagged back down into the bed as the nurse left the room. I was so tired, I just wanted to sleep. I didn't have the energy to go around and around in my head trying to figure out what had happened to make Damien sorry he'd kissed me. I was too tired to care.

I turned onto my side, facing away from Damien, and closed my eyes. There was a scrape of a chair and the sound of what I assumed to be Damien sitting down. After a few awkward minutes of silence, I felt the painkillers take effect and the pain in my body began to ease, and in my pain-free bubble I began to drift off to sleep.

It was early evening when I woke up.

I was sleeping on my side facing Damien, who was paging through a magazine. When he saw movement, he closed the magazine and leaned closer.

"How are you feeling?" he asked anxiously.

"I'm fine," I answered, rubbing my eyes. I didn't feel any pain and I felt better now that I'd had some sleep. I had no idea that the simple task of bathing and washing my hair would tire me out.

"Chris came by to visit but you were fast asleep," he told me. Disappointment flooded through me. I'd been looking forward to his visit all morning and I couldn't believe I'd missed it.

"The nurse came to check on you," he went on. "She said you might have done too much and tired yourself out."

I remained silent as I let my gaze wander past him.

Would he talk about what had happened? Or was the kiss going to be swept under the rug and never mentioned again? The problem with sweeping it under the rug and not talking about it was that the awkwardness between the two of us would continue, and I didn't want that. I'd been through so much, and I needed him.

Would I need to be the one to bring it up so that we could hash it out and then once we'd discussed, it would be better? Then we could move on and it would never happen again. I'd sorted this all out in my head and now it was time to take the bull by the horns and sort it out with Damien.

"Damien," I said as I sat up and faced him.

"Listen, about that kiss," he said. I could see he was anxious and nervous as he clasped his hands together. His eyes held mine. "I wanted to explain why I shouldn't have done that."

He said it like he'd been the only one taking part in the kiss, but that kiss, my first kiss, had involved both of us. I dropped my gaze, unable to look at him while he told me all the reasons why that kiss shouldn't have happened. How could something that felt so good be so wrong?

"You deserve better than me," he started, and then paused for a few moments. I glanced at him and I could see that he was struggling to find the words to explain what he needed to.

Patiently, I waited for him to resume speaking. He sighed and ran a hand absentmindedly through his hair.

"You have been through so much and you deserve nothing but love and happiness from here on out. I'm not good for you; you need someone who can love and care for you the way you should be loved. I can't give you what you deserve," he explained with a pained expression on his face, like this talk was hurting him just as much as it was hurting me.

It hurt to hear those words from him. My heart felt a little raw and bruised. I'd never been interested in anybody, and then Damien had come along and somehow I'd started to feel things I'd never felt before. He'd been the first boy to make me want to do normal things like kiss and date—all the things girls my age were doing.

Like in the fairy tales I'd read as a child, Damien had swooped in and saved me. He'd been my knight in shining armor. And in the fairy tales, the princess and the knight kissed and then lived happily ever after.

The reality was my knight was telling me our kiss had been a mistake and that he couldn't love me the way I should be loved. I bit down on my lip to keep it from trembling. It was bad enough getting hurt by the idea that he couldn't love me, and I didn't want to show him how much it hurt me.

"Why did you kiss me?" The question had been on my mind since he'd ended the kiss.

"I wanted you," he answered honestly and shrugged. "But… you deserve better."

He didn't think he was good enough for me.

"You know about my reputation at school. You've heard the rumors," he insisted. "They aren't rumors… it's all true."

His wide eyes searched my face for a reaction to what he'd just said. I knew about his reputation. I'd seen it for myself when he'd had made out with Angela against the lockers at school. Nothing he was telling me was something I didn't already know.

"I don't do relationships or commitment. I don't get attached."

I couldn't help but wonder why he was that way. There were plenty of guys that had a phobia about commitment, but Damien seemed to have an extreme case of that, because I heard that he went through women faster than I'd ever seen. Why was he so scared of getting attached? I knew there was a lot more to this than he was telling me, but I wasn't going to push it. He was right, though. Even though I liked him and that kiss had literally swept me off my feet, I deserved someone who was capable of loving me.

I closed my eyes and took a deep breath to try and clear my thoughts. A slight ache in my head had begun to grow. I was getting a headache and I was beginning to feel tired again. But this time I knew it was the emotional strain that was making me tired.

When I opened my eyes, he was sitting in the chair beside me, watching me closely, waiting for my reaction.

I'd just managed to escape the nightmare that had been

my life for the last seven years and I needed time to deal with everything that had happened. Somehow I needed to try and pick up the pieces of what was left of my life and try to carry on. With so much going on, the truth was I didn't have the emotional capacity to include someone else in my life and worry about them as well. Dating and relationships needed attention, and I needed to concentrate on myself. I needed time to try and deal with everything that had happened while trying to navigate through my new life.

For all I knew, Grant would succeed in another attempt to kill me before the police found him. I had a lot more important stuff to worry about than my heart and the butterflies in my stomach. It was probably best that we didn't get involved. If something more had developed between the two of us and things didn't work out, I wasn't sure if it would be possible to go back to being friends.

It hurt that he didn't think he was capable of giving me what I wanted, but now that I'd actually thought about things, it was probably for the best.

"I need you," I whispered softly. His eyes connected with mine and I knew my words were pulling on that inner part of him that I knew wouldn't let me down.

"I can't," he whispered back as he shook his head gently.

I shook my head at him. He hadn't understood me correctly.

"I need you to be in my life. I need you to be there for me when I'm about to fall apart or when things get too tough to handle. I need you to be there to pick me up and put me back together."

His eyes held mine.

"I need you to be my friend," I explained, trying to keep his gaze, but scared he might reject me outright. I couldn't cope without his friendship.

I couldn't lose him completely. After everything that had

happened, I needed him. He was one of the few people I felt safe with and that was what I needed right now. Relief flooded through his face and he stepped forward and enveloped me in a hug. I breathed him in, musk and spice— it was comforting and soothing. The anxious feeling began to fade and I started to feel content.

"I can do that," he whispered hoarsely into my hair.

I sighed with relief. I'd been so scared that he would pull away from me totally. At least I still had him as my friend. He pulled back and tucked a stray piece of my hair back behind my ear.

"I will always be there for you. Anytime you need anything." He said it with such conviction that I knew he meant every word. His words warmed my heart.

"Thank you," I whispered hoarsely, overcome with emotion.

He sat back down.

"Mom told me that you're going to come and live with us," he said, smiling and looking a little more relaxed than he had before.

"Yeah," I answered, starting to fidget with the end of the blanket.

Talking about moving in with his family made me nervous and stressed. What if they didn't like me once I'd moved in? I was so used to trying to be invisible that I didn't know how I was going to try and integrate into a 'normal' family when I had no idea what 'normal' was.

"What's wrong?" he asked when I refused to make eye contact with him and continued to fidget with the blanket.

"I'm just nervous about it," I answered, looking up at him.

"Don't be nervous. Everything will work out," he assured me. "Dad's started on the paperwork. He wanted me to talk to you about something."

My eyes flew to his. This didn't sound good, and from the tone of Damien's voice it didn't sound like he was looking forward to talking to me about this something.

"My dad has held off the cops and social workers for as long as he could, but they are insisting on seeing you," he revealed softly.

I understood that I would need to answer the cops' questions, and in doing so I was helping them. I had to remember that.

"When?" I asked, hoping I would have some time to prepare myself for it. I wasn't looking forward to taking a trip down this particular memory lane. It was bad enough every time I looked at the cast on my arm, or the bruises all over my body, and remembered what he did to me. Now I would have to sit and relay every moment of my ordeal. I wasn't even sure if it was something I could do.

I looked expectedly at Damien.

"Tomorrow."

CHAPTER FIFTEEN

Haven

That night I was restless. I barely slept a wink. I knew exactly what was bugging me enough to keep me tossing and turning the whole night. It was the thought of meeting with the cops and having to answer questions about my ordeal. It wasn't something I wanted to think about it.

I spent most of the night watching Damien sleep in the chair beside me. He slept with his arms crossed over his chest and his legs straightened and slightly crossed. It looked uncomfortable, but it didn't seem to bother him.

I felt guilty that I'd been sleeping in a comfortable bed and he'd spent every night since I'd been admitted to hospital sleeping in a chair. No one had watched over me like he had and I couldn't help the warm and tender feeling that spread inside me as I watched him sleep peacefully.

He had a bad reputation with girls and I knew he had issues, but I'd seen for myself that deep down, where it counted, he was a good and caring person. I didn't want to think about what I would have done if I hadn't been able to lean on him like I had. It was hard to believe that in such a short space of time he'd become the most important person in my life.

My thoughts turned to the other important guy in my life, Chris. After missing his visit yesterday, I was looking forward to seeing him later today.

I glanced down at the message he'd written on my cast. After everything that had happened, I was glad Damien hadn't seen the message. As soon as I had a chance I was going to write over it so that no one else would see it. I was lucky to have two special guys like them in my life, because I would be lost without them. I was hopeful that once I moved in with the Knights I would be able to form relationships with Amy and Steven. They were nice people. There weren't many people that would offer a home to an abused girl like me. It showed me that they were honest and caring, and I just hoped that it all worked out.

It was going to be a big change for me. I'd spent so many years in a soul-destroying environment, and I'd survived. I didn't know if I'd be able to cope with 'normal.' The doctor had told me I would recover from my physical wounds and the slight malnutrition I'd suffered from. I'd already noticed that I'd started to gain a little weight from my short stay in the hospital. The physical wounds would heal, but it was the emotional scars that I was more worried about.

At the moment I had more important things on my mind. The closer it got to meeting with the police, the more nervous I became.

"Morning." Damien's half-asleep greeting pulled me out of my thoughts and I gave him a weak smile as he rubbed his sleepy eyes.

"Hi," I greeted back.

He ran a hand through his hair and it fell back into place. Even first thing in the morning he was gorgeous, I thought again. I reprimanded myself—he was my friend and I had to stop thinking about him in that way.

"How did you sleep?" he asked as he pulled the chair closer to the bed and leaned a little closer.

"Not very well," I admitted with a shrug.

"Don't worry," he told me. "My dad and I will be with you when the police come to question you."

I gave him a slight nod. It wasn't having the meeting with the police that was worrying me, it was the thought of having to relive the ordeal that I scared me. He reached for my hand and squeezed it.

"It'll be all right," he reassured me. I gave him a weak smile.

I hoped he was right.

I was wound tight by the time the two policemen walked into my hospital room later that morning. The slightly overweight cop was dressed in a uniform and the skinnier one was dressed in a dark brown suit. I darted a nervous look to Damien who was standing beside me, still holding my hand. He gave me a reassuring smile and squeezed my hand.

My eyes flickered to Steven who was standing on the other side of my hospital bed. I was nervous.

"Good morning," greeted the policeman dressed in the suit with a friendly smile. He was tall and lanky with shaggy light brown hair that reached his ears. "I'm Detective Green and my colleague is Officer Smith."

Officer Smith looked like your typical short and overweight police officer. He looked a lot older than Detective Green because he was going bald. As I waited for them to start with the questions, I held onto Damien's hand a little tighter.

"We have some questions to ask you," Detective Green explained as he stood at the foot of my bed beside Officer Smith. His eyes went to Steven first and when Steven gave him a brief nod, he opened up a notebook.

"We know this has been difficult for you, but we need

you to answer some questions so that we can get a clearer picture of what happened the day you were attacked. We're going to try and keep this short and sweet, okay?" he said to me.

My throat felt dry so I just nodded my head.

"We know from our discussion with your doctor that you were being physically abused at home," he informed me. "Was there any sexual abuse?"

I felt embarrassment heat my cheeks as I shook my head.

"We've managed to piece together what happened up until you arrived home," he informed me. "What happened when you got home?"

"Grant…my stepfather, was waiting for me when I got home," I began to explain. "He was mad at me."

"Why was he mad?" he asked, scribbling something into his notebook.

My gaze flickered to Damien and then I looked back to the detective.

"He'd seen me with Damien," I answered.

"Damien told us he gave you a lift home that day."

"Yes, it upset Grant," I revealed without thinking. It was only when I uttered the words did I realize the mistake I'd made. My eyes flickered to Damien's and I realized it was too late. Damien gave me a horrified look as he released my hands.

"Why did seeing you with Damien upset him?" the detective asked interrupting us.

I swallowed hard as my eyes went back to the cop.

"He'd seen Damien drop me off before and he told me if it ever happened again, he would kill him," I answered as I looked to the detective, hating the fact that now Damien knew what had set Grant off. The thickness in my throat grew as I tried to swallow again. I couldn't look at Damien but I could feel his eyes on me.

"So Grant was angry that he'd seen Damien drop you off?" the detective asked. I nodded my head.

"What happened next?" he asked.

I could still feel Damien's eyes on me but I couldn't look at him. No matter what I said next the damage had been done, Damien knew that Grant had beaten me because he'd seen the two of us together, despite my attempts to keep my distance from him. He would blame himself.

"He began to hit me," I answered, keeping the emotion I felt out of my voice.

The detective remained silent.

"Then he said something about me going to join my mom." It was all a bit fuzzy and I couldn't remember his exact words.

"Your mom died a few days earlier?" Detective Green asked calmly.

I nodded my head.

"Then what happened?" he prompted.

"He went to the kitchen and came back with a knife," I began to explain, dropping my eyes to my hands in my lap so that I wouldn't see their reaction.

"Does she really need to go into all the details of the attack?" Damien demanded. I looked up. He looked visibly upset by what he'd heard so far, but I knew it went deeper than that.

Steven shook his head at the detective.

"What happened after the attack?" Detective Green asked.

"He left me..." I answered, but as I said the words all the emotion I'd been able to suppress bubbled to the surface and I couldn't finish the sentence. I tried to calm myself down, but a sob broke loose and I felt Damien wrap me in his arms.

"Shh," he soothed softly.

"I think that's enough for today," Steven said to

Detective Green and Officer Smith.

"I think we have all we need," Detective Green informed Steven as he closed his notebook. "I'll let you know if we have any more questions."

Tears slid down my face. Damien held me close, trying to ease my pain. Steven showed the cops out of the room, while Damien remained with me.

I cried until my tears finally dried up. Damien had held me the whole time whispering soothing words while he stroked my hair. Finally emotionally exhausted, I pulled away from him and brushed the tears from my face.

"I'm sorry," I muttered, upset with my lack of control over my emotions.

"You have nothing to be sorry about," he whispered as he tucked a stray piece of hair away. It was the tone of his voice that made me look at him. He looked so upset.

"Damien—" I said before he cut me off.

"I'm the one who needs to say sorry," he spoke softly. I could see the guilt was eating at him.

"But no amount of words can erase what happened to you because of me," he stated. I wasn't sure if he was saying it to himself or to me.

"Damien—" I started, trying to reason with him, but he shook his head.

"It was my fault," he declared. The look in his eyes pulled at my heart.

I shook my head. It was heartbreaking watching him try and wrestle with the knowledge that Grant had nearly tried to kill me because he'd seen me with Damien.

"Oh my God, he nearly killed you," he gasped as he fisted his hair. I could see the he was beginning to spin out of control as it hit him full force.

"Damien," I whispered, trying to explain to him that it hadn't been his fault.

"How can you even stand to look at me?" he asked, as he bent down so our gazes were level, his hand on his chest. He was beyond upset now.

"I'm so sorry," he apologized to me with an edge of desperation that scared me. Then he pushed away from the bed. He didn't say another word; instead, he stalked out of the hospital room, slamming the door shut.

I sat, staring at the closed door of the hospital room. How had things gotten out of hand so quickly?

Not once since the attack had I ever thought for one second that it had been Damien's fault, because I didn't blame him at all. Grant was angry that day and seeing the two of us together was just a justification to him, not that he needed a justification hurt me. I wanted to kick myself for telling the cops about it because I hadn't thought about the effect it would have on Damien. I should have known better, but what was done was done and I wasn't sure how or even if I could fix it.

He was so upset. He hadn't given me a chance to explain that I didn't blame him and that it hadn't been his fault. I dropped my head into my hands. He thought he was to blame, but he wasn't.

Irrespective of the facts that he'd told me that he couldn't love me and that we'd agreed to be friends, I was falling for him. It was hard not to. I'd lectured myself, telling myself that I had too much to deal with to also deal with feelings for a boy I had no idea how to handle. That it would only end in heartbreak, mainly my heart breaking; but the heart wants what the heart wants, and no logical reasoning was going to change that.

I wanted to go and look for Damien, but I had no idea if he was still even in the hospital. I wanted to tell him that I didn't blame him at all.

By the time Steven returned, I was exhausted and

emotionally raw. He stood beside me.

"Where's Damien?" he asked, a little confused that Damien would leave me alone.

"He left," I answered, while I fixed my eyes on my hands in my lap.

"Are you okay?" he asked gently.

I shook my head.

"Can you tell me what happened?" he asked softly as he sat down in the chair beside me.

"He blames himself," I whispered. I hated that I'd hurt him.

I looked up and saw Steven study me for a moment, and then he let out a sigh.

"Damien cares about you and I'm sure he's upset that he thinks he is the reason why you are here," he explained. I already knew. "Give him some time to deal with it."

I nodded my head. There wasn't much I could do to rectify it if I couldn't even find him.

"Do you want me to stay with you?" he asked me kindly.

"No, I'll be okay."

The lack of sleep and the stress from the last hour had taken its toll on me, and I was tired. I just wanted to be alone to sort through my thoughts.

"Are you sure?" he asked. "I don't mind staying if you want me to."

I gave him a weak smile that didn't reach my eyes.

"I'm sure."

He was sweet. It was nice to know that I had other people I could depend on.

"I nearly forgot," he remembered. "This is for you."

Out of his pocket he pulled a brand-new iPhone and handed it to me.

"You didn't have to," I protested as my hands clasped around the new phone. It was sleek and smart, I'd never owned anything this beautiful.

He smiled at my obvious awe.

"I want you to be able to call us if you need to. I've programmed our numbers in," he informed.

"Thank you."

I would need to play around with the phone to figure out how to use it. The only other phone I'd ever owned had been the one Damien had given to me.

"The social worker is coming later this afternoon. She wants to see you alone, but I'm going to be just outside in case you need me, okay?" he told me.

"Thank you."

"You're welcome," he assured me just before he left.

Finally alone with my thoughts, I set the phone down on the side table and slumped back into the bed.

I closed my eyes and tried to make sense of what had happened with Damien. My heart hurt when I remembered the look on his face. I wondered if I should try and call him, but then I decided against it. Irrespective of how desperately I wanted to talk to him, I had to respect the fact that he needed time alone.

It was hard, but somehow I stopped myself from reaching for the phone. I really hoped that Damien would come back soon, but minute after minute ticked by and an hour later he still hadn't returned. Exhausted, I rolled onto my side and closed my eyes. I had just wanted to rest for a few minutes, but I drifted into a deep sleep.

CHAPTER SIXTEEN

Haven

I honestly thought that by the time I woke up a little later that afternoon Damien would have been back, but he wasn't.

After the cops' questioning, I wasn't looking forward to meeting with the social worker, but I was thankful when Steven appeared in the doorway of my hospital room half an hour before the meeting was scheduled.

"Damien still not back?" he asked casually as he stood beside the bed.

"No," I answered. My heart felt heavy. I didn't want Damien to feel guilty, irrespective of what had set Grant off. It had been inevitable. I just wished Damien would show up so that I could explain it to him.

"He'll be back," Steven assured me confidently. I felt a whole lot less confident that Damien would return.

The closer it got to the meeting with the social worker the more nervous I became. Thoughts of Damien were forgotten as my thoughts turned to what the social worker would ask. I'd already relived the attack earlier with the cops and I didn't want to have to do that again.

By the time the social worker arrived for our meeting I was a nervous wreck. I just hoped it went quickly so that I could get rid of the sickening feeling in my stomach. The social worker was younger than I expected; she looked like she was in her late twenties, neatly dressed in a skirt and jacket with a white blouse.

Once Steven had a few words with her, he reminded me that if I needed him he would be outside the room, and then he left the two of us alone. The social worker gave me a friendly smile as she sat down beside the hospital bed. She pulled out a notepad and a pen before she gave me her full attention.

I tucked a piece of stray hair behind my ear.

"Hi, Haven," she greeted me. She looked like a kind person, so the nervousness I'd been feeling began to dissipate.

"Hi," I mumbled.

"My name's Sarah," she introduced herself. She scribbled something down onto the notepad and then looked back to me.

"I know you've been through a lot and I'm not going to take up too much of your time," she informed me.

At least the meeting was going to be quick. I was ready for this day to be finished.

"Cases like yours have to be handled with care," she began to explain. "The police have given me all the information they have and I've been updated by your doctor on your medical history and wellbeing. Between them I have all the information I need, so I don't believe there is a need to go into a lot of detail."

I breathed a sigh of relief. She was letting me off the hook, and I was grateful.

"Mr. Knight has filed the correct paperwork to gain

custody of you, so it will all be sorted out soon," she assured me, then she scribbled some more notes on the notepad. I wondered what she was writing because I had yet to say a word.

"I'm still going to keep in touch to see how you settle in with the Knights."

Then she linked her hands and her eyes settled onto me. It was like she was building up to something and I was pretty sure that I wasn't going to like it.

"I think that after everything you have been through you need someone to talk to about it. I'm going to give you some contact details of a therapist I suggest you go and see."

The thought of talking to an absolute stranger about what had happened to me over the last seven years made me sick to the stomach.

"I really do think it will help."

I gave her a slight nod to speed up this meeting. There was no point in arguing the point that no amount of therapy would erase all the things that had been done to me. Frankly, I thought it was a waste of time. The meeting didn't last long. As she was about to leave she handed me her business card and the details of the therapist.

"I'll be seeing you soon," she said before she left.

I remained silent and stared at her business card. It was hard to think that her job was to deal with kids like me on a daily basis. It must be a pretty depressing job.

"Hi," Steven greeted when he stepped into the room.

"Hi," I replied, shoving the cards into the drawer in my side table.

"How did it go?" he asked, watching me. I think he was trying to see if I was upset.

"It went...okay," I answered with a shrug.

"I've got to get back to the office," he told me. "When

Damien makes an appearance, tell him to call me."

And then he left.

I slumped backward onto the pillow and lay on my side. After the day I'd had, and even after having had a nap, I was still tired. I lay on my side with my gaze fixed on the window. It was nice just to lie there and stare at the view. There wasn't much, but through the blinds on the windows I could see some trees.

For a moment I just concentrated on the scene outside trying to push thoughts of Damien from my mind.

At least I'd gotten the meeting with the cops and the social worker over and done with. My thoughts went straight to Damien. I wished he'd come back. The doctor would be around in the morning but so far I was on track to be discharged tomorrow. I was beginning to feel nervous.

Not only was it nerve-wracking moving into a new home and trying to be 'normal', but I was also worried about Grant. The cops didn't have him in custody yet and the fear that he'd finish what he started petrified me. Now that I had a new lease on life I didn't want it cut short.

I must have dozed off for a while because the next moment I opened my eyes it was dark. I yawned and rubbed my tired eyes as I sat up. It was then I noticed Damien leaning with his back against the wall, watching me. For a few moments I just quietly returned his stare. He looked stressed and upset. I wanted to put my arms around him and hug him close.

"I'm sorry," he whispered hoarsely.

"You have nothing to be sorry about," I reassured him.

"Of course I have to be sorry. I'm the reason why he hurt you...the reason he nearly killed you..." Emotion clogged his voice. The pain in his features made my heart ache.

"But if it wasn't for you I wouldn't have had a phone,

without you I would have bled to death," I reminded him. He'd saved me.

"If it hadn't been for me you wouldn't have been in that situation to start off with," he tried to explain. I could see the guilt as clear as daylight in his eyes.

"Grant was going to do what he wanted, whether he had an excuse or not," I said. Silence descended as I tried to think of the right words to explain to him that he'd saved me in more ways than one. "And besides, if the attack hadn't happened, I would still be living with him, completely helpless. He would still be hurting me."

Sympathy and anger mixed together radiated from him. It was hard for him to hear it, but he needed to know that he was my hero.

"I'm free because of you," I said. I bit my lip to keep the tears at bay. "Thank you."

"Don't cry," he said softly as he closed the distance between us and I felt his arms reach for me. He was warm and comforting and I clung to him.

He soothed me as he held me in his arms. His hand made small circular motions on my back as he held me close. Just the smell of him was enough to make me feel safe. I sniffled and he gently looked down at me.

He shifted me over slightly and climbed onto the hospital bed, and then lay down on his side. Gently he shifted me so that I lay on my side with my head on his chest like a pillow, my one arm wrapped around his waist.

"I'm sorry I left you earlier," he apologized while I felt him soothe my hair gently as he held me closer.

"To think I was the reason why he did this to you was...heartbreaking..." he said, his voice choking from the emotion. "From the moment I laid eyes on you I wanted to protect you and keep you safe, and I failed."

"You didn't fail. I've never had anyone try and protect like you did. What happened wasn't your fault and you need to accept it and move on. I'm here, alive, because of you, and that's what you need to remember. If anything, you're the knight that saved the princess from evil."

Grant wasn't in police custody, but he was out of my life for the moment and I could finally breathe without having to worry if something was going to set him off, and I no longer had to hope that he wouldn't hit me hard enough to leave marks I would have to try and explain.

"I'm no knight," Damien said.

"You might not think so, but you saved me. You're my hero. You've given me hope and that is more than I've had in a long while."

I expected him to say something, but he held me close. I relaxed in his embrace, feeling safe and happy.

For a while we lay together in silence.

"How was the meeting with the social worker?" he asked.

"She was nice and friendly." It was the only information I was going to give him. I didn't want to tell him that she'd suggested I got into therapy. He might look at me like was a nut case. I didn't want to spill my deepest and darkest secrets to a stranger—just the thought of doing that made me physically sick.

"I'm sorry I left you," he apologized again. I could feel his breath in my hair.

"Stop apologizing," I insisted as I lifted my head to look at him and our eyes connected.

There was something that sparked inside me every time his eyes met mine. He brushed his knuckles over my cheek gently while I remained transfixed by his deep gaze. I licked my lips nervously. I knew I was playing with fire. His eyes flickered to my lips and then back to my eyes.

Maybe it was the fact that we decided we shouldn't date that made it something forbidden, something that we both now wanted even more. Or was the physical attraction between the two of us too strong to resist?

I didn't know.

But what I did know is that we leaned into each other and I felt his lips touch mine. It was like fireworks going off inside of me at the magical touch of his lips against mine. My mind was telling me to stop, but my body wasn't listening, it was just reacting to the chemistry and attraction between us. It would only end in heartache, but at that moment I didn't care. The world would be falling apart around me and I would have been oblivious to everything except for the feel of his lips against mine.

His hand cupped the back of my head as his lips moved more intensely against mine. I groaned and opened my lips slightly, and he didn't need any more invitation than that. His tongue swept into my mouth and explored my mouth, tangling with my tongue.

My hand clutched at his shirt, holding him desperately while I felt myself spinning out of control as the kiss intensified. It was like a hurricane around us, and I clung desperately to him. I even felt my toes curl and the tingling from his kisses spread through my body.

He pulled me closer. His lips moved from my mouth to press a trail of kisses to my jaw. I wanted him so badly and I held onto him as the effects of his touch vibrated through my body like electric shocks.

"I want you," he whispered hoarsely. He pressed a kiss to my collarbone.

His words broke the spell that had held me captivated by him. He only wanted my body—it was a physical thing for him, but I wanted more. I wanted it to be more than just a physical thing between the two of us.

I pulled away from him.

"I can't," I said breathlessly.

Thankfully, we were no longer touching, so I was able to think straight and keep him at a distance. It was one thing to be wanted by someone, but I needed more. I didn't want to just be wanted in a physical sense, I wanted to be loved. I needed the emotional connection he wasn't able to give me.

"We can't keep doing this to each other," I insisted as he sat up and faced me. "We want different things. There can't be anymore slipups."

He remained quiet while he watched me. I could see that he was struggling with the need to pull me into his arms and finish what we had started.

"No more touching, at all," I instructed him. I could keep him at a distance if we didn't touch each other. Once our skin met I threw caution to the wind and I lost all self-control. "No more hugs, or holding each other."

My fingers touched my slightly swollen lips, the physical remains of our heated kiss. I blushed at my reaction to him and his kisses. Living under the same roof wasn't going to be easy, but we would have to make it work.

"Okay, no touching," he agreed breathlessly. His eyes were still dark with need. It was nice to see that I wasn't the only one struggling with the effects from our kiss. I affected him as much as he affected me.

It would be so easy to say 'fuck it' and do what I wanted, and see what happened, but I deserved more. I didn't want to be some player's girl of the week, I wanted to love and be loved. In keeping with our new rules he moved off the bed and sat down, keeping his distance.

It was at that moment, while I was still trying to catch my breath, that Chris walked into the room. His perceptive eyes didn't miss my slightly swollen lips or the uncomfortable way Damien couldn't look him in the face and kept his gaze glued to the floor.

He smiled.

"Hi," he greeted me, still grinning.

"Hi." It was good to see him, because I'd missed his visit yesterday.

"I've got to go and call my dad," Damien muttered, and then left me alone with Chris.

The traitor.

CHAPTER SEVENTEEN

Haven

"Spill," Chris instructed me when he sat down next to the bed, grinning at me.

"I..." I started.

"Kissed Damien Knight, the hottest guy in our school?" he offered, with a mischievous smile.

I rolled my eyes at him and then sighed. "Yes."

"I knew it!" he exclaimed, getting all excited. "It was just a matter of time."

I shook my head at him and he gave me a confused look.

"We've decided to keep things platonic," I revealed. He didn't look convinced.

"And how's that going for you?" he replied as he pointed out my still slightly red and swollen kissed lips.

"We're trying," I argued. The operative word was trying, not succeeding.

"It seems to be working," he replied sarcastically. He was voicing what I already knew. Trying to keep things between us platonic was going to be difficult. If we could just make sure we didn't get too close to each other, we might just be able to resist the pull we each felt to the other.

Chris spotted my phone on the side table and picked it up. I didn't need to ask what he was doing—I knew he was programming his number into my phone. He handed me my phone when he was done. I still needed to learn how to work the phone properly, but I managed to find the contacts. I scrolled through them; there weren't many, and I had to suppress a giggle when I spotted a contact listed as "Hot Friend."

"Really?" I asked him.

"It's the truth," he shot back, pretending to be upset that I even questioned the description.

That was the thing about Chris: he was a person that was just so addictive to be around because he always lightened the mood.

"So are you going to tell me the reason why you and Damien are going to remain friends instead of giving into your hormones and getting it on, which, I might add, is inevitable?" he asked. I hoped he wasn't right, because I would be the one getting my heart broken.

"He doesn't date, and I need more than that."

My answer was simple.

"You do deserve someone who is emotionally capable of loving you," he told me softly. He didn't act seriously often, but his words and the lack of a smile on his told me that he meant every word. It touched my heart.

"Thanks," I whispered as I put my hand on his. He linked his hand through mine.

"Any idea when they're going to let you out of here?" He gazed around the room in distaste. "I hate hospitals."

"Maybe tomorrow," I murmured. I didn't want to think about that yet. It gave me a whole new set of problems that I would be deal with.

I yawned. It was hard to believe I was still tired even after the nap I'd just had.

"If you need to sleep, I can go," he offered.

"No, please stay. I'm okay," I insisted.

He stayed for a while longer, and there was no sign of Damien. I wasn't sure if it was because Chris was visiting me or if he was trying to avoid me.

Despite trying to stay awake, I started dozing off while Chris was giving me a rundown of all the gossip at school.

***

When I woke up, it was early evening. The first thing my eyes searched for was Damien, and I found him sitting in the chair beside me.

I was relieved. He had come back.

"Hey," he greeted me when he noticed I was awake.

"Hi," I replied, rubbing my eyes.

I sat up.

"Chris?" I asked. I must have fallen asleep while he'd been visiting.

"I saw him on his way out. He said you were so tired you drifted off in the middle of the best school gossip," he informed me, a smile tugging his lips.

"I've slept so much but it just never seems to be enough."

"You're healing, your body needs time to recover," he explained gently.

He was right. I glanced down at my arms. The bruises, which had once been black and blue, were turning a light yellow color. Soon they would be gone. My stab wound on my stomach was much better as well.

"The nurses came around with your food while you were sleeping. I'm going to tell them you're awake."

When he left, I noticed the pen on the side table. It hadn't been there before.

Chris hadn't. I glanced down at my cast and realized he had.

Underneath the previous message he'd written he wrote 'I love Damien's hot kisses.'

I was going to kill him.

As soon as I got a chance I was going to get a big black marker and write over it with a black line. I was mortified and I felt the telltale heat in my cheeks—I was blushing. I was careful to keep my cast away from Damien when he returned a little while later. It would be so embarrassing if he saw the messages that my so-called best friend had written.

The nurse appeared with my dinner and I began to eat.

At least with my stab wound healing I was more mobile, and I insisted on going for a shower before I went to bed. Damien, being his usual overprotective self, stayed outside the bathroom door the entire time. He was so scared that I'd fall or accidentally hurt myself.

After my shower, he helped me back to the bed. It was then, as we stood by the bed, that he glanced down at my cast and read the messages.

"Chris?" he asked with a smirk on his face, pointing to the penned messages on my cast.

"Who else," I replied, feeling the heat in my cheeks again. It was mortifying.

"So my kisses are hot?" he asked with a teasing tone. He was enjoying every second of my embarrassment.

I glared at him and he just laughed.

"Those were Chris' words, not mine," I replied as I got back into the hospital bed with his help.

"So you don't think my kisses are hot?" he asked, his eyes darkening as he held my gaze.

"Your kisses were okay," I lied, because they were totally hot. I didn't need to feed his ego, even though my toes curled at the memory.

"Just okay?" he asked with a raised eyebrow. The playful tone was gone.

"I don't want to discuss it," I told him, trying to steer the conversation away from the current topic.

"Well, I do," he said as he stood with his arms crossed over his chest. Was it an ego thing? Why wouldn't he just let the subject slide?

He got a dangerous glint in his eye and he stepped closer. Before I could utter anything, his lips covered mine. Any coherent thought disappeared and all I could concentrate on was his lips against mine. I groaned and my lips opened slightly. His tongue swept into my mouth. I grabbed for his shirt as his tongue touched mine. It was so hot.

Then he was gone. I looked at him, confused, as he stood a few feet away from me with a smirk on his face.

"So that was just 'okay'?" he asked smugly. He'd done it on purpose just to prove a point.

"It was fine," I said breathlessly, underplaying the truth. I put a hand to my chest to slow down my heart that was beating rapidly.

"Just fine?" he asked as he stepped closer.

"It was hot," I finally admitted as I held my hands up, stopping him from trying to prove that his kisses were as hot as he said.

"I thought so," he smirked.

That night I didn't sleep well again. This time I was worried about leaving the hospital. For the few days I'd been here I'd felt safe and the idea of having to leave that safety scared me. I knew logically that I'd be safe in my new home with the Knights, but I couldn't help the fear of the unknown that kept me awake and studying the ceiling.

Beside me Damien slept in the chair, his arms folded and his legs stretched out in front of him. He was complicated. I couldn't understand why he was unable to commit. There had to be a reason why. Despite the fact that he wanted me and I wanted him, we were at a stalemate. He was unable to give me the commitment I needed and I was unable to just be the girl of the moment for him.

He made me feel things I'd never felt before and I couldn't deny that I liked the way he made me feel. Another thought popped up in my mind—I knew it was inevitable, given his reputation: soon I would have to watch him with other girls and I knew I wasn't ready to see that. I pushed all thoughts of Damien out of my mind, unable to deal with the pain they brought me.

Tomorrow the doctor was going to discharge me and I'd be going to live with the Knights. I couldn't help the nervous knot that formed in my stomach. I was one of those pessimistic people that thought about all the things that could go wrong. What if they changed their mind after a while? I was pretty screwed up, and what if I was too much to handle?

Damien was with me all of the time, I knew I would have to start to develop some independence and start to do things on my own, but that would take time. I couldn't expect Damien to keep doing what he was, it wasn't fair. He never complained. He still felt responsible about what happened to me and it was probably the guilt that kept him glued to my side.

I knew what I wanted to accomplish, but I had no idea how. I wanted to be able to be independent and do things on my own, but the fear that I felt kept me from taking those steps. I considered what the social worker had suggested. Maybe going to see a therapist might help me build up the courage to be able to be my own person and not to lean on Damien or his family too much.

Sometime after two in the morning I finally fell asleep.

The next morning was a flurry of activity as the doctor discharged me. He'd offered to prescribe me pain medication but I'd declined. Damien packed up my stuff for me as I fidgeted nervously, waiting for his parents to arrive.

"Don't be nervous," Damien said with an encouraging smile as he zipped my bag closed. "Everything will be okay."

"I know, I just can't help feeling anxious."

Twenty minutes later, the Knights arrived to take me to their home—my new home.

Amy and Steven were casually dressed, which meant they'd likely taken the day off work to help me settle in. Damien and Steven took my bags to the car and Amy walked beside me as the nurse wheeled me to the hospital entrance in a wheelchair.

Outside, the sun was shining brightly. It was a beautiful day but it did nothing to help the building anxious feeling in my stomach.

Amy held my elbow as I stood up. As we walked out of the hospital I saw a luxurious red car parked in the front. Damien was standing beside it. Amy steered me toward the car and Damien helped me in, and then closed the door. He jogged around the back, opened the door and slid in beside me.

The car smelled new, and there was a distinct scent of leather. I'd never been in a car this nice.

Nervously, I clutched my hands together and kept my gaze on the scenery as we pulled away from the hospital that had been my sanctuary up to now. I felt Damien's eyes firmly on me the entire journey to their house.

We drove into a nice, well-off neighborhood that had huge houses and well-kept gardens. I was in awe. I'd never seen houses as big as these. Some of them looked like fortresses with high walls to protect their privacy.

Even though Damien had told me his parents were loaded, I was open-mouthed shocked when the car pulled up into their driveway. The outside walls were high, but I could see a massive house that looked like a mansion inside. A black gate swung open and we drove up the driveway.

My mouth was still slightly open as I got out of the car once it pulled up in front of the house. It was so much to take in.

Damien took my bag as Amy ushered me into the house.

"I can't wait for you to see your room," she exclaimed as we entered the house.

The reception area was huge. Amy didn't give me a chance to look around before she steered me up the stairs to the first level.

"This side has Damien's room and yours," she explained as she indicated to the left of the stairs. Damien's room was close to mine. I wasn't sure how I felt about it. On one hand, I felt safer with him around, but on the other hand it was going to be difficult to be near him all the time.

"On the other side is a guest bedroom and a game lounge," she explained. A game lounge sounded interesting.

The house was beautifully decorated with large, flowing curtains and beautifully crafted furniture and ornaments. I wondered if Amy had done her own decorating or if she'd paid someone to do it.

Her excitement built and her smile grew as I followed her down the hallway. She stopped in front of a set of double wooden doors.

"I hope you like it," she said as she grinned from ear to ear.

She opened the doors and I saw my room for the first time.

It was beautiful.

The room was massive. It was probably the size of two standard bedrooms. In the middle of the room was a huge oak-wood bed. The bedding was a pale baby pink color with scattered lilac cushions.

To the side of the bed were a couple of sofas almost side by side that faced a flat-screen TV with a small coffee table in between. On the other side of the bed was a table and chair with a laptop. Beside the table was a walk-in closet.

"I bought you some clothes, but when you're feeling up to it I want to take you shopping," she told me as I peered in the closet.

"You don't have to," I said, seeing that there were more than enough clothes. I didn't need any more.

"I want to," she insisted, grasping both of my hands in hers.

My room was beautiful. I felt the sting of tears as emotion clogged my throat. I'd never owned much, so things had never meant a great deal to me, but I would be lying if I didn't admit that I was touched that Amy had done so much for me.

"Thank you," I managed to whisper to her when I turned to face her.

"You're welcome," she replied as she gave me a brief hug. I hugged her back. Slowly but surely, she was winning my trust.

"Let's go take a look at your bathroom," she suggested. I couldn't believe it—I had my own bathroom?

A door adjoining my bedroom opened up and I followed Amy into the bathroom. There was a corner bath and shower next to it. The towels and bath mat were the same baby pink as the bedcovers.

I was speechless. I wasn't sure if I would ever feel completely comfortable with all of this. Damien was placing my bags next to the bed when we stepped back into my room.

"I'm going to give you a chance to settle in," she told me as she followed Damien out of my room and left me alone.

I sat down on my bed and looked around my new room.

This would take some getting used to.

CHAPTER EIGHTEEN

Haven

I was still sitting on the bed ten minutes later, still a little shell-shocked, when there was a soft knock against the door.

"Come in," I said. I remained sitting on my bed, still trying to take everything in.

Damien stepped into my room.

"So what do you think?" he said when he sat down on my bed beside me.

"I'm a little overwhelmed," I admitted, flickering my gaze to the flat-screen TV and the laptop.

"You'll get used to it," he assured me, but I wasn't convinced.

"They bought me a laptop. I haven't even figured out how to use my new phone properly," I explained, indicating the laptop on the desk. I felt like such a failure.

"Don't worry about small things like that," he told me. "I'll teach you."

He'd already done so much for me.

"What do you want to do today?" he asked.

I wasn't sure, but when my eyes swept around my room and settled on the TV I knew what I wanted to do.

"I want to watch a movie."

If I were anyone else, it would be a normal to sit and watch a movie and eat popcorn, but I was anything but 'normal.' I couldn't remember the last time I'd done either of those things.

"You have a look through the DVDs and I'll go and make the popcorn," Damien suggested as he left my room.

Inside the cabinet below the TV I found a whole bunch of DVDs. I sat cross-legged in front of the cabinet and looked through the titles, but I had no clue what any of them were about. There were a couple of titles that I'd remembered hearing about from other people, but I'd never watched any of them.

When Damien returned with two sodas and two bowls filled with popcorn, I still hadn't decided on a movie to watch.

"Too many choices?" he asked, when he saw I still hadn't picked one.

"Something like that," I muttered, feeling self conscious.

He set the popcorn and sodas down on the coffee table and bent down in front of the cabinet beside me. His finger trailed over the spines of the DVDs until he selected one.

"How about *Pretty Woman*?" he asked.

"Okay."

I had no idea what it was about. I wasn't even entirely sure what I liked. He took the DVD out of the box and slipped it into the DVD player while I sat down on the one sofa with my feet tucked underneath me. Instead of sitting on the other sofa, he sat down next to me and handed me my popcorn and soda.

"Thank you," I said. I set my soda back on the coffee table in front of me.

He pushed a couple of buttons on a remote, and the movie started.

I munched on the popcorn with my eyes glued to the TV. I was hyperaware of every movement Damien made beside me and no matter how hard I tried to ignore him, I failed.

While we watched the movie, I couldn't help but root for a happy ending between the two main characters. The whole story line was so unrealistic, it was laughable. There was no way a rich, good-looking guy goes looking for a hooker and ends up falling in love with her. Even though the plot was unbelievable, I was on the edge of my seat, nearly biting my nails, hoping he'd come back and sweep her off her feet.

And when he did I sighed with contentment and settled back to watch. I felt Damien's eyes on me but I ignored him as I popped some more popcorn into my mouth. By the time the credits began to slide up the screen I set my bowl of popcorn down onto the table.

"Have you ever watched it before?" he asked quietly. I shook my head. There was no point in lying about it.

"Why?" he prodded further when I didn't elaborate. He set his empty bowl on the coffee table as he turned to face me.

I released a sigh. He wasn't going to let it go.

"It's the first movie I've watched in seven years," I explained, and then I waited for the disbelief. His eyes widened with surprise.

"No movies in seven years," he repeated softly. He stared at me, trying to comprehend what I'd just told him.

"What about TV?" he asked after a little silence.

I shook my head. I felt like a freak. Most of the things my peers took for granted, I'd gone without. All of this stuff was new to me.

"I'm sorry," he said softly.

"It's fine, it's just movies and TV," I said with a shrug.

"It's not just movies and TV you went without," he stated softly. He knew how badly I'd been treated. A heavily emotional silence descended as I averted my gaze from his. I didn't want his pity.

"I'll make sure you make up for everything you missed out on," he insisted, sitting forward.

My gaze met his. He smiled at me, his somber expression gone.

I nodded my head at him. "I'd like that."

"Come on, let me give you a tour of the house," he offered as he pulled me to my feet.

"Sure," I replied. This house was so big that I might need a map, not just a tour.

I followed Damien out of my room.

"That's my room," he indicated the room across the hall from mine. The doors to his room were open, so I got a glimpse of his room. It was messy, but I could see that he had a bed similar in size to mine with a dark-blue bed cover.

I wondered if his room smelled like him. I shook my head to dislodge the inappropriate thoughts about Damien that were beginning to develop in my mind. I glanced further down the hall and saw another door.

"What's down there?" I asked, pointing down the hallway I had yet to explore.

"Storage room, nothing important," he explained vaguely, but I saw the sadness in his eyes.

He was lying, but I let it slide for the moment.

The tour of the house took over an hour, and by the end of it I had asked Damien to draw me a map. He laughed and told me I would get used to it. I didn't agree. I'd lost count of the number of bedrooms and bathrooms the house had. There was a game lounge, a formal lounge, an informal lounge and another lounge (I couldn't remember what they used it for.) At least I could find the most important rooms in the house: my bedroom and the kitchen.

The outside was stunning. There was a massive garden

with beautiful flowers which had a path to another building, the pool house, which housed an Olympic-size swimming pool. It was heated. The last time I'd swum was before my dad had died—I'd just gotten the hang of swimming back then. I stayed a safe distance away from the pool. I wasn't sure if I could still swim. Maybe swimming was the same as riding a bicycle: once you learned how to, you never forgot.

"Can you swim?" Damien asked, watching me look at the water with a little fear in my eyes.

"I used to be able to swim, but I'm not sure if I still can," I revealed to him, my eyes still glued to the sparkling blue water.

"I'll help you," he offered as he walked me out of the poolroom.

"I know you want to help me, but I don't want to take up all of your time," I told him. I couldn't monopolize him anymore; he had to have a life of his own. Besides, I'd promised myself that I would start to try and become more independent, even if it meant I had to go into therapy.

He stopped and I turned to face him.

"I want to help you," he stated firmly with his hands in his pockets.

I changed the subject by asking some questions about the garden.

By the end of the tour I was exhausted as I opened the door to my room. The bed looked so inviting.

"Are you going to lie down?" Damien asked when he followed me into the room.

"Yeah, I'm a little tired," I admitted. "I think I overdid it today."

"Are you hungry?" he asked, checking his watch. "It's lunchtime."

"A little," I admitted. My stomach began to grumble slightly at the mention of lunchtime.

"I'll bring you up something to eat," he offered.

"Thank you," I said.

"I won't be long," he assured me before he turned and left.

I climbed onto the massive bed and pulled the blanket over me as I lay down. My room was so big compared to what I was used to and I felt a little lost and out of place.

Damien returned twenty minutes later with a tray for me. He set it down on the side table next to my bed.

"Sorry, my mom went a little overboard," he warned when I glanced at the amount of food that he'd brought me.

There was a sandwich and a side salad. There was a packet of crisps and a bowl of some sort of dessert. On closer inspection it looked like chocolate mousse. There was a bottle of water and a glass of juice as well.

"There is no way I'm going to be able to eat all of that," I warned.

"Eat what you want and then I'll take back the rest," he offered.

"Thanks," I said as I took the one half of the sandwich and took a bite.

"Because we've been off for a while, my mom went past our school and picked up our homework so we can try catch up before school on Monday," he told me.

I nodded my agreement as I finished chewing the bit of my sandwich.

"Is there a lot?" I asked once I swallowed the mouthful.

"Yes." He grimaced. "It's probably going to take us most of the weekend to work through it."

"Do you want to start now?" I asked, feeling a little better now that I had some food in my stomach.

"Aren't you tired?" he asked.

"I'm feeling a little better now that I've eaten something," I answered. I pushed the blanket off myself and slid out of the bed.

"Okay," he said. "You make yourself comfortable at the desk and I'll go and get the homework and our books."

It was only when I sat down at the desk that I wondered how his mom had gotten my books. He returned a short while later carrying them, and sat them down on the table.

"How did your mom get my books?" I asked.

"I think she organized it with the principal. They got them from your locker."

I couldn't help but think about the books in my schoolbag that I'd left in the flat. That specific thought brought back the memories of the attack that I'd been trying to forget.

"What about my books at the flat?" I whispered. I knew it wasn't a big deal, but I couldn't help but ask.

Damien regarded me for a moment.

"For any of the books that we didn't find in your locker, my mom got new books for you," he answered softly. I gave him a nod and focused my attention onto the books in front of me.

"The cops will be busy with the apartment for a few more days and then I can go around and get some of your stuff if you want me to," he offered.

I nearly started to laugh hysterically, because I didn't have a lot of stuff. The only valuable thing that I had in the apartment was the only photo I still had of my dad.

"Okay," I said with a shrug. "Let's get started, it looks like it is going to take us forever."

I had successfully steered the conversation into another direction. He pulled up a seat next to me and we started to get stuck in the homework we'd missed. Somewhat luckily it was my left arm that had been broken, because I was right handed. It would be hard trying to do schoolwork if I couldn't even write.

I tried my hardest to concentrate on the homework we had to get done, but it was so difficult when Damien was sitting so close to me. The slightest touches, like his arm touching mine, or his knee brushing against mine, kept me hyperaware of his being next to me.

After a couple of hours I couldn't take it anymore. I closed my book and dropped my head into my hands.

"I can't do any more," I moaned. I felt a headache start up and I rubbed my forehead to ease the slight pounding in my head.

"Okay," he said as he stretched his arms above his head. The action hitched his shirt up and I got a peek at his taut stomach muscles.

I stood up and averted my eyes from him. It was getting harder and harder to be around him. I heard a phone start to ring and he reached into his pocket and pulled out his phone.

"Hi…I can't, maybe sometime next week," he said after a moment. His eyes flickered to mine and I turned to busy myself with the stuff I had yet to pack away.

Thoughts of who was on the phone began to gnaw at me while he continued his phone call. I couldn't help but wonder if it was his girl of the week that was trying to meet up with him. I felt jealousy stir within me. I took my bag of clothes from the hospital to the walk-in closet so I didn't have to hear any more of his conversation. To think he was on the phone with another girl hurt—I knew I had no right to feel that way, but I couldn't help it.

I folded the clean clothes from my bag as best as I could, considering my one arm was in a cast, and put them away in my cupboard. The rest of the clothes I took to my bathroom to put in the wash basket. Damien was still on the phone when I passed him on my way to my bathroom.

"I'll call you later," he whispered into the phone as he watched me walk into the bathroom.

It was times like this that I wasn't sure how I was going to stay just friends with Damien. If I couldn't stand to listen to him talk to a girl over the phone, how on earth was I going to handle seeing him with a girl? I dumped the dirty clothes into the wash basket.

"Sorry about that," Damien said from the doorway.

"It's fine," I said casually. I couldn't let him see how much it affected me.

"I'm just going to leave the books and stuff on your desk so that we can pick up where we left off tomorrow," he told me.

"Sure."

An awkward silence descended and then I turned to him while I rubbed my forehead.

"I'm a little tired, I think I'm going to try and have a lie down," I lied to him. I wasn't really tired, but just to get some space from him I would lie down on my bed and pretend to nap.

"Sure, no problem," he replied. He studied me for a few moments before he turned and left.

I let out a deep sigh when I walked back into my room. I took a sip of orange juice and then I climbed onto my bed and pulled the blanket over me.

How on earth was I going to live with Damien and be able to keep him at a distance? How was I going to avoid getting hurt when I saw him with different girls? It was going to be impossible. I was screwed either way. If we kept things purely platonic between us, I'd get hurt watching him with other girls and, if I let things happen between us, he'd hurt me when he finished with me and moved onto another girl. I was going to get hurt irrespective of which choice I made.

A little later I was still lost in my thoughts when I heard a soft knock on my bedroom door. I closed my eyes and pretended to be asleep.

"How is she?" I heard Damien ask softly.

"She's sleeping," Amy replied, and I heard the distinct click of the door closing.

I didn't know what I was going to do, because I couldn't hide in my room forever. At some point I would have to get up and face my problems.

CHAPTER NINETEEN

Haven

The first night in my new home, I woke up in the middle of the night screaming. My whole body shook with fear as the door to my bedroom flew open.

"It's okay," a voice soothed, and strong arms held me gently to a firm chest. It was still dark and frightening in my room with only some light from my open doorway filtering in.

Still half asleep and with the fear of my nightmare still fresh in my mind, I began to struggle against the arms holding me.

"It's me, Haven," Damien said, trying to get me to calm down. He kept me firmly in his arms, refusing to let go.

Relief flooded through me at the realization that it was him holding me. Feeling safe, I slumped against his chest. My body was shaking. He held and soothed me for a while before I began to calm down.

"I'm sorry," I said. I realized he didn't have a shirt on and that I was being held against his bare chest. I pulled away from him, trying to stop my hands from shaking. His strong and warm hands covered mine and he held them gently. I didn't know if it was the warmth from his hands or the aftereffects of the nightmare wearing off that stopped my hands from shaking.

"You don't have to be sorry," he said softly. "It was just a nightmare."

"It felt so real," I whispered, sorting through the horrors of what I'd just dreamed. Grant had cornered me in my new bedroom. This time he'd used a gun to kill me. I'd tried to scream for help but no one had come. I could still hear the gunshot ringing in my ears.

"Do you want me to stay with you?" he asked.

I hesitated.

"I'll sleep on the couch," he clarified.

I knew I should have been strong and told him no, but I couldn't. I was so scared and he made me feel safe. I needed to feel safe.

"Please," I whispered, my voice still hoarse from all the screaming.

He reached for the blanket at the bottom of my bed and walked over to one of the sofas. I felt bad because it was only a two-seater sofa and Damien was tall. There was no way he was going to get any sleep tonight if he slept there.

"The sofa is too small. You can sleep in my bed," I quietly offered.

He stood watching me for a moment, still holding the blanket in his hand.

"Are you sure?" he asked.

I nodded.

He was doing me a favor by staying the night in my room to ease my fears; the least I could do was let him sleep in my bed so that he could get some sleep.

I lay back down and pulled the bed cover to my chin as he walked over to the other side of the bed with the blanket. Instead of pulling back the bed cover, he climbed on top and spread the blanket over him. Restless, I tossed and turned for a while before I felt Damien reach for my hand in the darkness and hold it in his.

That small gesture was enough to settle me down and I began to relax. Having him sleeping in my bed might help me sleep for the night, but it was only going to make my feelings for him deepen, and it would only bring me heartbreak.

We spent the rest of the weekend catching up on our schoolwork. Damien didn't go out the whole weekend—he spent most of it with me showing me things, like how to use my new laptop and my new phone. I was starting to get the hang of it.

He even came with us when his mom took me shopping for some clothes and other things. No guy liked to go shopping, so I assumed it was to make me feel safer. I tried to keep her from going overboard with the shopping, but she was on a mission so I let her have free reign. It seemed to make her happy. Damien, like a typical guy, moaned and groaned the entire time, muttering about how shopping was as boring as watching paint dry.

It was hard not to like his parents. They were such kind and loving people and after all they'd done for me I was very grateful.

After the nightmares returned the following night, Damien started to sleep in my bed every night. His presence kept the nightmares away. I wasn't sure what why I was having nightmares. Maybe it was the stress of trying to fit in. I hoped that after I settled down in my new home the nightmares would stop, and then I could keep Damien at a safe distance.

It was nearly impossible to keep my feelings for him platonic when he slept in my bed half naked every night holding my hand. It was hard to believe that the kind and thoughtful person that slept in my bed every night to keep my nightmares away was the same person who couldn't commit and was trying to sleep his way through all the senior girls at our school.

Steven had kept in touch with the cops but there had been no new developments. They were still looking for Grant. As much as I wanted to stay home and keep hidden until the cops caught Grant, I couldn't stop living my life because of him. I needed to go to school, I had to pick up the pieces to my life, despite my fear.

The first day back at school was nerve-wracking. From the moment Damien drove us to school and everyone watched me get out of his car, I'd had everyone's attention. I wanted to fade into the background like I'd been doing for the last seven years, but that was impossible when I was around Damien.

There were plenty of rumors going around the school about what had happened to me, and why I was living with Damien. Chris had given me a rundown of all of them at lunchtime. Some of them were ridiculous.

The most ridiculous was that I'd been orphaned, which I supposed was technically true, but then I'd been involved in an accident and somehow it had been discovered that I was the long-lost sister given away by Damien's mom when she had been a teen. Now I'd been reunited with my family, and Damien was my brother.

It was the type of stuff soap operas were based on.

Damien had invited me to join him for lunch, but I'd declined. I was trying to put some space between us. Besides, I'd had enough of the glares for all the jealous girls trying to audition to be his girl of the week. Thankfully for my fragile heart, I hadn't seen him with any girls—yet. I knew it was only a matter of time, so I had to keep my distance from him so that when he finally went back to his usual self it wouldn't hurt too much.

I depended on him too much and I needed to change that; but, like the saying goes, Rome wasn't built in a day, and I couldn't expect to change overnight. I got a few sympathetic looks from my teachers, but I tried to ignore them. I hated that they knew the truth about what had happened to me. It made me feel vulnerable.

By the end of the day I was physically and emotionally tired. In the passenger seat of Damien's car I slumped backward and rubbed my forehead. The ride was quiet but I could see Damien's eyes glance my way a couple of times on the way home.

I kept my eyes closed, trying to fight the headache I felt pounding in my head.

"What the fuck?" I heard Damien say suddenly, and then his hand was on mine.

"Keep your eyes closed," he instructed fiercely. I kept my eyes closed but sat up straight as the car stopped.

"What's wrong?" I asked as I began to panic.

What could have happened at the house that was so bad he didn't want me to see?

"Keep your eyes closed," he reminded me before I heard his door slam shut.

Moments later, I heard the passenger door open and he helped me out the door.

The fear in me made me open my eyes slowly while he tried to steer me to the front door past the garage doors.

Oh. My. God.

The scene in front of me made me fall to my knees.

Damien tried to pull me up, but I pushed him away, my eyes glued to the horrific scene in front of me. It was too late, I'd seen it and there was no way to erase the heart-stopping sight.

"I told you not to look," he scolded softly as he bent down to put a protective arm around my shoulders.

The word "Whore" was painted in red on the white garage door. I knew who was responsible. Grant had called me a whore when he'd first seen me with Damien.

I began to shake when the realization set in that Grant knew where I was. It was only when I took a closer look that I realized that what I initially had thought was red paint was in fact blood.

"Oh my God," I whispered when I spotted the source of the blood. Lying on its side was a dead cat that had been gutted, its insides spilled out onto the brick pavement.

I felt my stomach heave at the sight and I rushed to the bushes just by the doorway before I lost the contents of my stomach. Bent over in the bushes, with my head pounding and my hands clutching the grass, Damien knelt beside me. I closed my eyes again while I heaved again, he held my hair away from my face.

I wiped my mouth with my sleeve and sat back for a moment. I heard the echo of my heartbeat echoing in my ears as the fear took hold of me. Suddenly I started to feel dizzy.

"I've got you," Damien whispered into my ear when he picked me up and walked me into the house.

My mind began to shut down and I felt disconnected from my body. It was too much to deal with. Damien carried me upstairs to my bedroom and set me down gently on the bed, but I just lay there, staring past him. I felt numb. I saw Damien talk to me, but I heard nothing. All I could hear was the echo of my heart beating in my ears.

In my peripheral vision I saw him talking on the phone while he paced up and down beside my bed. Grant knew where I was. The fear that gripped me nearly took my breath away, because I knew he wasn't finished with me. The message had been received loud and clear: he was going to come back and finish what he'd started. I began to shake so violently that my teeth chattered.

"I don't know what's happening to her, mom… I think she might be in shock," Damien said frantically into the phone.

He paused, listening. "Okay," he said, and then he put his phone back into his pocket.

I felt the bed dip as he sat on the bed beside me and pulled me into his arms.

"I won't let him get you," Damien quietly promised as he rubbed my back gently. Desperate to believe his words, I closed my eyes.

The next few hours passed in a blur. Damien made me drink sugar water, and it eased the shaking. Amy was the first one to arrive home.

"Haven," she gasped with frantic concern when she entered my room. Damien let go of me and shifted off the bed as she sat down on my bed and hugged me. It was a warm and loving hug, a mother's hug. I sank into her embrace and took the comfort she offered. When she pulled back, she scanned my face.

"It'll be all right," she assured me. Her wide, expressive eyes made me believe her.

By the time Steven arrived home I was exhausted. Amy gave me something to help calm me and it began to make me sleepy. She pulled my curtains closed and said she'd check on me a little later.

Damien stayed with me. I was too scared to be on my own. He lay on his back and my head rested on his chest as his arm wrapped around me and held me protectively. In his safe arms, I fell asleep, but my dreams made me restless and a couple of hours later I woke up sweating and twisted in my bed covers, alone.

I climbed out of my bed and went to look for Damien. A

soft knock to his bedroom door went unanswered. He had to be downstairs. When I went downstairs I heard his voice coming from the kitchen. As I approached, I heard Amy say my name. I stopped, wanting to hear what they said about me.

"The cops can't give her the protection she needs," said Damien, clearly upset.

"We'll organize something," Steven murmured.

"What did the cops have to say?" Damien asked his mom.

"Detective Green said they are working as hard as they can to find him."

"I can't believe it's been nearly two weeks and they haven't got any closer to catching him!" Damien exploded.

"Calm down, son," barked Steven. Then, in a more gentle tone, he said, "Getting upset about it isn't going to help things."

"Your father is right," Amy reinforced gently.

"Detective Green thinks that when Haven's mom died suddenly, it was too much for her stepfather to deal with and he had some sort of mental breakdown. It could explain why, after years of abusing her, it had suddenly escalated."

"They are following up all the leads they have but he said it takes time. It also doesn't help that the stepfather isn't mentally stable, so it's hard to predict what he'll do next."

I nearly laughed hysterically. It just didn't end. I dropped my head into my hands, feeling defeated.

"We will keep her safe," Steven assured Damien.

Having heard enough, I crept back to my bedroom.

Not only was I scared to death of Grant and what he was capable of, I was scared of all the trouble I was causing the Knights. What if having me in their home caused them more trouble than they were willing to deal with? Would they get rid of me? I'd started to ease into life with them and I had begun to care for them, despite my fears. I wouldn't recover if they decided I was too much trouble.

When I heard Damien creep back into my bedroom a little later I pretended to be asleep as he climbed into my bed and I felt him pull me into his arms. He pressed a soft kiss to my forehead and tightened his hold on me for a moment. I was wound up so tight with all of my fears that I doubted I would sleep a wink even when I was nicely cocooned in Damien's embrace all night.

Another growing fear that ate away at me was that I was spending more and more time with Damien, and it was getting harder to keep my heart closed off from him.

CHAPTER TWENTY

Haven

A new level of fear set in after the incident. It didn't matter what I was doing, I couldn't help the thought that Grant could be watching me, and I was always on my guard.

The next day Amy pleaded with me to stay home, but I refused. I wasn't going to let the incident keep me a prisoner in my new home. It felt like if I let the fear rule me, then, in a way, Grant was winning, and I couldn't let that happen. As scared as I was, I got dressed, got my schoolbag and went to school with Damien. If he was protective before, he was practically smothering me now. I couldn't blame him, but I felt like my whole situation was taking over his life and I didn't think it was fair.

He'd slept in my bed that night, holding me close. I knew what was happening, but I couldn't pull myself away from his warm embrace. Instead, I burrowed deeper, trying to ignore the warning signs going off in my head. It was like watching an accident unfold and being unable to pull my gaze away from it.

Damien walked me into the school and to the lockers, where I spotted Chris leaning against mine.

"Hi," I greeted as he straightened up and flashed me a warm smile.

"You kept me waiting this morning," he said with a teasing tone.

"Yeah, sorry about that," I replied as I opened my locker. Normally when Chris was around, Damien would leave, but today he stayed by my side.

I turned to face him and told him, "I'll be fine, I'm with Chris."

His eyes rested on Chris for a moment and then he looked at me. I could see that he was wrestling with his decision.

"Okay," he finally relented. "I'll see you later."

I watched him turn and walk down the hallway, disappearing in the crowd of students filtering into the school.

"What's that all about?" Chris asked when I turned back to my locker.

I let out a heavy sigh. I just wanted to be able to forget about what had happened yesterday, but it wasn't going to happen.

"When I got home yesterday, there was a message from Grant on the garage door," I said calmly, even though I felt the fear creep in.

"A message from Grant?" he gasped. I had his undivided attention.

"Yes. He wrote 'whore' on the garage door with the neighbors' dead cat's blood," I answered with a calmness I didn't feel.

"Oh. My. God," he said as he touched my arm.

"Yeah," I replied, keeping my attention on my schoolbooks in my locker.

"He knows where you live." He said it more to himself than to me.

I nodded my head. If it wasn't for the fact that the Knights had state-of-the-art security inside the house, I wouldn't be able to sleep at night. The fact that Damien slept beside me helped.

Amy had mentioned to me that they were looking into installing extra security on the property and the surrounding wall to keep intruders out. I wasn't sure that would be enough to keep Grant away from me, but I appreciated the thought. She also said something about the cops making arrangements to watch over me.

"Why are you so calm? If I were in your shoes, I'd be freaking out," Chris asked, watching me carefully.

"I might sound calm, but I'm not... I can't just give up and hide out in my room hoping he won't get me."

I stuffed the books I needed into my bag as I closed my locker and turned to face Chris.

"If I give up, he wins," I stated feeling a little emotional.

"You're right," he said as he looped his arm around mine and we started to walk to class. "If you need anything you can phone me anytime, even if it's just to talk."

He'd offered countless times but I wasn't ready to talk about the stuff that had happened with Grant. I'd never talked to anyone about it, and I wasn't sure if I would ever be ready.

"So when can I come visit?" he asked, which made me feel relieved because he'd effectively changed the subject.

He'd been dying to visit since I'd moved in. Everyone knew the Knights were loaded, and he wanted to see the house.

"I'll need to speak to the Knights first," I replied. I needed to make sure it was okay with the Knights before I started inviting people around.

"Sure, no problem," he replied when we came to a stop outside my first class for the day. "I'll see you at lunch."

He gave me a hug and hurried down the hall to his class. Walking into my class and sitting down, I noticed some people still staring at me. I still couldn't get used to the jealous glares from some of the girls. I was still getting some sympathetic looks as well, but I wished people would just ignore me like they had before.

Students filtered into the class as I gazed outside the window. I heard the chair next to me scrape, and I turned to see a guy I'd never seen before sit down in the seat next to me. When he caught my eye he smiled as he dropped his bag next to the table.

My breath caught in my throat. He was gorgeous. He had dark brown hair that reached just below his ears and the most beautiful emerald green eyes, surrounded with long dark eyelashes. His smile widened as I gaped at him. As his smile widened, dimples appeared in his cheeks. It was a lethal combination and I struggled to swallow when I felt the full effect of his eyes on me. I pulled my eyes away from him and tucked my hair behind my ear, nervously trying to ignore the hot guy still staring at me.

"Hi, I'm Mark," he said, introducing himself.

My eyes shot back to him.

"I'm Haven," I replied softly.

"Nice to meet you, Haven," he said before he sent me another devastating smile.

I shifted in my seat, letting my gaze drop to my textbook in front of me, trying to ignore him, but I could still feel his eyes on me. I sighed with relief when the teacher finally entered the classroom and started the lesson. Even through the lesson I felt his eyes on me more than a couple of times. I used my hair like a curtain to keep myself hidden from him.

When the bell rang I shoved my book into my school bag and dashed out of the class to get away from him. It was all for nothing because in my next class I looked up and saw him sitting a couple of seats away from me. It was impossible to ignore him. By the time the lunchtime bell went I was looking forward to escaping him for a while.

Chris was seated in our usual spot when I dropped down to sit next to him.

"Have you seen the new student?" he said, beginning to gossip.

"Let me guess, dark brown hair and dimples and his name is Mark," I replied dryly.

"I take it you've met him already," he said. "I saw him briefly and I have to admit, I think he is going to give Damien some competition with the girls."

My stomach dropped. I didn't want to see Damien with another girl.

"Damien's worried about you," he revealed softly as he opened up his lunch bag.

My eyes shot to his.

"How do you know that?" I asked, wanting to know the details.

"He told me. He also asked me to keep an eye on you when he wasn't around," he answered.

I wasn't sure how I felt about that. On one hand I got a warm and fuzzy feeling inside at the fact that he felt worried and protective about me; but then, on the other hand, I felt disappointed because no matter how much he cared it would never be enough.

"I haven't seen Damien with any other girls, you know," Chris said. It was like he could read me like a book.

"It doesn't matter, he can't give me what I want," I said, reinforcing myself. "So he can do anything he wants with, with whomever he wants."

It didn't matter how many times I told myself I didn't care; the fact was that I did more and more every day.

"What do you think about the new guy?" Chris asked,

steering the subject away from Damien. I gave him a questioning look as he broached the new subject.

"He seems nice," he added. My forehead furrowed when I realized what Chris was getting at.

"I'm not sure I'm ready to put myself out there yet," I said with a shrug. Damien was the one that made the butterflies flutter in my stomach. He was the one that held me in his arms at night and made me feel safe.

"You were ready to try with Damien," he reminded me softly.

He was right, but Damien was different.

"I know Damien." It was a weak excuse and even I knew that.

"There was a time when you didn't, and now you do. I'm not telling you to run off and marry Mark, but try have a conversation with him," he advised. "You can't keep yourself closed off from everybody. Look at us. When we first met, you weren't interested in allowing yourself to interact or feel for other people, and look at us now. If I hadn't persevered, we wouldn't be friends. I'm not telling you to stalk the guy like I stalked you," he teased lightly.

I couldn't help but smile, because that was how he'd wormed his way into my heart.

"Just keep yourself open to the idea, " he continued. "Have a conversation and see where it leads."

"Okay," I relented. "I'll try."

I wasn't good with people. The only reason I had Chris and Damien in my life was because they'd practically barged in, set up shop, and refused to leave.

Honestly I had no idea how to interact with people, and just the thought of talking to Mark made me feel nervous, but Chris was right—I had to learn how to interact with people.

I spent rest of lunchtime quietly contemplating what I

would say to Mark. By the time I left Chris to walk to my next class, anything that I'd thought up sounded pathetic.

Chris was right, Mark was the only boy in the school to give Damien competition when it came to the girls, so it didn't surprise me when I saw him talking to Angela as I passed them in the hallway on the way to my next class. I felt a little disappointed, because there was no way I could compare with a girl like Angela, so I decided there was no point in trying to start up a conversation with him.

I was the first one in the class, so I sat down and got my schoolbook out. I began to doodle on the paper with a pen while I waited for the teacher.

"Hi." I turned to see Mark sitting at the desk next to me. He flashed me that devastating smile of his which accentuated his dimples. I felt nervous.

Damien made me feel hot and cold at the same time and my stomach fluttered every time he looked at me or touched me. When Mark looked at me I felt nervously aware of him and nervous that there was no doubt that he was gorgeous.

"Hi," I replied, taken a little off guard because I hadn't even heard him sit down next to me. All the things I had prepared in my mind before evaporated, and I stared at him blankly.

"You're not much of a talker, are you," he said, leaning back in his chair, his eyes still firmly on me.

I blushed slightly at the directness of his stare. His confidence would make most girls go weak at the knees. I shook my head in response to his question and, unable to hold his gaze, I dropped my eyes back to the doodle I'd been drawing with my pen.

The teacher entered the class at that moment and began the lesson. I tried to concentrate on what the teacher was saying, but I was hyperaware of the fact that Mark was still watching me. As much as I wanted to dash out of the class as soon as the lesson ended, I made myself take my time putting my stuff into my bag as Mark did the same beside me.

"Can I walk you to your next class?" he asked as I hitched my bag strap over my shoulder.

"Sure," I replied softly, and we walked side by side out of the classroom.

"I hear you were the new girl not so long ago?" he asked casually.

"Yes," I mumbled. I didn't want to be reminded of a time that I was living in fear on a daily basis.

"What happened to your arm?" he asked. I glanced down at my cast. I couldn't exactly tell him the truth.

"I had an accident," I lied.

"Who was the guy you were sitting with at lunch?" he said, continuing his questioning.

"Chris," I replied, feeling more nervous.

"And Chris is…?"

"My friend," I answered, shooting him a glance. He smiled at my answer.

"Good."

He had all the same classes I had, so he walked me to each class, asking me more questions. Did I have any siblings? Where had I lived before I'd moved here? Some of the questions made me feel uncomfortable, but I tried to answer them as best I could. School had finished and I was standing at the entrance waiting for Damien and Mark had been standing with me when he asked me one particular question that I didn't know how to answer.

"So, what does your mom do?" he asked, an innocent question.

I couldn't even remember what her occupation had been before she'd spiraled out of control.

"I don't like to talk about my family," I answered softly, dropping my gaze.

"Sorry, I didn't mean to pry," he replied. "I just want to get to know you better."

My eyes flickered to his and I felt a little hot and cold under his serious stare. Why would he want to get to know me better?

"Haven."

Damien saying my name snapped me out of my moment with Mark.

"Hi," I said to Damien, but his attention wasn't on me, he was looking at Mark—well, glaring at him.

"Hi, I'm Mark," Mark said.

Damien continued to glare at him and then muttered, "Damien."

"I've got to go," I said to Mark.

"Sure, I'll see you tomorrow," he replied, flashing a smile.

"See you tomorrow," I replied. Mark walked down the stairs to the car park.

"Let's go," Damien said to me before he stalked to his car. I followed quietly behind him.

"What's wrong?" I asked him as I climbed into his car, but instead of answering, he slammed the door closed.

He wouldn't even look at me when he got into the driver's side and started up the car. I bit my lip, trying not to let his behavior upset me, but it was hard. He was important to me, and he was clearly upset with me.

I'd just been talking to Mark. Then I had a sudden thought—could Damien be jealous?

"Why are you mad at me?" I asked softly when we were halfway home.

"I don't want to talk about it," he snapped, keeping his eyes on the road in front of him.

I didn't want to presume that he was jealous. Maybe he wasn't, so I let him ignore me for the rest of the ride home. It hurt. I was used to the caring, protective, understanding Damien. The boy sitting next to me in the car was a stranger.

He was quiet for most of the journey and I didn't try and start up any conversation. I wasn't used to him acting like this and he was hard to read, so I kept my mouth shut and stared out the window.

It was beautiful where the Knights lived. Even the sidewalks were wide with beautiful, lush, green trees. Thinking back to my old neighborhood, there hadn't been much beauty.

I couldn't help but hold my breath as we pulled up to the driveway, but thankfully there were no more messages from Grant. The bloodied message from the previous day had been cleaned up, so there were no remnants of what had happened. There were no messages, but it didn't make me feel any safer.

Grant knew where I was and for all I knew he could still be watching me right now. I couldn't help scanning the bushes surrounding the outer wall as Damien drove up the driveway. Once he parked, we got out of the car and walked to the front door. I walked in first, and Damien followed behind. Amy greeted us as we entered the house. She smiled and hugged me.

"How was school?" she asked while we walked to the kitchen.

"It was okay," I replied as I took a seat by the counter.

"I've got some stuff to do," Damien said as he stood in the doorway to the kitchen. "I'll see you later."

"Okay," his mom said and I nodded.

"Would you like something to drink?" she asked before she opened the fridge.

I shook my head. I remembered Chris asking when he would be able to come visit.

"Would it be okay if my friend Chris came to visit?" I

asked nervously.

"Of course, any time, you don't have to ask," she replied with a smile on her face. "I want you to feel comfortable here, this is your home. You can invite friends over any time you want."

"Thank you," I replied. It was so strange, living in a house where I was given so much freedom after living with so many restrictions for years.

I stayed in the kitchen talking to Amy and then I went back to my bedroom to finish my homework. I was almost done when there was a knock at my door and I looked up to see Damien standing in my doorway.

"Mom wants to talk to us," he said. I closed my books and slid off the bed.

Silently, I followed him to the kitchen. It was the place Amy spent most of her time when she was at home. Were we in trouble? I couldn't help the negative thoughts from entering my mind as an anxious feeling settled in my stomach. Amy was quiet when Damien and I entered the kitchen. She smiled at me and the smile didn't reach her eyes.

CHAPTER TWENTY-ONE

DAMIEN

I snuck a glance at Haven as I drove us both to school. It was the morning after discovering the bloodied message Grant had left for Haven on the garage door. My mom had tried to get her to stay at home, but she'd been determined to go to school and carry on as normal.

I admired that in her. Most people would have stayed at home.

Just the thought that the man that had been physically abusing her, and who had tried to kill her, was still watching her made my blood boil. If I ever met him I'd kill him with my bare hands. I'd seen what he'd done to Haven and anyone who could do that shouldn't be allowed to live.

The details of what had happened to her over the last few years were still a mystery. She wasn't ready to talk about it and I wasn't going to push it. The doctors had been horrified at the amount of abuse they'd discovered when they'd examined her, so I knew it had been bad. I was already protective of her, but after the message I just wanted to keep her locked in her bedroom away from any potential harm.

Once we got to school I walked her to her locker where

Chris was waiting for her. He was a good friend to Haven. I knew he cared about her and that he'd do anything for her, and that alone made me like him. There weren't a lot of people I trusted to look after Haven, but I trusted him.

I left Haven and Chris to go to my locker. When I got to my locker, I opened it and swapped some books around for my first few classes when I turned to see Nicole standing beside me with her chest pressing against my arm. Her cleavage was fighting to get free of a top that looked two sizes too small.

"Hi," she whispered huskily into my ear.

Before Haven, I wouldn't have even thought twice; but as much as I wanted to deny it, I wasn't the same person.

"Hi, Nicole," I greeted her as I stuffed my books into my bag and closed my locker.

"You've been quiet lately," she said with a pout. She was a cheerleader, so she was popular with the boys, and I knew she'd give me whatever I wanted—but I wasn't interested.

I didn't have time for this. I had more important things to worry about than girls and sex.

"Yeah, I've had a lot on my plate," I said, not wanting to reveal too much. She was right—normally I was out at every party with some girl, but I hadn't been out since Haven's attack.

And for some reason I couldn't explain, I hadn't been with a girl since the day I'd seen the damage in myself reflected in Haven's eyes.

"Are you going to Evan's party tonight?" she asked as she trailed a red-polished nail down my shirt seductively. She was beautiful on the outside, but there wasn't much to her on in the inside. She was exactly the type of girl that I would have taken to bed and left the next morning. If she was good in bed, I'd keep her around for the week, but that was all I ever offered.

I shook my head.

"Maybe another time," I mumbled as I walked away, leaving her standing open mouthed in front of my locker.

"What the hell, man?" said a shocked voice. I glanced to see Shane, the source of the voice, join me as I walked down the hallway. "Did I just hear you tell her that you weren't coming to the party tonight?"

"Yeah, you heard right," I said. I didn't have to explain my actions to anyone.

"Does this have to do with Haven?" he asked. I'd told him that Haven had moved into my house but I'd been tightlipped about the reasons why, and he'd stopped asking. Haven's story wasn't mine to share, even with my close friends.

"Yes, there is a lot going on and I don't have time to party at the moment."

There was no way I was going into more detail than that.

"If you need anything all you have to do is ask," he offered. That was one of the reasons why he was my best friend.

"Thanks, man," I replied, running an agitated hand through my hair.

"Just think, you'll have more girls to pick from," I teased him. He was my wingman and it helped that the girls loved him as well.

"Whatever, man," he said as he shook his head. "I don't need any help getting laid."

Thoughts of Haven consumed me for most of the day. I struggled to push the image of her horrified look when she'd seen the message from my mind.

Every broken look she expelled to the world pulled at something inside of me. There were times she looked so fragile and all I wanted to do was hold her close and keep her safe. A couple of my teachers had to pull me out of my thoughts to concentrate on their lesson.

Today had been a waste. I was in no mood to sit and pretend everything was okay, especially when the cops were still searching for Grant. I couldn't believe they hadn't caught him yet. It didn't ease my fear that my parents were taking extra precautions to ensure her safety.

In between classes I couldn't prevent my eyes from searching for a glimpse of Haven in the sea of students walking in the hallways trying to get to their next class in time. My happiness at spotting her was cut short when I spotted a guy walking beside her.

They were talking, and I swear I just saw her give him a smile. It felt like someone had punched in me in the gut. Jealously pierced through me like a hot knife and I wanted to walk up to her and yank her away from him. A feeling of possessiveness I'd never experienced wanted me to make it clear to her new friend that she was mine, but I stopped myself.

Who was I kidding? I held myself back, but stood still in the hallway with students walking around me, my eyes glued to the retreating figures of Haven and her new friend. I'd told her that I couldn't give her what she deserved, and irrespective of my jealousy and possessiveness, that hadn't changed. Against the instinct pulling inside of me, I turned around and kept my head down as I rushed to my next class.

As much as I tried to block thoughts of Haven from my mind, I couldn't. We had chemistry, and I'd felt that when I'd kissed her. I wanted her more than I'd ever wanted any girl, but I could only offer her the physical side of me. I didn't do emotions. There was no doubt that I did care for her, but for my own survival I couldn't allow that to deepen or become something stronger.

It was hard trying to keep my distance from her when all I wanted to do was keep her close and keep the world from hurting her. The gut-wrenching feeling that settled in my stomach when I thought of all the years that bastard had been hurting her for was unbearable.

Death had taught me that the more you loved, the more you had to lose, and I'd already lost enough. I couldn't go through that again, so I made sure I kept my emotions closed off. Sex was the closest I got to anyone, but there was no emotion in it, and once it was finished I walked away. The emotionally damaged side of me stopped me from sticking around and making deeper attachments.

I'd been good at it until Haven had stepped into my life. After everything she'd been through she deserved someone who was capable of loving her without holding anything back, she deserved the type of love that I couldn't give her. I was emotionally scarred and all I'd do is hurt her.

I carried the ache in my chest throughout the entire day. Seeing Haven with another guy wasn't sitting well with me but I wasn't going to interfere. She deserved a chance to be happy, and I knew it was something I couldn't give her. How on earth was I supposed to make her happy if I couldn't even make myself happy?

Thoughts of her plagued me for most of the day and no matter how much I tried I couldn't stop picturing her walking beside the new guy. Every time I saw the two of them together and her smiling at him my chest ached a little more.

Fuck!

This was exactly the type of pain I'd worked so hard to avoid. I cared about Haven too much. Somehow, and without even being conscious of it, I'd started to care deeply for her. For my own sake, I had to pull back and start putting up walls, otherwise she'd have the power to hurt me.

She wouldn't hurt me on purpose, but hurting went hand in hand with loving someone. I'd told her I couldn't give her what she needed, so I couldn't blame her for opening herself up to someone else. It hurt to see her with him, but if I didn't let her go so she could move on I might be tempted to throw caution to the wind. I was only human and there was only so much I could stand before I gave in. That's why there had been moments of weakness, like when I'd kissed her and I'd wanted so much more.

Maybe if I took that conscious step to move on then it would stop the growing attachment I was forming with Haven, like ripping a band-aid off quickly. The sooner I got on with it the sooner my life could return what it had been before Haven.

It was the end of the day and I was walking to the entrance of the school when I saw Haven standing with the boy from before. Unbridled jealously tore through me. I stopped and took a deep breath to get my temper under control.

"Haven," I said, tightlipped, when I reached her side. I tried to ignore the guy standing with her but I couldn't help but glare at him.

"Hi," Haven greeted me, but my eyes were still glued to the stranger.

"Hi, I'm Mark," he tried to introduce himself as I glared at him.

"Damien," I muttered.

"I've got to go," Haven said to Mark.

"Sure, I'll see you tomorrow," he said, giving her a smile. I wanted to punch his face. Had they made plans to meet up at school?

My chest began to ache at the realization that there might possibly be something starting up between the two of them, and I didn't like it one bit.

"See you tomorrow," she replied with a weak smile and I had to grip my hands tightly to my side as another urge to hit him gripped me. I wanted to be the only one to make her smile.

"Let's go," I told her coldly. I couldn't control the anger that had begun to build up inside of me. Logically, it made no sense, but that was the thing about emotions: they made no logical sense.

I walked to the car and Haven followed quietly behind me. I opened the passenger door and she climbed in.

"What's wrong?" she asked but I ignored her and slammed the door shut.

I couldn't exactly tell her I was angry because I was jealous so instead I kept my eyes glued to the road as I drove us home.

"Why are you mad at me?" she asked softly. I knew I was hurting her but I just couldn't help myself.

"I don't want to talk about it," I snapped. The hurt on her face made me feel like the asshole I was. My emotions wouldn't allow me to follow the logic my mind dictated.

She cast her eyes downward and kept quiet and I ignored her until we got home. I noticed the police car stationed across the road from our gate. Even though I was angry I was still relieved when we drove to the home that there weren't any messages from Grant. We got out the car and I followed Haven into the house. My mom greeted us as we entered.

"How was school?" she asked when we walked to the kitchen.

"It was okay," Haven answered as she sat by the counter.

"I've got some stuff to do," I lied while I stood in the doorway to the kitchen. "I'll see you later."

"Okay," my mom said, and Haven nodded absentmindedly.

Even in the sanctuary of my room I struggled to deal with my anger that seemed to build every time I pictured Haven smiling at Mark. It felt like every time I saw her today, he was with her. It was like he was glued to her and it annoyed me.

I was still trying to wrestle with my anger when my mom called me and told me she needed to talk to Haven and me. She sounded anxious, so I knew whatever it was it couldn't be good. I knocked on Haven's door and told her my mom wanted to talk to us. She followed quietly behind me to the kitchen. My mom looked a little nervous as her eyes flickered to Haven. She tried to mask it with a smile, but we weren't fooled.

CHAPTER TWENTY-TWO

Haven

"Detective Green called," Amy revealed.

Damien looked at me as he took a step closer to me. It's almost like he knew whatever his mom was about to tell me would upset me.

"They haven't been able to find Grant yet. He assured me that they are still following up some leads, and he is confident that they will catch Grant soon," she explained. "He called me today to tell me that the forensic investigation and evidence collection has been completed at the apartment."

She paused for a moment as her eyes flickered to Damien and then she looked back to me.

"He said if we needed to go and get any of your stuff, we could," she said.

I didn't have much, but there was the photo of my dad that I wanted. It was one thing, but it was the only photo I had of him.

"If it's too much, Damien or I can go and get what you need," she offered gently.

I shook my head. I wanted to go. It was going to be

tough, walking back into the apartment where I'd nearly bled to death, but I had to.

"I'll take her," Damien told his mom.

"Can we go now?" I asked, wanting to get it over as soon as possible.

"Sure," he said. Gone was the stranger from before. I saw the concern in his eyes.

This time I was quiet and subdued in the car. Damien kept glancing in my direction as we drove to my old apartment. It hadn't really been a home; a home was filled with love and family. The closer we got the more nervous I got. When we arrived outside the apartment and he cut the engine he looked at me.

"Are you sure you want to do this?" he asked softly.

I gave him a nod as I opened the car door. The thickness in my throat kept me from trying to talk. Once outside the front door of the apartment, Damien opened the door. I stepped inside and I was transported back to the day Grant had tried to murder me. An array of emotions hit me as my gaze fell on the dark red mark on the carpet. Staring at the physical evidence of what had happened to me was hard. I knew I'd come close to dying, but seeing the amount of my blood was in the carpet made me realize what a close call it had been.

The stale smell in the air reminded me of all the bad memories that I wanted to forget about.

"You don't have to do this," Damien spoke to me softly.

I ignored him and took a couple of steps into the room. This place held no good memories for me. It was hard to think about the hard times when I'd wondered if I would ever escape the abuse. I took a deep breath, pushing the old memories from my mind. I was here to get the one thing that meant so much to me and had kept me going through those dark days.

With Damien following closely behind I made my way up to my bedroom. I hesitated for a moment before I pushed the door open and stepped inside. He remained in the doorway as I walked over to the mattress. I stuck my hand underneath the top corner of the mattress, and I felt the photo. As soon as I saw the photo of my dad and me, I felt a wave of emotion before I suppressed it.

I stood up and turned.

"I'm done," I said as I walked to him. He looked confused but he didn't say a word as he followed me out of the apartment.

For as long as I lived, I never wanted to step foot back into that apartment again. He helped me into the passenger side and then he jogged around the car and got into the driver's side. He started the car and pulled out into the road.

I looked at the photo and I took a deep breath as I brushed my finger over my dad's smiling face. He'd be happy for me now. The rest of the journey home was quiet. I didn't want to talk and Damien seemed to sense that because he didn't say a word.

Amy didn't bother me with questions when we got home, and I just wanted to be by myself, so I went upstairs to my room.

That night, instead of sleeping in the bed with me, Damien slept uncomfortably on the sofa. I slept restlessly, so the next morning I was still tired. He was still being standoffish around me and I didn't have the patience to deal with it. Chris was his usual cheerful self and managed to make me smile a few times.

"I did what you suggested, and when Mark started up a conversation, I spoke to him," I replied.

"You actually had a conversation with him?" he gasped as he grabbed my hands. I nodded my head.

"I knew you could do it," he replied. He knew how hard

it had been for me to take that small step.

"He's nice."

Mark walked with me to all of my classes. He was really friendly, and I liked him. At lunchtime, I was sitting with Chris when Mark appeared beside me.

"Do you mind if I join you guys?" he asked.

I looked to Chris, unsure. Chris nodded and said, "Sure."

He dropped down to sit next to me and opened his lunch. I introduced him to Chris and the three of us had lunch together. There was another person creeping into my little circle, and I was happy that I was making another friend.

Mark was easygoing, so he and Chris hit it off immediately. Every time Mark wasn't looking, Chris would wiggle his eyebrows at me while looking at Mark. I had to stop myself from laughing at him. He was terrible. At the end of lunch, when the bell rang, we stood up and dusted the grass off of ourselves. I looked upward and just a few feet away I saw Damien scowling at us. Before I could confront him, he stalked off.

"Everything okay?" Mark asked when he saw my worried expression.

"Yeah," I lied. Everything wasn't all right.

I didn't see Damien again until it was time to go home. Mark insisted on standing with me until Damien showed up, which didn't help with Damien's growing anger at seeing me with Mark. I said goodbye to Mark as I followed Damien to the car.

I kept glancing in Damien's direction as he drove us home, but he refused to look at me and kept his eyes on the road in front of us. He ignored me the entire journey. When he pulled up in front of the house he jumped out of the car and without a backward glance he walked straight into the house. I slid out of the passenger side and closed the door. He was acting like he was jealous.

Like Chris had said, I needed to put myself out there. When I'd needed someone to lean on, Damien had been there for me, and he'd become my security blanket. So now that he was acting so out of character, I felt vulnerable without him. Slowly my sadness began to turn to anger. He was being an asshole.

"What's wrong with Damien?" Amy asked me as I walked into the house. She could obviously read her son well.

"I don't know," I muttered with a shrug. I had a good idea why he was so cross but I wasn't about to try and explain it to his mom.

Damien was nowhere to be seen when I walked through the house to my bedroom. His bedroom doors, which were normally open, were shut. I hesitated outside his door. I wanted to knock and get him to talk to me, but I decided that maybe he just needed some time. I sighed as I turned and entered my bedroom, dumping my bag on the floor. Sitting on my bed, I rubbed my face. I didn't know what to do.

I thought about Chris. I got my phone and dialed Chris and waited for him to pick up.

"Hi," he answered cheerfully.

"Hi," I greeted.

Before I could contemplate or change my mind I blurted out, "Do you want to come over?"

"Sure, just give me the address and I'll be over as soon as I can," he replied, then he ended the call. I sent him a message with the address.

I mulled around my room until I heard a car pull up. Looking out of my window, I saw Chris get out of his car. By the time I made it downstairs, Amy was already ushering him into the house.

"Hi," I said when I reached the bottom step.

"Hey," he replied. Just seeing him was already making me feel better.

"It's nice to meet finally meet you," Amy said to Chris, giving him a warm smile.

"It's nice to meet you too, Mrs. Knight."

"Shout if you guys need anything," she said before she went back to the kitchen, leaving us alone.

"This place is awesome," Chris gasped as soon as Amy was out of earshot. "I bet your room is huge."

"Come on, I'll show you," I said as I waited for him to follow me up the stairs.

"Do you think they'll adopt me too?" he whispered while he took in the vastness of the house.

I couldn't help but smile. Before he'd arrived I'd felt so alone and sad, and after just a few minutes in his company I was already feeling so much better.

"Wow," he whispered when I opened the doors to my bedroom. His jaw looked like it would hit the floor when he looked around my new room.

"This is awesome!" he said as he stood in the middle of my room, taking it all in.

"Yeah, it's nice," I replied.

"Nice? This is more than 'nice'," he stated incredulously.

I shrugged and sat down on the bed.

"So what's up?" he asked, seeing that there was something bugging me.

"I think Damien's mad at me."

He sat down beside me on the bed.

"What happened?" he asked.

"Damien saw Mark eating lunch with us today," I explained.

"So let me get this right—Damien is mad at you because he saw you and Mark together at lunch?" he asked.

"I think so."

"He's jealous," he stated factually. I'd already gathered that much.

"That's what it seems like," I replied. "What am I going to do?"

"He's an idiot," he said as he pulled me into a hug. "He can't give you what you want but he doesn't want anyone else to."

I was disappointed in Damien, and I couldn't help the nervous and anxious knot that began to form in my stomach at the thought of sleeping on my own tonight. I slept every night with Damien in my room. I didn't think I'd get any sleep tonight if he wasn't there.

"Enough about Damien," Chris said, moving the subject along. "Mark seems like a nice guy."

"Yeah, he is."

His grin widened at that as he wiggled his eyebrows. I laughed.

"I think the new boy is interested in you," he stated.

"I don't know," I replied. I didn't have enough experience with boys to know when a boy was making moves or just having a friendly chat.

Chris spent the rest of the afternoon keeping my mind off Damien, but when it was time for him to leave I didn't want to let him go.

"You'll be fine, and if you need to talk, you can call me anytime," he assured me.

"Thank you," I said softly.

"You're my friend, and that's what friends are for," he said.

I thanked my lucky stars that I had a friend like him.

After Chris left I kept busy with my homework and tried to keep my mind off Damien. His door was still closed, and I hadn't seen him since he'd stormed into the house earlier. Just before dinnertime, I heard his door open and close, and then about ten minutes later I heard him drive out of the driveway. He'd gone out.

I was lost in my own thoughts at dinnertime, so I just listened to Amy and Steven talk about their days. The anxious knot in my stomach had grown so I didn't eat much. Amy raised an eyebrow, but didn't say anything when I pushed my plate away and asked if I could be excused.

"Sure," she said and I went back to my room.

I had tried everything I could to keep my mind from drifting to Damien, but I couldn't stop thinking about him. Where had he gone? A nervous knot tightened in my stomach.

In the darkness, I stared unseeing up at the ceiling. I wondered if he was with a girl. At about midnight I was still wide awake, unable to sleep without Damien. Then I heard him come home. The sound of an additional car told me that he hadn't come home alone.

The relief I felt when he got home was cut short when I heard a feminine laugh in the hallway outside my bedroom. I heard his door close. It felt like someone had ripped out my heart out, and I don't know how long I sat there, knees pulled to my chest, staring at my bedroom door.

I couldn't be angry with him, because he'd been honest with me from the beginning. He couldn't give me more than what he was prepared to give any of the other girls revolving in and out of his life. Seeing me talking to Mark had pushed Damien to retaliate, and it saddened me. He'd accomplished what he'd set out to do: he'd hurt me.

Not much later, I heard his door open and then after another couple of moments I heard a car leave. I grabbed my pillow and put it over my head, unable to deal with the pain any more. Another sob tore from me and I wept quietly.

CHAPTER TWENTY-THREE

DAMIEN

"Detective Green called," my mom revealed. That protective instinct I had for Haven came out in full force and I took a step closer to her. Even though I was still angry with her, I wanted to protect her.

"They haven't been able to find Grant yet. He assured me they are still following up some leads and he is confident that they'll catch Grant," she explained further.

They hadn't caught Grant yet—so what did she want to talk to us about?

"He called me today to tell me that the forensic investigation and evidence collection has been completed on the flat," she revealed, watching Haven closely.

She paused for a moment, her eyes flickering to me and then back to Haven.

"He said if we needed to go and get any of your stuff, we could," she said.

I watched an array of emotions pass over Haven's face while she processed what my mom had just told her.

"If it's too much, then Damien or I can go and get what you need," she offered gently.

Haven shook her head. I could see the determined glint in her eye.

"I'll take her," I told my mom. Irrespective of how I felt at the moment, I needed to push it aside to be there for Haven. Walking back into the apartment where she'd nearly been murdered was going to be hard.

It was going to be difficult for me as well. Finding her so close to death covered in blood on the floor had hit me hard. It hadn't just been the fact that she'd nearly died that had affected me so badly—it had brought back my own memories of death as well.

"Can we go now?" Haven asked my mom, pulling me back the present.

"Sure," I said.

On the way to the apartment I kept glancing at Haven but she kept her eyes downcast. She was lost her in own thoughts as we neared our destination. Honestly I didn't want to go back to the flat, and I was tempted to just keep on driving.

But some things you couldn't run away from. By the time I switched off the engine outside the flats I could see that Haven was nervous. She fidgeted with her hands as she looked at the building that held no good memories for her.

"Are you sure you want to do this?" I asked her softly.

She gave me a nod as she opened the car door. A somber silence settled over us as I followed behind her up the stairs. Outside the door to the apartment she hesitated, so I stepped forward and I opened the door for her.

We stepped inside and her gaze fell on the dark red mark on the carpet. An image of her lying in a pool of blood, barely hanging on, flashed in my mind, making my chest ache. If this was hard for me, I couldn't imagine what Haven was going through.

"You don't have to do this," I said softly to her. I wanted her to turn around and walk out the door with me, and never step foot back into this apartment ever again. There were no good memories in this hellhole.

She didn't reply as she took a couple of steps further into the room. Quietly, and deep in thought, she looked around the room before she headed for the stairs. I followed closely behind her as she went up the stairs. Outside the one door she came to a stop and hesitated for a moment before she pushed the door open and stepped inside.

I remained in the doorway as Haven walked over to the mattress. I'd never been in her old bedroom before, and the scene in front of me filled me with anger. She didn't even have a proper bed—she'd been sleeping on a bare mattress. My jaw tensed and my hands fisted while I struggled to contain the anger I felt.

Haven walked to the mattress and bent down. It looked like she was searching for something under the mattress. I could see an old, tattered photo in her hands and I couldn't help being curious about it. Her eyes glistened as she stared at the photo for a moment and then she stood up and turned to face me.

"I'm done," she said, her voice hoarse with unspoken emotion as she walked to me. I wanted to put my arms around her, to give her my strength and take away some of the sorrow in her eyes, but instead I kept quiet and followed her out of the apartment. I hoped I would never have to step another foot back into that flat.

When we got to the car I helped Haven into the passenger side and then I walked around the car and got into the driver's side. I started the car and pulled out into the road. I glanced in her direction. She was quiet and subdued as she looked at the photo and took a deep breath as she brushed a finger over the smiling face of the man in the photo. I assumed it was her dad.

The rest of the journey home was quiet. That short trip back to the apartment had affected her deeply. As soon as we got home Haven disappeared into her bedroom.

"How did it go?" my mom asked.

"I think it was hard for her," I said, putting my arm around my mom and giving her a squeeze. "I think she just needs some time to herself. She'll be okay."

My mom gave me a kiss on my cheek.

"You're right," she said. "Come and help me with supper."

Helping my mom took my mind off Haven for a little while. That night I knew she needed space, but I didn't want her to have nightmares, so instead of sleeping beside her in her bed I took the couch.

I didn't sleep well—the sofa was damn uncomfortable—but at least Haven was nightmare-free that night. The next day, a sinking feeling settled in my stomach at the thought of watching Mark and Haven together again. I wasn't looking forward to it, so for the entire trip to school I kept to myself.

It was hard to try and pretend everything was okay when it wasn't. I was jealous and there was no hiding it. I'd managed to avoid seeing Haven and Mark together in the morning, but I wasn't so lucky at lunchtime. Just before the end of lunch I left the cafeteria to get something out of my locker when I saw Mark sitting beside Haven on the grass. It felt like someone had punched me. They were getting closer, and it hurt to watch.

Just as the bell rang I watched as Haven stood to dust the grass off her pants when her eyes met mine. I couldn't help but scowl at her, just as she was about to take a step in my direction, I stalked off. Seeing the two of them together had soured my mood dramatically. The last straw for me was when I went to find Haven after school and I found her standing by the entrance with Mark again.

He made her smile and I wanted to do him some serious bodily harm. It was then that I'd decided I'd had enough; it was time to move on, otherwise watching this would end up tearing me apart.

When Haven noticed me she said goodbye to Mark and followed me to the car. I ignored her the entire trip home and once we arrived I jumped out of the car and, without a backward glance, I walked straight into the house. Once inside my room I closed my bedroom door and leaned against it. I needed to make a plan to move on and the sooner I got on with it the better off I'd be.

I needed to go out and hook up with someone. There wouldn't be any way to entertain any ideas about Haven if I were screwing someone else. I dropped my school bag on my desk and got my phone from the back pocket of my jeans and called Shane.

"Hey," he greeted when he answered.

"Hey," I greeted back as I sat down in the chair.

"What's up?" he asked.

"I need to get out," I answered. In other words, I needed to get laid.

"A few of us are having a get together at Kirsten's, there will be plenty of girls," he informed me. Nicole was a friend of Kirsten's, and chances were she would be there. She'd already made it blatantly clear she was interested in me, and she knew me well enough to know the score and that after I was done, I'd walk away.

"What time?" I asked.

"Just after seven," he answered.

"I'll see you there," I replied. I knew where Kirsten's house was.

It was hard to concentrate on my homework but I managed to get it all done. A couple of times I looked up at my bedroom door, wondering what Haven was doing. I shook my head. I needed to stop thinking about her.

I knew my behavior was hurting her, but I just couldn't stop. It wasn't her fault I felt more for her than I should; it also wasn't her fault that I couldn't do relationships and dating. None of this was her fault. I was the one that should have known better. I should have kept my distance from her and protected both of us because we were both going to hurt. It hurt me to see her with someone else, and it would hurt her to see me with someone else.

After my homework was done I had a quick shower and then stood in front of my wardrobe. I pulled a pair of dark jeans off the shelf and pulled them on. I looked through my shirts and found a red one with some logo on it and pulled it over my head. I pulled my sneakers on before I got my wallet and phone.

I hesitated outside my bedroom for a moment; Haven's room was quiet. I took a deep breath and walked away. I had to do this for both of us.

My mom was in the kitchen cooking supper when I walked in.

"Where are you off to tonight?" she asked, noticing I was dressed to go out.

"There's a get-together at Kirsten's house," I told my mom.

"Don't you want to eat before you leave?" my mom asked.

"I'll get something when I get back," I replied. There was no way I could sit through dinner across from Haven. If I saw her now I wouldn't be able to do what I needed to.

"It's a school night so don't be back too late," my mom

warned me as she stirred something on the stove.

"I won't," I promised her. I gave her a peck on the cheek.

My parents were super cool. I could pretty much do what I wanted as long as my grades at school didn't suffer. An anxious feeling of foreboding settled in my stomach when I left the house and got in my car. It didn't take me long to get to Kirsten's house. When I got there, there were already a couple of cars parked outside.

"Hey, man," Shane greeted me as I stepped through the doorway. The front door had been open.

"Hey," I greeted him. "How did you know I was here?"

"I heard your car," he answered. "Everyone is in the basement. Do you want a beer?"

Normally I didn't drink much, but tonight I needed some.

"Sure," I replied and followed him to the kitchen. He grabbed a bottle of beer and handed it to me.

"Thanks," I said to him as I opened it, and I took a swallow.

I followed him from the kitchen down the stairs into the basement. A soft hum of music played in the background. There were about fifteen people scattered across the room. Some were playing pool, others were seated and talking, and some people looked they were doing the deed fully clothed in front of everyone. I scanned the room looking for Nicole, and when my eyes locked with hers, I gave her a lethal smile and her eyes lit up. This wasn't going to be hard at all.

A few hours later I was leaving with Nicole's hand in mine.

"Follow me," I instructed her.

She nodded. By the time I got into my car and pulled out in the road I saw Nicole in her car behind me. I tried not to think about Haven and her reaction to me bringing a girl home. It would hurt, there was no doubt about it. I didn't want to, but I had to do this.

Nicole was attractive but when I kissed her it felt almost mechanical. There was no deep lust wanting to break to the surface like there had been with the girls before I'd met Haven. Since I'd met Haven and formed some sort of bond with her, all the girls that I usually went for had lost their appeal. But I'd fix that. Once I fucked Nicole, there would be no going back, and irrespective of how much I cared for Haven, she wouldn't forgive me for this. It would push me to let her go and carry on like I had before.

When I pulled up in front of my house Nicole parked next to me and got out of the car.

"You've got a nice house," she said as she walked to me.

"Thanks," I replied. I walked to the front door. I opened it and held it open for her to enter.

I put my finger by my lips to indicate to her to keep quiet. Honestly, I didn't want to wake up my parents—my mother wouldn't be happy with me. She knew what I was like with girls. Moms just knew this stuff, and I knew she wanted me to find something more meaningful than one-night stands. I think that when Haven entered my life I'd started to change, and my mom had noticed.

Secretly, I think she wanted Haven and I to get together. But I was too damaged, and Haven deserved better.

Nicole let out a nervous giggle when we got outside my bedroom door. I couldn't help my eyes flickering to Haven's bedroom door opposite mine. I felt like an asshole, but I knew I was doing the right thing. I opened my bedroom door and pulled Nicole inside. She gazed around my room.

"Your room is huge," Nicole said.

"I like the space." I knew I had a lifestyle that most of the teenagers my age didn't have, and on top of that I had great parents.

She wondered around my room, running her finger along some of my books in the book shelf.

I sat down on the sofa and she turned to face me. She walked seductively over to where I was sitting and leaned over and kissed me. I pulled her down on top of my lap and she straddled me as our lips touched. I kissed her hard, trying to get into it, and she moved her lips against mine following my lead.

I stood up and held her against me as our kiss became more heated. Her lips opened under mine and my tongue swept into her mouth and touched hers. She groaned when I lifted her by the butt and she wrapped her legs around my waist. I pushed thoughts of Haven out of my mind as I carried Nicole to my bed. I lay her down and lowered my body onto hers. It felt so wrong but I kept my eyes closed and tried to go with it. I pushed my hand up her top and she groaned and pressed herself harder to me.

We kissed for a while and I felt her up but no matter how hard I tried, it wasn't working. I couldn't go through with it. Letting out a frustrated sigh, I pulled away from her and rolled onto my back.

"What's wrong?" she asked breathlessly, peering over me.

"I've got a headache," I lied to her. I rubbed my temple, trying to figure out what had gone wrong. I'd never had this problem before.

Haven. That's what had happened to me: I'd met Haven.

For a few silent minutes I lay there trying to get my breathing under control before I turned to face Nicole. She'd straightened her clothing and was standing in front of me.

"I'll let you out," I told her as I sat up and ran a hand through my hair.

"Sure," she said. I could see she was disappointed, even

though she was trying to hide it.

Quietly, she followed me out of my room and I tried to make as little noise as possible when I opened the front door and walked her to her car. I was preoccupied with thoughts of Haven as I waited for her to get into her car and leave. She started up her car and gave me a smile before she drove down the driveway. I took a deep breath and returned to the house.

Well, that hadn't gone as planned.

CHAPTER TWENTY-FOUR

Haven

I didn't sleep at all that night. At around two in the morning I curled into a ball and tucked the comforter around me. A few hours later I heard Amy knock on my door.

"It's time to get up," she told me.

I lifted my head to see her looking at me from my doorway.

"I'm not feeling well," I told her. I couldn't face Damien.

"What's wrong?" she asked, looking concerned as she walked over to me. The first thing she did was put her hand to my forehead to feel if I had a temperature.

"I've got a splitting headache and I didn't sleep well," I fibbed. I hadn't slept at all.

"Okay, I'll bring up some painkillers," she told me as she walked out of my bedroom, closing the door behind her.

It didn't take her long to return with a couple of tablets and a glass of water. I drank them and slumped back into my bed, relieved she wasn't going to make me go to school in my fragile state.

"I need to go into the office this morning, but I'll be home this afternoon to check on you," she said with concerned eyes, and it made feel a little guilty.

I gave her a brief nod before she left.

A little later I heard a car leave. It was probably Damien going to school. I was relieved that I wouldn't have to face him yet, I'd have some time to try and get myself together. Although I wasn't sure if I could put myself back together; my heart still felt so fragile and it felt like the pain would never ease.

Exhausted but unable to sleep, I finally got out of bed and ran myself a bath. I thought maybe lying in a bubble bath would help, but nothing eased the pain in my chest.

I had a text message on my phone from Chris when I got out of the bathroom.

Damien told me you're home sick. Everything okay?

I wasn't ready to talk about the real reason I was hiding, so I just said I felt a little unwell today, but that I would be back at school tomorrow. I didn't want him to worry.

Bored and unable to sleep, I opened my door. It still physically hurt to even look at the door to his room. I wandered downstairs to get something to eat. I wasn't really hungry, so I grabbed an apple and took a few bites before I threw it in the trash can.

I stood looking out of the window. The weather outside matched my mood. It was dark and overcast. It looked like it was going to rain, but I didn't have any more tears to shed.

On my way back to my bedroom my eyes settled on the door at the end of the passage. I remember Damien telling me that the room was used for storage. It was what he hadn't said but what I'd seen in his eyes that encouraged my curiosity. I felt terrible for snooping around, but I couldn't help myself as I put one foot in front of the other. I paused for a moment when I stood in front of the door. Curiosity won over the guilt and I opened the door.

The room was dark, so I flicked the switch and I was

shocked at what I found when the light flooded through the room.

Damien had lied. It wasn't storage. It was a bedroom, a boy's room. I stepped inside the room and quietly closed the door behind me.

A neatly made bed stood in the middle of the room. On the one side was a bookcase with a desk. On the top couple of shelves of the bookcase were various trophies. I stepped closer to see what the trophies were for. I picked one up, and it looked like a trophy for soccer.

I took a look at the gold label on the trophy. It read 'Awarded to Dylan Knight.'

Dylan Knight.

Then everything began to fall into place. The reason why Damien was broken like me. He'd lost his brother.

Oh. My. God.

How was it possible that he had lost a brother and nobody at school had said anything about it? Especially Chris, who always knew what was going on at school; how had he not known about this? I couldn't help but wonder what he'd looked like, and how old he'd been when he died.

Then my thoughts turned to Amy and Steven. It must have been horrible to lose a child. It then dawned on me that maybe having lost Dylan was what had made them open their home to me. Overwhelmed, I sat down on the bed for a moment and my eyes drifted to the other side of the room.

On the wall were dozens of pictures of the family I'd come to know with their lost family member. I slid off the bed and took a step closer as I studied the first picture. It was a professional photograph of the family with Amy and Steven in the middle. Damien stood by Amy and then I looked at the face of the other son.

Shock set in when I realized that, not only did Dylan look like Damien, he was in fact an identical twin. Dylan had been Damien's *twin*.

In the photo, I couldn't tell them apart. It was sad to be looking at a moment when he'd been alive and his family had been happy and whole. It looked like the photo had been taken about five years ago. My eyes drifted from one photo to another. They looked so happy in the photos; some were professionally taken and some looked like they'd been snapped at family gatherings, possibly birthdays.

The one that haunted me was a photo taken of Damien and Dylan in their soccer uniforms. They had their arms around each other's shoulders as they smiled into the camera. It looked like the most recent photo, and it looked like it had been taken a couple of years ago. I couldn't help but feel the sadness that settled over me at the thought that his brother had died, leaving his family behind to try and pick up the pieces.

Whatever had happened to Dylan had happened a couple of years ago. I couldn't help but wonder what had happened. The pain that Damien had endured when he'd lost his twin must have been devastating.

He'd been sympathetic and understanding when he'd found out I'd lost my mom because he'd understood what it felt like to lose a close family member. The difference between us was that I hadn't really cared about losing my mother, but I knew that hadn't been the case with Damien and his twin.

Feeling like I was being nosy, I backed out of the room and switched the light off. I went back to my room and climbed into my bed. I was still so upset with Damien, but I couldn't help feeling sympathy for him and his parents. Losing someone so close must have been hard.

Exhausted, I drifted off to sleep.

When I woke up, it was dark. I must have slept for most of the day. I felt numb, maybe the result of the overemotional morning I'd had. Hiding out in my room for the rest of my life wasn't an option. At some point, I would have to face him. As much as it hurt now, I knew it would hurt worse when I saw him.

I pulled myself from my bed and dragged myself through a shower, hoping it would make me feel a little better. It didn't. I got dressed into a new pair of pajamas and climbed back into bed.

There was a knock at my door.

"Come in," I said when I sat up in my bed.

"Hi, how are you feeling?" Amy asked as she walked to my bed. She was such a kind and a caring person, and I felt guilty that I'd been snooping around her dead son's room. Losing someone close was hard, but losing a child went against the cycle of things. Parents weren't supposed to bury their kids, it was meant to be the other way around. Having a little insight into the pain she had to deal with, I wanted to put my arms around her and hold her close.

"Better," I lied.

"Are you hungry?" she asked with concern.

"A little," I answered. I knew I should be hungry because I hadn't eaten all day, but the truth was I wasn't.

"I'll bring up some food," she said before she turned and left, closing my bedroom door quietly behind her.

I needed something to distract me from my thoughts, so I put the TV on and climbed back into bed. There were so many channels, but I flickered through half a dozen without anything capturing my interest.

When Amy returned with a tray of food, she set it down on my side table.

"Let me know if you need anything," she offered. I gave her a brief nod and she left.

I knew I shouldn't care, but I was curious to know whether Damien was home. It was none of my business what he did, but I couldn't help hoping that he was home instead of out with some girl.

The food Amy brought me made me feel obliged to try and eat something. I took a couple of mouthfuls of the spaghetti and meatballs, chewing it and forcing myself to swallow them. I didn't want to lose the healthy weight I'd to put on.

The silence across from my room made me believe Damien had gone out again. The thought of him with some other girl again made my heart sore. Feeling emotionally raw and tired, I got up and brushed my teeth, settling back into my bed after turning off the lights. I held the comforter up to my neck, staring at the darkness that surrounded me. The nights that Damien hadn't slept in my room I'd had horrific nightmares about Grant and the attack.

Unable to handle the darkness without Damien I got up and switched my bedroom light on again and then got back into bed.

The sound of activity outside my bedroom doors made me hold my breath. It had to be Damien.

I heard a gentle knock, but I wasn't ready to face him, so I closed my eyes and pretended to be asleep. My door creaked open as I held my breath. A few moments later a hand caressed my cheek and I felt a light kiss pressed to my forehead. I didn't need to open my eyes to confirm it was Damien. I recognized his soothing smell as he leaned over me. His soft footsteps exited my room and I heard the door close quietly behind him.

Why had he come into my room to check on me? Irrespective of what had happened last night he still cared about me. It didn't make me feel any better.

The hurt that he'd been with another girl right across the hallway from me was too strong to be glossed over by his affectionate actions. I couldn't help the thoughts that took over when I thought about him, which included a girl wrapped around him, kissing him. It made my heart ache. I needed time to be able to get over the hurt, before we could be close like we had been, but there was always the possibility that we would never be able to be as close as we were before.

Sometime during the night I drifted to sleep, and the nightmares started. The attack replayed in my dreams. I swear I felt the pain of the being stabbed again as Grant drove the knife into me.

I screamed.

"Shh, it's okay," I heard a familiar voice murmur.

My eyes blinked a couple of times, taking in his concerned face.

"I got you," he murmured while he held me.

A familiar smell of safety surrounded me and I began to relax. My eyelids grew heavy again as my heart steadied. I was still hurt and angry with him but I needed him, so I stayed in his arms until I fell asleep.

The sun filtered in through a gap in my curtain as I opened my eyes. I rubbed my eyes and yawned as I tried to remember if I'd dreamed of Grant last night. Vague memories of the nightmare flitted back, but then I remembered someone holding and soothing me. It had to have been Damien. I searched the room with my eyes, but I was alone. Did he stay with me for most of the night and then leave early so that he wouldn't have had to face me in the morning?

I dragged myself out of bed and started to get ready for school. After everything that had happened, things had changed, and I couldn't continue the way I had. I'd depended on Damien long enough, and I needed to take the steps to gain my independence, to learn to cope with my issues without having to lean on other people. I didn't want Damien to feel obligated to help me only because I couldn't cope without him. I didn't want his pity for me to glue him to my side.

My thoughts went back to what the social worker had suggested. Maybe it was time to go and see a therapist. They would be able to give me the tools to work through my issues and to help me put them behind me so I could look at the future with less baggage. There would always be permanent emotional scars that I would never get rid of, but I hoped that I would be able to work through some of it.

Amy was in the kitchen drinking some coffee when I entered.

"How are you feeling?" she asked when I sat down next to her at the kitchen table.

"Better."

She smiled and took another sip of her coffee.

"Would it be okay if I go and see a therapist?" I blurted out before I could change my mind.

"Of course you can," she replied as she set her coffee back down on the table.

"The social worker suggested someone," I said. I handed her the information.

"Sure, I'll make an appointment for you," she said as she took the piece of paper from me.

There, I had done it: my first step to getting better.

Damien entered the kitchen and I couldn't prevent my eyes from meeting his. I felt that awareness of him hit me immediately and I averted my gaze. The hurt that he had caused still ached inside of me.

CHAPTER TWENTY-FIVE

Haven

An awkward silence descended as Damien drove us to school. He kept glancing in my direction, but it was too hard for me to look at him. It still hurt too much.

Technically, he wasn't tied to me, so it wasn't like he'd betrayed me or cheated on me, but even knowing that logically he was blameless, I couldn't help feeling hurt every time I looked at him. All I could see was him kissing and making out with some random girl.

I wished I could turn off my emotions and never feel anything, but it was impossible, so I did the next best thing: I ignored him. As soon as Damien pulled into the school parking lot I got out of the car and walked swiftly into the school, leaving him behind. There was a group of cheerleaders gathered around a locker and I couldn't help my gaze drifting to them. I wondered if it had been one of them that had been with Damien in his room. The thought made me feel physically ill. I shook my head, trying to push the thought from my mind.

The sight of Chris leaning against my locker made me smile.

"Good morning," he greeted me, flashing me a smile when he spotted me walking toward him.

"Hi," I greeted as I came to a stop in front of him.

"You feeling better?" he asked with a little concern in his face.

"Um…yeah," I mumbled, remembering that I was supposed to have been sick yesterday.

"Are you sure you're okay?" he asked, watching me carefully as I opened my locker.

I paused for a moment, taking a deep breath. Clearly I wasn't hiding my heartbreak well enough.

"What's wrong?" he asked, his voice edged with concern, and I felt my eyes begin to water. He gently turned me to face him as the first tear slipped down my cheek and was closely followed by another as the dam of emotions in me burst open.

He pulled me into his arms and wrapped them around me as I burrowed my face into his chest, clutching at his shirt. Lost in my own loss of control, I didn't notice the crowd that had stopped to stare and whisper. He steered me out of the hallway and down to the field, where there was no one to witness my breakdown.

Quietly, he held me until I stopped crying.

"I'm sorry," I mumbled, still not used to losing control of my emotions like this.

"It's fine," he soothed as he took my face into his hands and angled my eyes to his.

"What happened?" he asked gently as he brushed the tears from my face.

I bit down on my lip, trying to get control over my raging emotions. Putting what I was feeling into words would make my heartache all that more real. I'd be admitting out aloud how I felt about Damien and how much he'd hurt me.

"If you don't tell me I swear I'm going to corner Damien

and ask him," Chris quietly threatened me.

"Please don't," I pleaded.

"Then tell me what happened."

I took a deep breath.

"He brought a girl home."

It was just five words but it was enough for Chris to understand why I was heartbroken.

"He brought a girl home?" he gasped again, not quite believing what I'd just told him.

I nodded my head.

"I never imagined he would actually move on," he said. "I always thought things would work out between the two of you."

I just shrugged. I had never believed that we would work out.

"It sucks," he said, trying to sympathize with me.

"It does."

But what was done was done, and I needed to pick myself up and carry on.

"He doesn't deserve you," he informed me as we started walking back inside the school.

I shrugged my shoulders. There wasn't a lot more to say about the subject. I cared for him more than I should and clearly Damien had moved on. It was time for me to do the same.

I felt a little better when I walked into my first class and Mark smiled at me. He wasn't Damien, but I liked him. He made me feel special and I liked to be around him.

"Hi," I greeted him as I slid into my seat beside him.

"Hi," he greeted back. "Are you feeling better?"

"Yeah," I said with a slight shrug of my shoulders, and I averted my eyes from his so he couldn't see the truth in my eyes. What I'd been suffering from wasn't going to be fixed overnight.

"Have you got plans for the weekend?" he asked, leaning forward.

I hadn't realized it was Friday already.

"No," I answered. It wasn't like I was a social person that had people lining up to spend time with me.

"Good." I was surprised at his comment and he flashed me that devastating smile again.

"Do you want to go to a movie this weekend?" he asked as he watched me.

I was speechless, I was pretty sure my jaw looked like it would hit the floor.

"If you want?" he added, looking a little nervous. He was normally confident and seeing him look a little nervous and unsure of himself made me feel good. I made him nervous. I'd never been on a 'date' before and I'd never been to the movies before.

"Forget I asked," he replied and settled back into his seat, looking a little disappointed.

"Yes," I finally managed to get out. His face lit up and he leaned forward with a big grin on his face. His green eyes sparkled with excitement.

"You sure?" he asked, seeing how nervous I was as I clasped my hands together.

"Yes."

I liked Mark, and what better way to get over my feelings for Damien? I was nervous but I knew that Mark was a good guy and he wouldn't hurt me, he wasn't a Grant. It was my second step in moving forward in my life. I was going to go and see a therapist as soon as Amy made the appointment for me and I was going to go on my first date with a boy. As nerve-wracking as the thought was, it was the right thing to do.

The morning flew by quickly and before I knew it, Mark was walking me to our usual spot where we had lunch with

Chris. Chris was already there waiting for us and he smiled when he spotted us. When the lunch bell rang, Mark shot to his feet and told me he needed to get something from his locker, leaving Chris and me alone.

"Why do you look so happy?" Chris asked as we walked, side by side, back into the school hallway.

"I'm going on a date," I said with excitement. He wasn't Damien, but I was still excited to be going on a date.

"With who? " Chris asked, a little surprised.

"Mark," I revealed.

"I knew he had a thing for you," he said smugly.

"I like him," I said with a shrug. I didn't want to say what I was feeling. I liked Damien more, but after what he'd done, there was no going back.

"When are you going on your date?" Chris asked.

"He said he'd call tonight to let me know," I answered as I hitched my bag more securely on my shoulder.

"You deserve to be happy," he told me. "And I think Mark can make you happy."

I thought so too.

A couple of times during the day I caught Damien watching me, but I ignored him. The knife in my heart got driven deeper when I was in the bathroom and overheard a group of girls gossiping about him.

"All the rumors are true. Damien is *that* good," the one girl declared, and it felt like something pierced my heart.

"We want all the dirty details," another girl squealed.

"I don't kiss and tell," the other girl replied as I heard the bathroom door open and close.

For a few minutes I remained hidden in the stall, making sure the girls were gone and trying to ease the pain in my chest. It felt like every tender kiss I'd ever shared with him had been tainted. I splashed some water on my face and dried my eyes before I left.

"Are you okay?" Mark asked. He stood waiting outside the bathrooms for me.

I gave him a brief nod as I walked to the entrance of the school, still preoccupied with what I'd heard. Had that girl been the same girl that he'd been with the other night?

"Is there something wrong?" Mark asked again with concern in his eyes.

"No, I'm fine," I lied. I wasn't fine—I was hurt.

Then the source of my hurt appeared by my side.

"Are you ready to go?" Damien asked as he watched Mark. It was almost like he was sizing him up.

"Yes."

"I'll call you later," Mark said with a smile.

"Sure," I said to him then he turned and left.

Damien was quiet until we got into his car. Instead of starting up the engine, he turned to face me. The way I was feeling, I wasn't ready to talk to him, so I shifted my gaze from him and focused on the scenery outside my window.

"Why is Mark going to call you tonight?" he asked softly.

No way. He was going around screwing girls all over the place and he had the audacity to question me about a guy calling me. I bit my lip to stop from yelling at him. Instead, I let out a sigh as I turned to face him.

"It's none of your business," I stated calmly. Surprise flashed in his eyes and he shut his mouth. His eyes held mine. He clenched his jaw. He wasn't happy with my response, but I didn't care. He'd hurt me.

Without another word, he started up the car and drove us home. The silence was filled with tension that rolled off him in waves. He was acting like he was jealous, but I had no sympathy for him. He hadn't thought twice about screwing some random girl across the hallway from me.

I spotted the cop car keeping watch outside the gates when Damien pulled into the driveway and the gates opened.

It was a reminder that Grant was still out there somewhere, biding his time.

Once Damien pulled up in front of the house I got out first and walked into the house. I went to my room and closed my door. I leaned against the door and took a deep breath. It had been a rough day. After everything I'd survived in the last seven years, this should have been a walk in the park, but I couldn't ignore the ache in my chest.

I heard Damien open his bedroom door across the hall. There were a few moments of silence and then I heard his door close. Guilt was what I began to feel when I got my books out of my school bag to try and do some of my homework. Damien had been there for me when I'd needed someone; if it hadn't been for him, I wouldn't be alive.

I hated that we were not getting along, because I needed him in my life. Without him, Grant came for me in my dreams and at this rate I would never get a good night's rest again. As hard as it was to concentrate on my homework, I forced myself to finish it.

Dinner was a little awkward. The four of us sat at the dining room table, where I continued to avoid Damien's gaze.

"I made the appointment with the therapist for Monday after school," Amy informed me when I took a bite of food. I gave her a nod and I felt Damien's gaze on me.

"Either Damien or I can take you," she offered.

"Thank you," I said, looking at Amy and avoiding eye contact with Damien.

"I'll take her," Damien offered. It was times like this that especially I wished I had a license, and that I didn't have a cast on my arm, so that I could drive myself.

It was another step toward my independence which I needed to take. As soon as the cast came off I was going to get my license. I couldn't expect Damien or Amy to drive me around forever.

"I'd rather have Amy take me," I said to Damien. Amy looked from Damien to me.

"Sure."

"Is it okay if I go out with someone this weekend?" I looked to Amy when I asked the question.

"Yes," she said, looking a little surprised.

"Mark, a guy from school, wants to take me to movies," I told her, and I couldn't stop my gaze from drifting to Damien to see his reaction. He didn't look happy at all. His jaw clenched as his eyes connected with mine.

"Do you know Mark?" Amy turned to ask her son.

"Yeah," he replied tersely. His mom's eyes narrowed at his tone.

"As long as I get to meet him before you guys go out," she told me. It was a reasonable request.

"Sure," I replied. I wanted to be excited that I had permission to go on my first date, but all I could concentrate on was Damien and his reaction to my news. Anyone with two eyes could see that he was upset.

His gaze dropped and his hands tightened into fists on the table. My appetite vanished and I looked to Amy and asked to be excused. I pushed back my chair and left the dining room, feeling a new wave of anger rise up in me.

I was agitated and angry. I paced my room, trying to make sense of my feelings.

My phone rang a little later that night when I was lying in my bed trying to fall asleep.

"Hi," I answered nervously. It was Mark.

"Hi," he greeted back. "I'm just calling to ask if you want to go to movies tomorrow night. There is a new movie on and everyone is raving about it."

"Sure, that sounds… great," I replied. He had no idea that I had never done this before. I wondered if it would freak him out if he knew what I'd been through. But I wasn't ready to share that with him.

"I'll pick you up at seven," he said.

"Okay," I said.

We spoke for a little while about school. I liked talking to him.

"See you tomorrow," he said. I said goodbye and he ended the call.

I got ready for bed. A nervous knot settled in my stomach at the apprehension of the nightmares I would have. With my bedroom lights still on, I drifted off to sleep sometime after one in the morning. Nightmares gripped me and I tossed and turned, frantically trying to escape Grant.

With a scream, I shot up in my bed, breathing erratically.

"It's okay," Damien soothed as he pulled me to his chest. The relief I felt at his presence outweighed the anger I felt toward him. I rested my head against his chest as he held me in a protective embrace. My mind told me it was a bad idea when Damien climbed into my bed and pulled me close, but my fear of the nightmares made me hold on tightly to him.

Safe in his arms, I drifted off to sleep. Just before I dropped off to sleep, I thought I heard him say something under his breath.

"I'm not giving up."

CHAPTER TWENTY-SIX

Haven

For the first time in a while, I woke up feeling warm and safe. I opened my eyes to see that Damien hadn't left yet. Normally he would be gone by the time I woke up. His chest rose and fell as he slept peacefully by me. I was warm and safe cocooned in his arms. A deep breath of his scent made my heart ache, so I closed my eyes and for a few moments I imagined a different life for us, one where we weren't so broken.

Lying in his arms, facing him, it was easy to imagine a different life to the one we'd lived. Even though I had some insight into why he was afraid to open himself up and love someone, it still hurt that I wasn't enough to make him at least try. His arms tightened around me and he pulled me closer. I closed my eyes to the reality and pretended for a few more minutes that I was enough for him.

I kept my eyes closed when I felt him stir beside me. It was just easier than being faced with the awkwardness of him holding me so close to him while we slept. I waited for him to shift off the bed and leave, but he didn't. His finger trailed down my cheek and I felt him tuck a stray hair behind my ear. His soft lips pressed a light kiss to my forehead as I pretended to be asleep.

Perhaps he was trying to imagine the same as I had. Maybe we were both trying to hold onto something that wasn't meant to be. After a few minutes I felt him shift out of my bed and then moments later I heard my bedroom door close.

I rolled onto my side and let out a sigh.

I spent the day lazing around the house. A couple of hours before my date with Mark, I began to get nervous. There was a knock at my door and I opened it. I couldn't help the grin that spread across my face at the sight of Chris.

"You do realize that a girl friend or even a gay friend would be better at this than I'm going to be," he informed me as he stepped into my room.

"You're my only friend, so you're going to have to help me," I insisted. I pushed him to the sofa. With a sigh he dropped into the seat and crossed his arms.

"Damien's your friend, too," he threw back.

"Damien is not just a friend… he's complicated," I said, trying to move the conversation away from him.

I didn't want to ruin getting ready for my first date thinking about Damien.

"Are you sure you're ready to move on?" he asked, watching me.

"I have to," I insisted. "For both of our sakes."

"Okay, enough about Damien, let's have a look at what you're going to wear." He stood up and walked over to my walk-in wardrobe.

Although Amy had insisted on buying me tons of clothes, I wasn't comfortable wearing dresses and skirts, so it limited my outfit to a pair of black slacks or dark jeans.

"Which one?" I asked as I held up both items, showing them to Chris.

"The slacks are too formal for a first date," he informed me with his arms crossed over his chest.

"Jeans it is, then," I said, laying the jeans down on my bed. I folded the slacks and put them back neatly in my wardrobe.

Chris stood in my closet, looking through some of the tops. I was glad he was helping me, because I honestly didn't have a clue.

"How about this?" he asked, holding up a red baby-doll shirt with thin straps.

I looked at the shirt. The color was bold and it was sexy, so unlike me. I chewed on my bottom lip as I tried to imagine what I would look like in it.

"Why don't you go and try it on?" he suggested. As much as he loved me and wanted to help, I could see he was starting to get bored. A guy could only be so interested in clothes and shoes.

"Okay," I said, grabbing the shirt and the jeans as well as some underwear and headed into my bathroom.

Once I got dressed, I stepped out of my bathroom.

"So what do you think?" I asked while I stood in front of Chris as he lounged on the sofa.

"You look... hot," he assured me.

I felt a little uncomfortable in the revealing top. At least my bruises were gone and the only thing that still remained from my attack from Grant was the cast on my arm.

"How much longer do you still need to wear that?" Chris asked, pointing at my cast. He'd seen my gaze lingering on it.

"Another few weeks," I answered. I couldn't wait to get rid of it because then I wouldn't think about the attack every time I saw it.

"What did Damien have to say about your date with Mark?" he asked when I sat down beside him and put my feet up on the small coffee table in front of us.

"He isn't happy about it," I said, shrugging my shoulders.

"I know you have feelings for him, but in the long run Mark will be better for you," he told me. "I've known Damien for a while and I just don't think he is capable of committing to just one girl."

Someone knocked on my door.

"Come in," I said.

"What are you guys doing?" asked Damien as he walked into my room.

"I'm getting ready for my date," I told him. Damien's smile disappeared. His eyes scanned me.

"You look beautiful," he said softly while his eyes held mine.

"Thanks to my good taste," added Chris, looking at me like I was his masterpiece.

"I'll see you later," Damien said to me before he turned and left.

"He feels more for you than he is willing to admit," Chris said softly, his eyes where Damien had been a few moments ago.

"Maybe," I said.

He'd moved on, and I was going on my first date with a boy. We were moving on. It didn't matter how he looked at me or how I looked at him, what mattered was the action, of taking hold of something and never letting go. That was what mattered. The secret looks, the mistaken kisses, the hidden longing just wasn't enough.

When Mark arrived to pick me up for our date, Damien was nowhere to be seen.

"Hi," Mark greeted me as his eyes slid over me, making me feel nervous. "You look beautiful."

"Thank you," I replied, giving him a weak smile as I clasped my hands together to keep them from shaking.

"Mark, this is Amy," I introduced. Amy stood beside me.

"Hi, Mark," said Amy. "It's nice to meet you."

"You too," he said, flashing his signature smile, which showed off his dimples.

I could see from Amy's reaction to him that he'd won her over. We spent a few more minutes getting our pictures taken by Chris.

"This isn't prom, you know," I reminded my overeager friend. He was snapping photos like he was shooting a fashion shoot.

"It's your first date and I want to make sure you remember it," he insisted. I felt a slight blush tint my cheeks at the thought that Mark now knew this was my first date. My eyes met Mark's, and he smiled at me. He seemed to be easygoing and didn't seem to mind Chris going nuts with the camera. Even Amy seemed to be endeared by Chris as she laughed at my attempts to get him to stop taking photos.

"That's enough," I muttered, putting my hand up to the camera playfully.

"Okay," he relented with a grin. "I think I might have enough photos."

"Thanks for helping me get ready," I whispered to Chris as I hugged him.

"You're welcome, have fun," he whispered back, giving me a quick squeeze.

"Enjoy," Amy murmured as she hugged me goodbye.

"Are you ready?" Mark asked and I nodded. He opened the front door and he turned to say his goodbyes to Amy and Chris before we left.

I couldn't help but think about Damien as Mark opened the passenger door to his car and I slid into the seat. He walked around and got into the driver's seat and I pushed all thoughts of Damien out of my mind. I was on a date with a really nice guy and I was going to give him a chance. He kept the conversation light. He also didn't ask me questions that I didn't want to have to answer. I was sure he was curious to know why I was living with the Knights, but he never asked why. Instead, we talked about school.

"Chris is really a character," he stated with a smile as he drove us to the cinema in town.

"Yeah, he is. One of a kind," I agreed. I knew what a good friend he really was. He'd been the first to crack through the hard exterior I'd kept up to keep people from getting close.

I had to suppress a laugh when I remembered Chris trying to get near my cast with a pen again after I'd gotten ready, but there was no way I was letting him put any more little messages on my cast. I was pretty sure it would end up being something about Mark, babies and kisses.

Everything was going well and after getting the movie tickets and some food we walked into the cinema. Mark walked behind me as I found our seats and I sat down. I couldn't ever remember going to the cinema, so it was new to me and I could feel a nervous knot in my stomach. An apprehensive feeling settled in my bones as I glanced around the darkened room. I took a deep breath to try to calm my nerves but it didn't help.

The dark scared me.

"Everything okay?" Mark asked, picking up on my nervousness.

"I'm fine," I lied. I could do this. I wanted normal, and this is what normal girls my age did. They went out to the cinema and watched movies.

They didn't sit in fear of what the darkness would bring. An image of Grant flashed in my mind. I knew he'd been watching me and for all I knew he could be sitting in the darkness, waiting for another chance to kill me. Suddenly it got a little harder to breathe.

What if he was in the cinema? My fear kicked up into panic and my hands began to shake.

You can do this, I kept chanting over and over in my mind. Not once since I agreed to go out on a date with Mark had I thought about Grant, but now it was all I could think about. I managed to hold on until the cinema lights darkened and the screen in front flickered on. The darkness set something off in me and terror gripped me. I stood up, spilling my popcorn over.

"I can't," was all I managed to get out before I brushed past a confused Mark.

The cinema doors banged open and I stepped through them from the darkness into the safety of the light. I breathed in like I was starved for air. Mark was right behind me, looking at me with concern as the doors closed behind us.

"Are you okay?" he asked as his eyes scanned my face. There was no point in lying, he could see I wasn't okay. I shook my head.

Gently, he steered me to a bench and my legs wobbled a little and I sat down.

"I'm sorry," I managed to feebly mumble, trying to get my hands to stop shaking.

"It's okay," he assured me as he watched me struggling to contain my panic.

It was too much too soon. Taking another deep breath, I dropped my head into my hands. I didn't even want to think about what Mark thought about my little breakdown. He would think I was a freak. He had no idea what was behind my erratic behavior.

Damien.

With shaky fingers I pulled my phone from my bag. Under Mark's concerned gaze, I dialed Damien.

"Hey." Hearing his voice blanketed me with warmth that made me feel safe.

"I…" I stuttered, struggling to form a sentence.

"What's wrong?" he asked anxiously and I gripped the phone in my hand as the words got stuck in my throat and I struggled to get them out.

Gently, Mark pried the phone from my fingers and took over. Distantly I heard him talk to Damien for a few minutes before he ended the call. I dropped my head into my hands and rubbed my hands over my face, trying to calm my heart, which was thumping in my chest like it was going to explode.

"I'm sorry," I mumbled again when he sat down next to me again and handed me my phone. I felt so bad because I should have known I wasn't ready to try and move on with my life.

The only way I would be able to carry on with some sort of normality would be if Grant was firmly locked up. Until then the fear that he was going to succeed and kill me would stop me from living my life. We drew a few curious looks as some people walked past us but I ignored what was going on around us.

"It's okay," he assured me as his eyes softened.

"I can't explain this to you." I wasn't ready to let another person in on my secret just yet. "But I just want you to know that I'm not crazy."

"I don't think you're crazy," he murmured. It was like he understood without me having to tell him anything.

After what felt like forever, though it couldn't have been even twenty minutes, I spotted Damien walking across the cinema toward me. He looked upset and worried as my eyes latched onto him. I stood up on my weak legs as he swept me into his arms. For the first time since I'd freaked I felt a calmness envelop me as I leaned my head against his warm chest and closed my eyes, taking a deep breath as he held my protectively.

I heard Damien's increased heartbeat thumping under

my ear. I'd scared him and I felt bad that I'd overreacted like I had.

"I'm sorry," I mumbled against his chest.

"Shh," he soothed and held me closer.

"Let's go home," he suggested gently as he steered me protectively through the doors of the cinema and out into the night. My first date, Mark, was left behind watching us leave, still confused by what had happened.

CHAPTER TWENTY-SEVEN

Haven

I leaned my head against the cool window, looking into the dark night while Damien quietly drove me home. A suffocating silence had settled between us. I could see he was worried, but I wasn't ready to talk about it yet. In a daze I watched the streetlights pass us by.

The evening had started off so well, and I couldn't believe it had ended the way it had. I felt the heat of Damien's gaze on me but I couldn't look at him. I'd tried hard to be normal but I had to realize I couldn't just sweep what had happened to me under the carpet and carry on as normal.

My life had been anything but normal for the last seven years, and there was a chance I would never be normal. It was probably a good thing that Amy had scheduled my appointment with the therapist. There was no doubt about it, I needed therapy.

Mark would probably never look at me the same way again, he probably thought I was crazy. It didn't really matter anymore anyway. Deep down I'd known that Mark would never be able to replace Damien in my life. What had happened tonight had brought that truth to the surface. I took a deep breath and closed my eyes, allowing the realization to roll through me.

I was hopelessly in love with a boy who was too broken to love me back. It wouldn't be fair to lead Mark on when I knew my heart belonged to Damien. I let a sigh out.

This wasn't just a passing physical attraction and it wasn't a crush that would go away, it was so much more. He was the one I wanted to lean on when everything got to be too much. I wanted to wake up every morning beside him, wrapped in his arms. I wanted it so much.

I couldn't stand around while he screwed everything in a skirt, it would kill me. It hurt that he was able to switch off whatever he'd felt for me because it wasn't that long ago he'd screwed some random girl across the hall from me. Despite how understanding and caring he was being at the moment, I couldn't mistake that for something that it wasn't. It was sympathy for my situation. I knew he cared for me in some way—just not in the way I wanted.

I was kind of relieved when we finally arrived at home. He switched the car off and turned to face me in the darkness, but I still couldn't look at him. I was scared he'd see what I was feeling in my eyes, so I kept my gaze on the house in front of us.

"Haven," he whispered softly as he tugged me into his arms. I should have pulled away and gone into the house, because the more time I spent with him the more I seemed to love him, but I couldn't. I closed my eyes and lay my head against his chest as he held me close. I pretended that everything was fine like I had this morning. For just a few minutes, I wanted to be happy and in his arms.

He played with a strand of my hair before he tucked it behind my ear. My eyes lifted to his and I was lost. My breath hitched in my lungs as his eyes kept mine captivated. His eyes flickered to my lips and then back to my eyes. I felt so aware of him at that moment.

"Let's go inside," he said when he released me and got out of the car.

I put my hand to my chest to stop my heart from bursting out of my chest as he opened the passenger door for me and helped me out onto my shaky legs. He had such a physical effect on me.

Amy was waiting by the front door when we stepped into the house with Damien leading the way, holding my hand.

"Are you okay?" she asked with concern.

"Yeah," I mumbled. I didn't want to go into detail about what had happened.

A look passed between Damien and his mom before he tugged my hand and led me up the stairs.

It was still early evening, but after everything that had happened, I was tired. By the time we came to a stop in front of my bedroom door, I was suppressing a yawn.

"Go get dressed in your pajamas, I'll be there soon," he instructed softly.

I let go of his hand and pushed my bedroom door open. Events of the night kept running through my mind as I went and got ready for bed. I was tired but I remained wide awake with the bedroom light still on when Damien entered my bedroom about half an hour later.

He was dressed in sweats and a T-shirt. He switched the light off and in the dark walked to my bed and pulled the comforter back. After the night I'd had all I wanted was to cuddle safely in his arms and sleep. Tomorrow I'd deal with the consequences of getting closer to Damien and what it meant for me.

He climbed into my bed and I went into his open arms. I breathed him in deep and laid my head on his chest.

"You want to talk about what happened tonight?" he

asked softly while he felt and stroked my hair. I closed my eyes for a brief moment.

Tonight had been more than just lingering fear from nearly dying at the hands of my evil stepfather. Nearly dying had broken free my conditioned fear of the dark. Most nights I'd lived in fear—some nights I hadn't slept much because I was too scared to let my guard down.

It was the reason why I suffered from nightmares when Damien didn't sleep in the room with me. Even in my subconscious state, I felt safer with Damien around. I'd never talked about the horrors that I'd endured under Grant's brutal fists; it was still too hard to talk about them, and I didn't know if I would ever be ready to talk about them.

I hoped that talking about them to a stranger might be easier, but there was no way I was ready to talk to Damien about it.

"I was scared." I swallowed hard.

He waited patiently as he held me protectively against his chest.

"I didn't realize the cinema was going to be so dark and when the lights went out I kinda freaked. Mark probably thinks I'm crazy," I muttered.

"You're not crazy," he stated. "You're were just a little scared. There's nothing wrong with that."

I felt weak and hopeless. Even now that I was no longer being physically abused by Grant, the fear of him still dictated my life, and I hated it.

"It's okay, you're safe with me," he assured me softly.

"I know," I murmured as I held onto the warmth and safety he provided. Safe with Damien in the dark, I closed my eyes.

Every morning I woke up next to Damien made me feel happy and content. I never got tired of watching him sleep peacefully next to me.

He lay on his stomach, with his arm flung above his head. He was effortlessly gorgeous. There was something about watching someone when they were not aware they were being watched. It was like you were seeing them for who they were, not for who they were trying to be.

Or maybe it was just creepy.

I was pretty sure I was crazy after overreacting like I had last night. Maybe the next step in my downward spiral was becoming a creeper. As much as I wanted to hide out in my bed and forget about what had happened last night, I had to face another day. I got out of the bed, making sure I didn't wake up Damien.

Now that I realized I loved him, I looked at him differently then I had before. He wasn't just beautiful to me on the outside. He was just as beautiful and sweet on the inside; well, except for when he had slept with that girl across the hall. I wasn't sure how I was going to cope with loving Damien.

Loving someone wasn't a logical choice that was made by stacking the pros and cons together, it just kind of happened, and you couldn't choose the person you fell in love with.

In front of my bathroom mirror, I looked at my reflection. On the outside, I looked like a typical teenage girl. No one just looking at me would see I was damaged from years of abuse. Only if you looked deeper into my eyes would you see the sadness deep in the depths of my soul.

I couldn't help feeling guilty leaving Mark like I had on our first date. I'd call him a little later and apologize, if he would still talk to me. I couldn't blame him if he never wanted to talk to me again. If I sat him down and explained my life to him he would understand, but I didn't want to do that. There were enough people that knew about what had happened to me, and I didn't want more people to find out about it. How was I supposed to try and put my life back together if I kept getting those knowing and sympathetic looks? I looked into the mirror and saw Damien, awake and standing a couple of feet behind me.

"Are you okay?" he asked softly. He still looked half asleep as he rubbed his eyes. His bed hair looked made him look devastatingly handsome. How was it possible for someone to look that good first thing in the morning?

"Yeah, as okay as I'll ever be," I muttered, still feeling like a freak because of my mini breakdown the night before.

"Haven," he said in a slight tone of warning.

I turned to face him.

"I freaked out like a little kid who is scared of the dark," I said, feeling like a complete idiot.

"Haven, you're the bravest person I know," he said to me. "What you've been through, most people wouldn't have stuck it out."

Did I tell him there were times when I'd contemplated doing something drastic to get away from the abuse? Did that make me a little less brave?

"Maybe it might help if I take you," he suggested, and I looked at him a little surprised. I wasn't sure I ever wanted to try going to the cinema ever again.

"I'm going to take you out to movies tonight," he told me. He couldn't be serious. I looked at him like he was the crazy one instead of me.

"But, why? What if I freak out again?" I asked as my heart began to speed up at the thought of having another freak-out in public.

He stepped forward and took my face gently in his hands, tilting my head up so that my eyes looked directly into his.

"It will be okay, I promise," he assured me with a surety I didn't feel. My hands covered his.

He had a way of keeping me calm but I wasn't convinced that would be enough to keep me from freaking out in the cinema, where the dark could hide memories of Grant.

"I'm scared," I whispered, my eyes pleading silently with his.

"I know, but it will be okay. I wouldn't do this if I didn't think you could do it," he explained as he brushed my cheek gently with his finger.

His belief in me made me feel all warm and fuzzy inside. I felt myself give him a gentle nod.

Later that day, Chris phoned to find out how my date with Mark went.

"Come on, I want all the juicy details. Did he kiss you?" he began, starting the inquisition. It was so like Chris to get straight to the point.

"No. The date ended before the movie even started," I explained, not wanting to relive the embarrassing memories of rushing out of the cinema.

"What happened?" he asked.

"I freaked out and left just as the movie started," I revealed softly, hating the fact that I felt so weak.

"What freaked you out?" Chris asked with concern.

"The dark," I whispered. "I couldn't help feeling that Grant was hiding in the dark, waiting to hurt me."

I didn't mention to Chris that Damien was going to take me back to the cinema tonight to try and conquer my fear. He might get the wrong idea.

He soothed my fears and told me I just needed some time to work through it.

After my call with Chris, I held my phone in my hand, trying to build up the courage to call Mark and apologize. It took me a good half an hour before I dialed his number and held my breath as it began to ring.

"Hi." His voice was cheerful, not at all what I was expecting.

"Hi," I managed to get out.

An awkward silence descended for a few moments before I spoke again.

"I'm so sorry. I never expected to freak out like I did… I had no idea," I began to babble.

"It's okay, Haven," he said, his soft words putting a stop to the rest of my apology. "I know there is stuff that has happened to you and I know it's not something you want to talk about. I get it."

I held my breath as my hand, holding the phone to my ear, trembled slightly.

"I just hope you're okay," he said.

"I am," I reassured him.

"There is something going on between you and Damien." It wasn't a question, it was statement.

I kept silent for a few moments.

"It's complicated," I said.

I couldn't explain to him why Damien and I were close like we were. The only way he would understand was if I told him everything, and I couldn't.

"I hope everything works out for you," he said softly. "But if he hurts you, I'll gladly beat the crap out of him."

I let out a laugh.

"So, we're good?" I asked, worried he wouldn't want anything to do with me.

"We're good," he assured me. "See you at school."

"See you at school," I said before I ended the call.

This time when I got ready to go out I had a feeling of dread growing in the pit of my stomach. Even the encouraging smile Damien gave me when he knocked on my door to see if I was ready didn't make me feel any better.

"Are you ready?" he asked while he stood there, watching me put some lip gloss on.

"Yeah," I said. I couldn't stall any longer.

No matter how hard I tried not to think of what had set me off the previous evening, I couldn't get rid of the building fear as we got closer to our destination. As we arrived in front of the cinema I could feel the fear flood through me. I let myself glance at Damien as he parked his car.

"It will be fine," he assured me when he saw the fear in my eyes.

Before I knew it we had tickets and food and were entering the cinema. I followed Damien to our seats and slumped down in the seat, holding onto my soda and popcorn tightly.

"Here," Damien said as he took my soda and put it into the cup holder.

With one hand I held the popcorn and with the other I held desperately onto the armrest between us. I glanced at Damien as I felt his fingers pry my hand from the armrest and intertwine our hands.

He gave me a reassuring smile.

"Trust me."

I closed my eyes for a second and released the breath that had been stuck in my lungs, and then I looked back to Damien and said, "Okay."

CHAPTER TWENTY-EIGHT

Haven

I held Damien's hand in a death grip as I rested my eyes on the screen in front of us, waiting for the lights to go out and for the movie to start. The moment the lights went out and the screen lit up, I tightened my grip on Damien's hand, but I didn't freak out like I'd expected I would. I turned to see him watching me with a proud smile.

"You did it," he whispered and I eased my grip on his hand and gave him a weak smile.

"I did it," I said.

Having got over my initial fear of the dark I began to relax and let myself enjoy the movie. After it finished we walked out of the cinema.

"You wanna go for a milkshake?" he asked with a glint of playfulness in his eyes. It was nice to see him acting carefree for a change—most of the time he was serious and intense. I suppose the same could be said about me.

"Yes," I answered. I wasn't ready to call it a night. I wanted to spend more time with him, even though this wasn't a proper date.

He took my hand in his and led me back to his car. He

drove us down the road to an old-fashioned type diner where you expected the waitress to be roller-skating around, but there were no roller skates in sight. A waitress showed us to a table. We slid into a pink candy-colored booth, sitting opposite each other. The waitress came over and handed us each a menu.

I glanced through the flavors of the milkshakes. It took me a while to decide on a chocolate one and Damien ordered a strawberry one.

"I'm so proud of you," he said softly.

"Thanks."

"Did you enjoy the movie?" he asked.

"Yeah, it was nice."

After I'd managed to get over the initial fear, I'd enjoyed the movie, although I'd held onto Damien's hand for the entire time.

"The more time I spend around you the more you surprise me," he said. I wasn't sure what he was talking about, and I waited for him to elaborate. "You've been through horrors no one should ever have to endure, and it left a vulnerability in you. I saw it the first time I saw you, but I tried to push you away. I was scared when I felt a need to protect you and I didn't even know you."

His words swept over me. His hand reached for mine. I remembered him being a little mean to me, when I had bumped into him my first day at school. The soft touch of his fingers against mine made my skin tingle. I'd never understood why he'd acted the way he had and now everything was starting to fall into place.

"There are moments in life that are so profound there is no way you can walk away unscathed. Sometimes those moments are good and sometimes they're... bad, really bad. I had one of those bad moments a few years ago, it was so devastating that it had changed me," he revealed with an emotional hoarseness in his voice. "I went from an easygoing person who lived every day without fear to a shell of my former self that could barely function because of the fear that gripped me."

His eyes flickered to our hands and then back to look at me.

"I lost my brother."

The sadness in his eyes pierced right through me and I felt the loss reflected in his eyes. There was no way I was going to reveal I'd already stumbled across his dead brother's room. I didn't want to lie to him or reveal that I already knew about his brother, so instead I held his gaze and gave his hand a supportive squeeze while I waited for him to continue.

"Losing someone so close was almost impossible to comprehend. And he wasn't just my brother—he was my twin, my other half," he said softly.

"I'm sorry," I managed to mumble through the emotion beginning to thicken in my throat. I never knew his brother, and I'd never get a chance to get to know him, either, but while Damien talked about him, I mourned him.

"We were so close, practically inseparable. I was the easygoing one and Dylan was the more reserved one. One afternoon a couple of blocks from our house we were playing soccer in the park. Both of us had joined the soccer team that year and we were practicing…"

A small smile was on his face as he reminisced about his brother, and then it disappeared and he took a deep breath before he continued.

"I kicked the ball toward him but he missed it and it rolled into the street. Dylan didn't look before he ran out into the street to get it, and a car hit him."

I could tell that telling me this story was taking an emotional toll on him, I hadn't even been there and I could feel the sting of tears at his words.

"I was the eldest by four minutes, so I was there when he took his first breath and I held him in my arms when he took his last."

The emotion in me bubbled over into the surface as I felt a tear slide down my face. I watched the anguish on his face. I'd lost family before, but there was no way I could understand or comprehend the level of despair he'd felt. The emotions that flooded through me urged me to hold him and comfort him but I resisted it.

"One moment everything was fine, we were laughing and joking, and in one split second everything changed. I suffered the worst kind of pain I thought possible and it broke something in me, something I will never be able to fix. For a while, I blamed myself. There were days I didn't want to get up and carry on, but I forced myself to take life day by day. Slowly but surely I got back on my feet, but I was never the same." I squeezed his hand in support. "His death scared me. Afterward, it was hard getting close to people because I held onto that fear of losing them. If you don't open yourself up to feel, you can't get hurt, and I lived by that."

It all made so much more sense now, his reluctance to date or get too attached to anyone. I understood him. I could sympathize; I would have felt the same if I'd been in his shoes. He paused for a moment to allow his words to soak in. His eyes held mine. Even if I had wanted to, I wouldn't have been able to look away from him. I felt like he was baring his soul to me.

"The moment when I looked into your eyes, I saw that your soul was broken like mine." I remembered that moment. "I don't think that it happened with just one moment like with me; I believe it was a whole lot of bad moments that chipped away at you until you finally broke."

I felt the sting of tears again, and another tear slid down my face. Maybe there would come a time I would be ready to talk about what I'd lived through, but I wasn't ready to do that now.

"A collection of good and bad moments define us. The moment I met you was a defining moment." He gave me a weak smile while I wiped my tears away. He really had a way with words. "I knew I would never be the same again the moment I looked into your eyes. I'd been able to hold people at arm's length, I was good at not getting attached to people. Girls came and went but I never kept any of them around. I was too scared that I'd feel something for them and I'd have to live with the fear of losing them."

He paused for a moment.

"You had me at the first moment I looked into your eyes. I didn't stand a chance."

For a moment I just stared at him in shock as he held my gaze. My thoughts were going crazy inside my head. What was he trying to tell me? I remember him telling me once before about the moment he had first met me, and that he'd felt an urge to protect me.

The waitress arrived with our milkshakes. It broke the intense moment, and I wrapped my hand around my milkshake and took a sip, grateful for the distraction. As soon as the waitress left, my eyes lifted to meet his. The intensity of his stare made me shiver.

"There are times I wish I knew what was happening to you at home," he revealed softly with an anguished guilt in his eyes.

I shook my head at him.

"But what's done is done. There is no point in going back and wishing things had been different," I told him. "Who knows if I'd even still be here if you'd found out earlier. Things could have been much worse."

He swallowed hard.

"You're right," he said, reaching for my hand. I glanced

down to see his hand cover mine. It was like he needed to touch me to chase away the memories of me nearly dying.

We finished our milkshakes, and then Damien dropped a couple of bills on the table.

"Let's get out of here," he suggested as he stood up and pulled me to my feet. I saw the appreciative look he got from our waitress as he pulled me by the hand out the door.

"I want to take you somewhere," he said as we walked to his car.

I had a feeling that he wasn't done talking but didn't want to continue the conversation in a diner with an audience.

"Sure."

The truth was I'd follow him to the ends of the earth and back.

The drive was quiet. I think both of us were lost in our own thoughts. It wasn't long before he parked the car at the side of the road. There wasn't anything around, and only when I got out of the car and peered down did I realize why he'd brought me here.

It was beautiful. It overlooked the whole town and the stars shone brightly in the night sky.

"I come here when I need to think," he explained as he got a blanket out of the trunk and spread it on the grass in front of the car. He sat down and pulled his knees to his chest.

"It's beautiful," I murmured as I turned to face him.

I sat down beside with my legs crossed. I let my eyes drift over the scene in front of us as I took a deep breath. It was so peaceful that it was calming.

"You're beautiful," he whispered and I turned to find him watching me. I was mesmerized. There were times I didn't feel beautiful but I couldn't help but feel beautiful when he looked at me the way he was now.

"And amazing," he whispered hoarsely. I kept silent. I wanted to tell him he was, too, but emotion clogged my throat. The things he'd done for me had been unexpected and I appreciated it.

If it wasn't for meeting him I wouldn't have gotten out and there was the chance that things could have escalated, and who knows what would have happened. Grant might have succeeded in killing me, or it all might have gotten too much for me to handle and I might have just given up.

A few seconds passed before he started to talk.

"From the moment Dylan died I stopped myself from getting attached. Sex is a way of physically connecting with another person, but feeling something for that person is something else entirely. The moment I met you, I began to feel something for you."

He seemed to wrestle for the right words.

"I care about you."

I knew he cared about me. He didn't have to tell me, because I felt it every day. He was the one that chased the nightmares away, he was the one that made me feel safe and protected.

"I won't lie to you... caring for you and feeling something for you scared me," he tried to explain. He ran an agitated hand through his hair before he turned to face me, taking both my hands in his. "I don't just care about you... it's much, much more than that."

He took a deep breath and released it. He looked unsure and vulnerable, and I wanted to wrap my arms around him and hold him, but instead I remained still so that he could finish what he wanted to say.

"At first I tried to keep away from you, but I still couldn't stop thinking about you. No matter how hard I tried to fight it, I couldn't keep away from you," he said. His hands tightened around mine. "Falling for you didn't happen in just one moment."

I was speechless. My heart began to speed up as my eyes widened.

"I fell a little the day I met you. You were so fragile and scared. I fell a little more every time I was with you. The moment I realized I'd fallen in love with you was the afternoon your stepfather tried to kill you," he whispered hoarsely, and I tightened my hold on his hands. "The last time I'd felt that type of fear was when I held my dying brother in my arms. It was then that I knew I loved you. To see you like that nearly killed me."

I closed my eyes for a second. It was hard to think back to that memory because I'd come so close to dying. His hand caressed my cheek. I opened my eyes as a tear slid down my cheek.

"Don't cry," he murmured as he brushed the tear from my cheek.

"It's hard to think about that memory without feeling the fear and hopelessness I'd felt when I thought I was going to die," I explained with hoarseness in my voice.

"I know it's hard, but you didn't die," he reminded me.

A few moments of silence rolled into a few minutes as I held his gaze. He was waiting for a response to his confession that he loved me. It was hard to listen to him tell me he loved me when all I could think about was him with another girl cross the hall from me.

"I don't understand," I said.

"What don't you understand?" he asked softly.

"If you felt that way about me, why did you bring that girl home?" I had asked the hard question. Everything he was trying to tell me was marred by the one action that had broken my heart.

I'd had such a tough life and it was hard to let people in, so if the people I let in hurt me, it was that much harder to let them in again.

"I kept telling myself that if I just moved onto another girl that whatever I felt for you would go away. It also didn't help that I watched you and Mark get closer, and it made me... jealous."

"You're the one that I wanted," I tried to explain my actions to him. I didn't do it to hurt him.

"I get that, but that doesn't mean it didn't hurt," he released my hands.

"Well, you bringing that girl home... hurt me," I managed to say as I felt an ache in my heart.

His eyes held mine as I tried to stop myself from crying. He loved me and I loved him but I wasn't sure I could get past that little incident. If I let him in again and he did something like that, I wouldn't be able to recover. The question was, could I trust him not to hurt me like that again? And the answer was that I wasn't sure.

"Nothing happened," he began to explain. "That night I brought that girl home. I couldn't do it."

I was stunned.

"Nothing happened?" I asked.

"Nothing happened. She wasn't you," he revealed.

Relief and happiness rushed through me and I smiled.

"I love you and I want to be with you," he stated, taking my face into his hands gently, as if I were fragile.

"I love you," I whispered breathlessly, drowning in his beautiful eyes.

He smiled and leaned closer. His hands threaded through my hair and I felt his lips touch mine. In that moment I let myself open up to him and allow myself to feel the love I felt for him freely, without any reservation.

CHAPTER TWENTY-NINE

Haven

I lost track of time as we kissed and he pulled me closer. This was all I'd ever wanted, someone to love me, and he did. Finally, his lips left mine, and I opened my eyes, still feeling little dazed at his revelation. He smiled at me and my hands covered his, which were still cradling my face gently.

"So will you be my girlfriend?" he asked softly while his eyes held mine. Gone was the nervousness that had been there earlier; now he was confident.

"Yes," I whispered, nodding my head, I still wasn't convinced it was reality, but if it was a dream, I didn't want to wake.

He leaned his forehead against mine and took a deep breath.

"I don't know how to do this," he whispered and I heard the vulnerability in his voice as it wavered for a moment.

"Neither do I," I told him.

It had taken us so long to get to this point where we'd realized we both wanted the same thing: each other. For a few moments we remained with our foreheads pressed together before I pulled away gently. I wanted to say something.

"This whole dating thing is new for me." I couldn't help but think about how my first date had gone terribly wrong. "We'll figure it out together."

"Come on, it's time to go home. We have school tomorrow," he reminded me before he stood up and pulled me to my feet.

He pulled me into his arms and kissed me liked I'd never been kissed before. I swear I felt my world tilt. I was breathless and stood on weak knees when he pulled away and smiled at the visible effect his kisses had on me.

He led me to the passenger side of his car and opened the door. I would never tire of the little things he did, like opening the car door for me. I slid inside. I was deliriously happy as I watched him gather the blanket and disappear behind the car. The trunk opened and then closed. I was smiling at him as he got into the car. He started the car and backed out. During the drive home, we were both quiet. I kept sneaking glances at him, allowing myself to admire this broken boy that had stolen my heart.

"You're staring," he teased when his hand found my while he kept his eyes on the road.

"I'm totally stalking you," I teased back. I hadn't felt this happy and lighthearted in as long as I could remember, and it was nice for a change. My life had been painfully serious and it was nice to have something to make me smile.

"Stalk away, I'm yours," he stated playfully.

I'm yours. Such powerful words, and they made me feel loved, but it was more than that. He had brought more than just love into my life—he had brought friendship and family. It was so much more than I'd ever hoped to have. It was hard to think back to the life I'd led before Damien had stepped into it, and I was thankful every day that he had.

"What's wrong?" he asked, pulling me out of my deep thoughts. I brushed away the tears that had gathered in my eyes but hadn't fallen.

"I'm just feeling a little emotional," I replied, giving him a weak smile.

He squeezed my hand. It had been an emotional night.

When we got home, Damien got out of the car. He walked around to my side and helped me out of the car. Instead of walking me into the house, he pulled me into a hug and I leaned against him.

"Everything will be okay," he murmured softly while he held me. "I'm going to give you so many happy memories that there won't be any space for the bad ones."

My heart melted at the words and I was too overcome with emotion to speak, so I gently nodded my head against his chest.

"As much as I want to stay right where I am, it's getting late and we have school tomorrow," he told me as he pulled away and dropped a kiss on my temple. I loved it when he did that, it made me feel adored.

He ushered me through the front door first and then upstairs. The closer we got to our bedroom, the more nervous I became. I stopped outside my door and turned to him, nervously fidgeting with my hands. Now that we were officially dating, I wasn't sure how the sleeping arrangements would work, although I knew there would be no sleeping if he wasn't in my bed with me.

"Get ready for bed and I'll be there soon," he instructed gently, easing my fear.

Fifteen minutes later I was tucked into my bed as my bedroom door opened and he entered. My heart fluttered at the sight of him. He'd done this before, but this time it was different, this time he was mine. He switched off the bedroom light before he slid into the bed with me. Gently, he pulled me into his arms and I lay my head on his chest as I snuggled closer.

"You know that when Chris finds out about us, he's going to start planning the wedding," I informed Damien.

Considering Damien had issues with commitment, I'd expected him to freak out a little, but instead he surprised me. He laughed and shook his head.

"That friend of yours is one of kind," he said still laughing.

He was right. Chris was one of a kind. There wasn't another one like him, and I was so blessed to have in my life. Never when he'd first suggested we go out did I ever imagine it would have ended the way it had. It had been the best night of my life and I was convinced life didn't get any better than this.

Then something occurred to me.

"What would have happened if my date with Mark had gone differently?" I asked softly. The idea that if things had gone well with Mark then what happened tonight might have never happened scared me.

He squeezed me gently before he answered, almost like he had to confirm that I was real and that I was really lying in the bed with him.

"You don't know how grateful I am that your date with Mark bombed," he replied. "Don't get me wrong, I'm not saying it was good you freaked out, but it gave me the chance to man up and tell you how I feel."

He paused for a moment.

"But if things had worked out differently, I would have fought for you," he admitted. "I would have done whatever I had to."

I was so thankful that things had worked out the way they had. I wasn't naive or blind to the fact that our road together might not always be smooth, but I was prepared for the ups as well as the downs. I loved him and he loved me but this wasn't just about love, this was so much more. It was the person he was around me, how me understood me better than anyone. It was all of those things that made him the boy for me.

I woke up with soft lips brushing against my cheek. Still half asleep, I stretched lazily, feeling Damien's arms around me as I opened one eye and fixed it on him. He was so handsome, and I couldn't help but smile at the fact that he was mine.

"Come on, you need to get up or we're going to be late," he whispered as he watched me with a smile. He looked as happy as I felt.

"But I'm tired," I moaned, trying to cuddle back into this arms but he was already getting out of the bed. It had been an awesome night even though I was still tired, and I couldn't help the smile that tugged at my lips.

"I'm giving you thirty minutes or I'll come and dress you myself," he said with a suggestive tone.

"I'm getting up," I assured him as I sat up in bed. He leaned over and kissed me lightly on the lips, taking me by surprise. I liked it; no, I loved it.

"Thirty minutes," he warned with a smirk before he turned and left.

I sighed happily.

I had to pull myself out of my happy thoughts to drag myself through the shower and get dressed. I couldn't wait to get my cast off because showering with a plastic bag over my cast was a pain, and it still took me forever to get clothes on and off.

It was only now that I was alone and in my bathroom, brushing my hair, that the full impact of what had happened last night hit me. Damien was my boyfriend now. Damien, who liked to have sex with various nameless girls. Sex. He was that guy that had slept with a different girl every week. I felt my knees shake.

I felt an anxious panic swamp me at the thought. I was a virgin and had zero experience with guys. He'd been my first kiss. I took a deep breath to keep the panic from overwhelming me. He loved me, but he was a guy, and guys wanted sex.

As much as I loved Damien, I didn't think I was ready for that, not now anyway. And I wasn't sure how long it would take me before I was. Would Damien be willing to wait? I bit my nail as I became more agitated with my thoughts. I put the hairbrush down and started to brush my teeth.

Doubt began to gnaw at me. Would he love me less if I wouldn't sleep with him? Would it make him stop loving me? One doubt after another ran through my mind.

I rinsed my mouth out and walked back into my bedroom, sitting down on my bed for a moment while I contemplated my fears. I was so lost in my thoughts that I didn't hear Damien enter my room; it was only when he was standing directly in front of me that I snapped out of my thoughts.

"Are you okay?" he asked softly as he bent down to bring his eyes level with mine.

I wanted to say yes, but I shook my head as I bit my lip. There was no point in delaying this conversation.

"What's wrong?" he asked. His concerned eyes scanned my face for any clues as to why I was so worked up.

"I can't," I stated anxiously, twisting my hands in my lap. His forehead creased.

"You can't what?" he prompted.

He had no idea what I was going on about.

"Me and you…and…" I stuttered, feeling mortified at having to talk about it.

He waited patiently for me to finish the sentence.

"Sex," I managed to blurt out as I felt the heat of a blush on my cheeks.

His eyes widened in surprise and then he smiled at me.

"Why are you worrying about that?" he asked softly.

"You know why, you're a guy. And up until now you've been a man-whore sleeping with a different girl each week."

He shook his head, but he was still smiling.

"And you think I need sex from you," he finished for me.

I nodded my head at him as I continued to bite my lip. He laughed and I was a little confused. He straightened up and sat down next to me on the bed.

"This thing we have between the two of us goes way beyond sex," he began to explain to me. "Yes, I've had plenty of meaningless sex that left me empty inside. The way you make me feel and just being with you fills that emptiness. Being together isn't about sex, it's how you make me feel when I'm with you. Do you understand that?"

My throat was tight with emotion so I nodded my head.

"One day when you're ready we can take the next step, and I'm happy to wait."

How had I managed to find such an awesome guy? Feeling relieved, I threw my arms around him and planted my lips on his. I'd taken him by surprise, but he put his arms around me and held me as he kissed me back.

He pulled back and looked at me.

"You better?" he asked.

"Yes," I answered.

"Good, because we need to go or else we'll be late for school," he reminded me as he stood up and pulled me to my feet.

We made a quick stop in the kitchen to grab a couple of cereal bars for breakfast.

"Have a good day," Amy said as we dashed out of the

kitchen, trying to make sure we weren't late for school.

Damien got us to school with a little time to spare. I felt a little apprehensive when he took my hand in his and walked me into school. Most of the students were inside already, but the few that spotted us holding hands began to whisper amongst themselves. It wouldn't be long before it got around school. The attention that we'd attract wasn't something I was used to, but I had to find a way to deal with it. It was part and parcel of dating a popular guy in the school. I glanced at my boyfriend. He was so worth it.

Chris' face lit up when he saw Damien's hand joined with mine as he walked me to my locker, where Chris stood waiting for me.

"I so told you this was going to happen," he stated as we stopped in front of him.

"Yeah, you did," I said, rolling my eyes as I let go of Damien's hand.

"I'll see you later," Damien said before he dropped a kiss on my lips and turned and walked down the hall to get to his first class.

I turned to face Chris, who was still smiling smugly.

"I've never seen you so happy," he said.

"It's because I've never been this happy," I replied, feeling a little emotional.

He pulled me into a hug and then released me.

"I like you happy," he stated, a little more serious than I was used to him being. He'd been there when I hadn't wanted a friend and he'd forced his way in. And I was so lucky to have him in my life.

"Me too," I said before I turned to open my locker to get the book I needed.

"Give me the cast," he demanded with his hand open and a marker in the other hand. I shook my head with a smile as I put my arm in his open hand.

He began to write on the cast like he had at the hospital. I was still wondering if it was such a good idea. A couple of moments later, he smiled as he pulled the marker away from the cast.

"All done," he told me triumphantly.

Curiosity made me look at the message he'd written. I couldn't help but smile at my goofy friend after reading the message.

"Just in case someone doesn't know," he told me.

The message read, "Property of Damien Knight."

"You're terrible," I said, shaking my head at him, but I was smiling.

"What?" he asked, pretending he had no idea what I was talking about.

I was officially dating Damien, so I wouldn't have to hide the message. I couldn't help but wonder what Damien would say about it. I was so happy that I didn't care. I didn't believe life got any better than this.

CHAPTER THIRTY

Haven

My first day at school as Damien's girlfriend was a little daunting and surreal. There were plenty of jealous glares from girls he'd been with. I think although he'd been upfront with them they had all secretly hoped they would be the one to change him. I could see them look at me and wonder what he saw in me, but honestly I didn't see what he saw in me.

I was nervous when I saw Mark in my first class but I walked in and sat down beside him. Unsure of how to act around him, I gave him a weak smile when he turned to face me.

I wanted to tell him about Damien and me before he heard about it from someone else.

"I'm sorry our date didn't go well," I said to him.

"It's okay," he assured me.

"I also wanted to tell you that...Damien and I...are kinda..."

"Dating?" he offered.

The news must have gotten around the school faster than I'd thought. I nodded.

"It sucks for me, but I just want you to be happy," he

said.

"Thanks," I said. He was such a great guy.

He flashed me that killer smile with the dimples and I knew we were okay. I was relieved, because I didn't want to hurt him. I wanted to be happy but I wasn't about to stomp on other peoples' feelings to get that feeling.

Another good thing was that he treated me exactly the same way he'd treated me before. It was like my crazy freak-out from Saturday night had been forgotten, and I was grateful for that. There was nothing worse than someone watching you go mental.

People that had never spoken to me before began to greet me when I walked past them in the hallways. I didn't know most of the people. Shane, Damien's best friend, greeted me with a friendly smile when I passed him in the hallway while I was on my way to my second class for the day.

Mark walked me to every class just like he had before, and it was nice. I spotted Damien standing by the door of my next class. His face lit up when he spotted me. I wondered if mine did the same when I saw him.

"Hi," he greeted me and pulled me into his arms. His lips touched mine and I felt my knees weaken.

"Hi," I said breathlessly. It was like when the two of us were together, everyone else disappeared into the background.

"Um, I'll see you in class," Mark said, looking slightly uncomfortable.

I didn't miss the look that Mark and Damien shared before Mark entered the classroom. Before it would have been Damien glaring at Mark because he was jealous, but now he knew there was no reason to be jealous. He owned my heart and there was no room for anyone else.

"And that?" I asked, referring the look they'd shared.

"Nothing you have to worry about, it's a guy thing," he said. "How's your day going?"

"It's been a little weird with all the attention," I told him. I was used to blending into the background, so it was something I'd have to get used to.

"I'm sorry," he said. "I've got to go, or else I'm going to be late for my next class."

He pressed a quick kiss to my lips before he released me. I watched him rush down the hallway. *I'm a lucky girl*, I thought to myself as I turned to enter my second class for the day. I sat down in the desk next to Mark. He looked at me and smiled.

"He really makes you happy," he stated softly. It had to be written all over my face, how happy I was at the moment.

"He does."

We'd both had horrible things happen to us—maybe that was why we understood each other so well. Maybe it even made us love each other even more. We were both perfectly broken for each other.

I floated on my cloud of happiness for the rest of the morning. At lunch time, Mark and I walked down to meet Chris at our usual spot. I was a little surprised to see Damien and his friend Shane already sitting with Chris. Not that I minded, because every moment I got to spend with Damien made me happy. Damien got up and kissed me when I stopped in front of him.

"Hi," he said as he took my school bag off my shoulder and put it down for me. He sat back down on the grass.

"Hi," I greeted when I sat down in between Chris and Damien, my two favorite people.

"What's this?" Damien asked as he took my cast and read the message Chris had written this morning.

He laughed and looked to Chris.

"Thanks, Chris," he said.

"I was just making sure everyone knew," Chris stated, opening his sandwich with a cheeky smile on his face.

"I don't think there is anyone in the school who doesn't know," said Shane, sitting opposite us. "I think within the first half an hour this morning everyone knew."

Our little group had grown and everyone seemed to get on and the conversation flowed steadily. Damien held my hand and I couldn't stop the goofy smile from appearing on my face.

It was hard to remember the girl that had shrunk away from getting to know people when I'd first started at the school. I had a boyfriend, that itself was still hard to comprehend. And I had friends, new ones as well as older ones.

I was very lucky and so happy at the moment, I was convinced that things couldn't get any better than this. But no matter how happy I was I couldn't ignore the nagging reminder in the back of my mind. Grant was still out there somewhere. What if the police never caught him?

It was like a constant fear that stayed in the pit of my stomach, wondering when he was going to come after me again.

"What are you thinking about?" Damien asked softly against my ear.

I didn't want to tell him I'd been thinking about Grant.

"You were thinking about him, weren't you?" he asked softly, so the rest of the group couldn't hear.

I nodded my head. There was no point in lying and pretending that Grant didn't exist.

"The cops will get him," he said with a sureness I didn't feel. They hadn't managed to catch him up until now.

I tried to shake those thoughts from my mind. I didn't want my fear of Grant to ruin my happiness. Today I was going to enjoy the happiness I'd found, and tomorrow I would worry about Grant.

That afternoon after school I had my first appointment

with the therapist. Damien took me and waited in the waiting room for me. I'd told him I could call him when I was done, but he insisted on waiting.

I'd been nervous when I'd first walked into the office and eyed out the leather couch with a single chair beside it. By the time I had left my first session, I had been emotionally drained. The therapist was an elderly lady with her long, gray hair twisted into a bun and glasses resting on her nose. She'd smiled and tried to put me at ease, but nothing could lessen my nervousness.

She'd asked me a few questions that I'd answered. We'd started off the session talking about my life before the abuse. I didn't know what was harder, talking about the life I'd lost or the life I'd endured with the abuse; sometimes it was hard to tell. The hour had gone by quickly. She'd told me that we'd had a good session, and she'd scheduled another session for the next week.

Damien kept glancing my way on the ride home. I think my lack of conversation concerned him, but I didn't have it in me to pretend I was okay.

Opening up to a stranger about my life had been a lot harder than I had thought it was going to be. I wished I could keep everything that happened to me tightly sealed in a bottle that I could bury deep into the ground and never have to open, that I could just carry on with my life and pretend it hadn't happened. Dealing with the stuff Grant had done to me was an emotional roller coaster. The emotional scars were worse than the physical ones.

It was harder to deal with it and then push it the back of my mind to ignore it, but I needed to deal with it even if it hurt, because I knew in the long run it would be better for me. When we got home, Damien quietly walked beside me into the house. I wanted to go straight to my room, but I didn't want to be rude to Amy. I knew she would want to know how it had went.

"Hi," she greeted cheerfully when we entered the kitchen. The smell of cooking food filled the air.

"Hi," I greeted back with a fake smile on my lips.

"How did it go?" she asked, scanning my face to pick up what I wasn't saying.

"It was okay."

That was all I was going to say about it.

"Good," Amy said. Without saying it, she understood I didn't want to talk about it.

Amy didn't miss it when Damien reached for my hand and held it. She smiled. Damien led me out of the kitchen and upstairs. Outside my room, he pulled me into a hug and held me.

"Go have a shower and I'll bring up some food for you," he said. He knew the session with the therapist had taken a lot out of me.

I nodded my head against his chest. He released me but before I could open my door and disappear inside, he cupped my face and placed a gentle kiss on my mouth.

After I entered my room, I closed the door and leaned against it. I didn't want to spend too much time concentrating on my thoughts, so I did as Damien had told me and I went to have a shower. Once I got out of the shower, I got dressed in my pajamas and climbed into my bed.

It wasn't long before I heard a gentle knock at the door.

"Come in," I said as I sat up and leaned against the headboard.

Damien entered with a tray of food. It was so thoughtful, but I wasn't hungry.

"How are you feeling?" he asked softly.

"Tired," I answered as he set the tray down on my lap.

"Why don't you try and eat something," he suggested.

"I'm not hungry," I told him, and he picked the tray up and set it down on the desk beside my laptop.

"What can I do?" he asked. I knew he was feeling helpless.

"Will you hold me?"

He didn't say another word. He kicked his shoes off and switched the bedroom light off. I lay back as he slid into the bed beside me and he pulled me closer. I sighed as I rested my head against his chest as he held me. I lost track of how long we lay together in silence before I drifted off to sleep, where I dreamed of my new life with Damien.

The next morning was rushed. We'd skipped breakfast because we were running late, but somehow Damien got us to school on time.

Chris was waiting by the school entrance for me. Damien walked me to him.

"I'm going to miss you," he said as he walked beside me, holding my hand. I loved how he did these little things that meant so much to me.

"It's only half a day, and I'll see you later," I teased him.

"I'll pick you up after school," he said as he cupped my face in his hands and kissed me when we got to Chris. I loved his kisses and how they made me feel.

"After school," I replied and I pressed a quick kiss to his lips before I looped my arm through Chris' and we walked into the school.

"Why is Damien missing school today?" he asked.

"He has a dentist appointment," I answered.

"You guys are really all happy and loved up," said Chris as we walked down the hallway to my locker.

"Yeah, we are," I replied. It was weird. When we'd been apart, we'd just been living day to day trying to survive our demons; but now that we were together, we were happy and the burden we carried seemed lighter.

"So have you done the deed yet?" he asked, wiggling his eyebrows suggestively as he bumped my arm.

"No," I told him, feeling a little embarrassed to be talking about that type of stuff, even if we weren't doing anything. "I'm not ready for that yet and he said he'd wait."

"Wow," he commented, sounding a little taken aback.

"What?" I asked as I glanced at him.

"I never thought I'd see the day where Damien would change for the better," he said, shaking his head. "It's like he's a completely different person when it comes to you."

It was hard for me to think about Damien as the person everyone else saw him as, because from the moment I'd met him he'd been different with me.

"So can I start planning the wedding already?" he asked in a teasing tone.

"Hey, I think you're jumping the gun a little there," I said with a grin. "We've only just starting dating."

Marriage. I'd never thought that far ahead in my life before. It had always been about surviving Grant, and there had been plenty of times I didn't think I was going to make it.

"I see the way you guys look at each other. Mark my words, one day you're going to get married and live happily ever after," he predicted.

I wasn't sure I'd ever believe in happily ever after again, so I said nothing.

"I just need to get a book for my next class," I told him as I stopped in front of my locker.

"I need to talk to my teacher before class starts," he told me. "I'll see you at lunch."

"See you then," I said to him as he disappeared into the crowd, walking in the hallway.

I got the book I was looking for, although I struggled to open my locker. Mark was already seated and waiting in my first class.

The first couple of classes dragged by. For some reason I just couldn't concentrate on schoolwork. My thoughts were on Damien. I couldn't help the happy smile that touched my lips at the thought of him, and the fact that he was my boyfriend.

I wondered if I would ever get used to it.

Mark normally walked me from class to class but the teacher had called him back to talk to him, so I walked to my locker without him.

I struggled with my combination. The lock was old and I had to spin it a couple of times to get it open. I'd need to speak to someone in the school office about it.

Suddenly, I heard a loud bang, and then someone screamed. What the hell? It took my mind a few moments to comprehend what was happening. *It sounded like a gun shot.*

Then I heard another one.

Oh my god.

CHAPTER THIRTY-ONE

DAMIEN

We'd just gotten back from dentist appointment. My mom had taken the morning off to take me to the dentist. It hadn't taken long for him to check what he had needed to and send me on my way, saying he'd see me back in a year's time. Apparently I had good teeth. It was a good thing, because the sound of the drill in the dentist's office sent shivers of fear down my spine.

The good thing about going to the dentist today was the fact that I had gotten a day off from school. It didn't happen often. I'd only been apart from Haven for a couple of hours, but I was missing her already. I still couldn't believe how lucky I was to be dating her.

"You missed breakfast this morning," my mom stated, looking in the fridge. "I can make some scrambled eggs if you want?"

I'd missed breakfast this morning because I'd driven Haven to school and by the time I'd made it back it had been time to leave for my appointment.

"Sounds good," I replied to my mom. Any food was good—I was a growing boy.

I sat down by the kitchen counter as I watched my mom grab a couple of eggs from the fridge. She'd just cracked the second egg open when the phone began to ring. She wiped her hands and answered the phone attached to the wall.

"Hello," she answered cheerfully. It took only seconds for her smile to vanish.

I watched as my mom's hand tightened on the phone and her eyes shot to mine. Panic and fear filled her eyes as she held onto the phone like it was a lifeline.

"What's wrong?" I asked as I stood up and reached for my mom, but she was still listening intently on the phone as her eyes held mine.

"Okay," she said, her voice stunned.

Then she ended the call. It wasn't good.

"What?" I prompted as my panic began to build. She looked away when I tried to scan her features, trying to figure out what was going on.

Her dazed expression lifted back to mine. I saw the horror in her eyes and I felt my heart stop for a moment.

"It was Detective Green," she said softly. "He said there's a situation at the school…"

Haven.

My heart felt like it dropped right out of my chest and splattered on the floor below. I reached for the kitchen counter to keep myself steady as something inside me shook with fear.

Haven. Her name resounded in my head.

"There are people to protect her," my mother reminded me when she saw my reaction. It didn't matter. She was in danger and that was all that mattered.

I didn't stick around for my mom to explain the rest. I dashed out of the kitchen. I grabbed my car keys and ran out of the front door toward my car. If it had been Detective Green on the phone, it had something to do with Grant.

Fuck! Please let her be okay, I kept begging inside my mind frantically.

I broke every speed limit on my way to the school. The roads in front of me blurred from one into another. I wanted to call her, but I couldn't find my phone as I patted my pockets down.

Damn it! I'd left my phone at home.

This couldn't be happening, not again. All I could think about was Haven. I should have gone to school today. If something happened to her because I wasn't there to protect her, I would never forgive myself.

I held onto the little control I had. I couldn't help Haven if I fell apart now, so as hard as it was, I tried to keep myself together for her sake.

The sight when I arrived a block away from the school hit me like a ton of bricks, and I had to slow down to take it in.

It was chaos. Crowds of students littered the road a block away from the school. Some girls were wailing hysterically, some were just crying. Teachers and other students tried to console them.

Unable to get any closer to the school with the car, I pulled over to the side of the road and jumped out.

I wanted to look for her in the crowd, but I knew that if Detective Green had called my mom then chances were Haven was still inside the school. A sense of foreboding settled in my stomach at the sight of ambulances in the street closer to the school. Paramedics were tending to some injured students.

I glanced at the one student that lay on a gurney. There was so much blood I nearly heaved, but the thought of Haven pulled me forward. Now wasn't the time to fall apart, I had to be strong. The entrance to the school parking lot was blocked off. I pushed my way through the crowd to the yellow crime-scene tape.

How long had the situation been going on for? The thought that it had been going on long enough for the cops and paramedics to arrive nearly made me want to scream. It had been too long already.

I called to one of the cops guarding the scene.

"Tell Detective Green that Damien Knight is here," I said to the cop that was closest to me.

He eyed me for a moment before he turned and walked away. I think the fact that I knew the name of the detective was the only reason he'd followed my instruction. He walked up to a group of cops, standing behind the front row of student cars in front of the school.

I watched anxiously for a few minutes, running my hand through my hair, before the cop returned and allowed me to move past the tape, keeping everyone else at bay. Most of the cops that were spread across the front row of cars had guns and had them pointed at the school.

I felt the panic rise again. I knew it wasn't going to be good, but I'd never imagined it would be this bad, and this was bad.

"Damien." Detective Green stepped forward when he saw me. He was dressed in a suit.

"Detective Green," I rushed to him. "What happened?"

I asked the question, but I wasn't sure I was ready for the answer.

"We got called in when a teacher called the police station reporting gun shots."

No!

"It only took us ten minutes to get to the school, but by then most of the students were out, including a few who'd been shot."

I swayed.

"Haven?" I choked out, not sure if I was ready for the

answer.

"She is still inside the school."

Images of her lying in a pool of blood flashed through my mind, but this time there wasn't a knife in her stomach: the blood oozed from bullet wounds in her chest. Every image sliced through me like a knife.

I'd promised to keep her safe.

"I need to go inside the school to find her," I stated to the detective as I took a step toward the school, but he clamped his hand down on my shoulder, halting me.

"There is no way we can allow anyone to enter the school. We already have a hostage situation and I'm not handing him any more hostages," Detective Green stated firmly.

"It's Grant, isn't it?"

"Yes."

It wasn't something I didn't know already, but hearing the confirmation out loud made me drop my head into my hands.

Detective Green paused for a moment before he continued.

"The teacher reported the gunman calling out the name Haven. They knew immediately that it was her stepfather, so the cop that took the call informed me. That's why I'm here."

"What about the cop car that was always stationed outside the school?" I asked. I'd seen the cop car on more than one occasion. They'd also made sure to have a cop car outside the house as well.

"They never saw anything. Grant must have got in another way, and by the time shots were being fired, it was too late, he had hostages."

I closed my eyes for a second, wishing this was a bad dream that I would wake up from, but when I opened my eyes I was still standing in front of Detective Green, living the nightmare.

We'd failed her, all of us.

The cops that had been there to protect her had failed. I'd promised her countless times I'd protect her and keep her safe, and I'd failed her, too.

I could only hope that Mark was with her inside.

"The only reason I allowed you past the tape was because you are familiar with the case. If you make one wrong move I'll cuff you and put you in the back of a cop car," he warned. His eyes conveyed the seriousness of his threat.

"I can't just stand here and do nothing," I pleaded with both of my hands out to him, feeling my desperation rise.

"We are trying our best to get everyone out alive."

Grant wasn't going to hold Haven hostage—if he saw her he'd kill her on the spot. There was no negotiating with that, he wanted her dead. The hopelessness I felt was the same as when I had watched Dylan run out into the road and I couldn't stop the car from crashing into him; all I could do was stand from the sidelines and watch it happen.

"How many are still inside?" I asked, keeping my eyes fixed to the entrance of the school and wishing I could make Haven appear safe and sound.

The school was ominously silent.

"We don't have a definitive number, but we think there are about fifty students and two teachers still inside."

"Has he killed anyone yet?" I asked, remembering the paramedics frantically working on a couple of students.

"We're lucky in that there haven't been any fatalities, yet. There have been four students with serious gunshot wounds that have been rushed to the hospital and there have been a few superficial wounds. It's a good thing he's a crap shot."

I was silent for a few moments. I let my gaze drop and I took a deep breath, trying to take in all the detective had told me.

"We think he's having a mental breakdown," he explained. My gaze shot back up to the detective. "We think the death of Haven's mom triggered something in him that snapped."

One of the officers nearby called out.

At the entrance of the school, a student appeared. I blinked a couple of times, unable to believe what I was seeing, but I wasn't seeing things.

Relief flooded through me as I watched Haven standing in the entrance.

Haven

There was a person in the school with a gun shooting at students. Even though the reality was right in my face—panicked students running for their lives—it was hard for my mind to process.

I glanced in the direction the students were running from. I couldn't see anyone there, although I'd half expected to see a student with a gun randomly shooting.

My thoughts jumbled in my head as my panic began to rise. My heart began to pound in my chest and the adrenaline began to flow in my veins.

Students were pushing and shoving, trying to get the school's exit. Some girls were hysterical and screaming.

My first instinct was to get out as well, but I couldn't leave Chris behind. I tried to remember what class he had just been to, but I couldn't remember anything in my haze of panic.

I gripped my school bag and slipped into the first empty

classroom I could find. I needed a moment to pull myself together. My heart was beating so fast it felt like it was going to explode right of my chest. I took a breath and released it, trying to calm myself down.

I crouched down with my back against the wall beside the slightly open door.

My hands were shaking so bad. I tried to hold them together to steady them. I took another deep breath to keep the panic from overwhelming me. Chris. I needed a way to find out where he was.

My phone.

With shaky hands I searched my school bag. It took me twice as long to find my phone because I was nervous, and I felt relieved when I found it.

My heart pounded in my ears.

I searched for Chris' number and then called it.

Pick up, pick up, I chanted in my mind, willing him to answer it. If he didn't pick up I would have no way of knowing whether he'd gotten out or he was still stuck somewhere in the school, or worse. I shook my head, not wanting to even consider that possibility.

There were plenty of horrible things I could deal with— I'd dealt with a lot in my life—but there were just some things that were too terrible to even think about. Chris had to be fine.

With every ring that went unanswered, I lost a little bit of hope. It rang five times.

"Haven," he answered in a hushed tone. Relief flooded through me, he was alive.

"Chris," I whispered. "Where are you?"

I was praying for him to be outside the school. I wanted him to be safe. I was so relieved that Damien was far away from here. There was no way I'd be able to cope knowing he was in danger.

"I'm still inside the school," he answered. I felt my heart drop. He was still in danger.

"Where are you?" I asked, trying to hear what was going on outside the classroom.

"I'm inside my art class," he answered in a whisper.

His art class was in the same direction where the gunshots had originated from.

"Where are you?" he asked with concern. It was just like Chris to be in danger and worry about me.

"I'm near my locker in an empty classroom," I answered.

"What are you still doing inside the school?" he said, the disbelief evident in his voice. "Get out."

"I can't leave you," I said, shaking my head. I didn't know how I was going to help get him out, but there was no way I was going to walk to safety while he stayed in the school hiding from a mad shooter.

"I'll be fine," he assured me, but his words were empty. He couldn't guarantee he would make it out alive.

"I can't leave you," I repeated, my voice hoarse with emotion at the thought of something happening to him. I gripped my phone more tightly in my hand.

"You have to, Haven. I'll never forgive myself if you stay and something happens to you," he whispered. I felt a physical pain in my heart.

"The cops will be here soon and they will get me out," he reasoned with me. They hadn't even managed to catch Grant yet, so I didn't have a lot of faith in them.

"I'm not leaving you," I said with determination, making it clear that there was no way I was leaving him behind.

"Haven, please. I need to know that you're safely outside the school," he begged softly.

"No," I insisted in a whisper.

The hallways were quiet now. The students had gotten out or were hiding like I was in the classrooms, too scared to make a noise in case the shooter heard them.

I heard a beeping in my ear and looked down at my phone. The caller ID flashed on the screen—it was Mark trying to call me.

"Chris, I'll call you back. Mark is trying to call me. Make sure you put your phone on vibrate," I said.

"Okay," he said and I disconnected the call. The call from Mark was still beeping.

I answered.

"Mark," I whispered with fear and anticipation. Was he also stuck in the school?

"Are you still in the school?" he asked, sounding out of breath.

"Yes."

"Where are you?" he asked with concern.

"I'm in an empty classroom two doors down from my locker," I answered in a whisper.

"Stay where you are, I'm coming," he said, before he disconnected the call.

CHAPTER THIRTY-TWO

Haven

I put my phone on vibrate as well. I had no idea where the shooter was. For all I knew they could be standing right outside the classroom I was hiding in.

I didn't want Mark to come and find me, I wanted him to get himself out of the school, but I didn't even get a chance to argue with him and tell him it was too dangerous. I didn't want him to risk his life for mine even though I was doing the same for Chris.

I tried calling him back to argue with him but he didn't answer. Frustrated, I wanted to throw my phone, but I needed it to keep in touch with Chris. I dialed Chris again. He answered on the first ring.

"Hi," he greeted nervously.

"Hi. Is there any noise in the hallway by you?" I asked, keeping my eyes fixed on the slightly open gap in the classroom door. It allowed me to see into the hallway, but it was empty. I hoped that the mad person had moved to another part in the school and that Chris was out of danger.

"What did Mark say?" Chris asked.

"He asked where I was. He told me to wait where I was,

that he was on his way," I told Chris.

The soft tap of footsteps outside in the hallway caught my attention.

"I hear something," I whispered to Chris. Panic and fear made me creep to the other side of the wall to the doorway so that when the door opened I would be hidden behind it.

I held my breath with the phone still pressed to my ear, waiting for the footsteps to pass, but they didn't.

The fact that it might be Mark didn't ease my fear in the least. If I showed myself and it was the person running around shooting innocent people, I was as good as dead. I had no way to defend myself.

The door creaked open and I stayed as still as I could, pressed up against the wall. There was nothing I could do but hope it was Mark.

The sight of the gun filled me with horror. It wasn't Mark—it was the gunman.

I wanted to close my eyes and pretend it was a nightmare I was going to wake up from. But when I opened my eyes the sight of the gun made it very clear that I wasn't dreaming; it was real, and I'd run out of time.

A hand holding the gun appeared as the person took another step into the classroom.

All I could think about was Damien, and the precious few moments we'd had together, and I thought about Chris. I could just hope and pray he'd get out alive.

The gunman took another step into the classroom. Horror filled me when I recognized the person. It *was* Mark.

A new wave of fear swept over me at the realization that it was Mark, standing inside the classroom with a gun in his hand—and he was looking at me.

"Haven," he said, still holding the gun.

I expected him to shoot me, but instead he shocked me by pointing the gun to the floor and holding out his other hand to me as he said, "Let's get you out of here."

"I don't understand," I said to him, with my eyes still glued to the gun he held in his hand.

"We don't have time for this," he said. "There is a gunman loose in the school shooting people."

It took a moment for my mind to process what he'd said. If he wasn't the gunman, what was he doing with a gun?

"Why do you have a gun?" I asked, still not moving, not sure if I fully trusted him at the moment.

"It's my job," he stated as his eyes held mine.

"Your job?" I echoed. What was he going on about?

"I'm a bodyguard," he explained.

Bodyguard.

"The Knights employed me to protect you," he explained as he took a step closer to me.

They did what? A bodyguard, how was that possible?

"I know it's a lot to take in, but we don't have time to talk about it now. I have to get you out of the school," he insisted anxiously when he stepped closer to me.

My initial shock had worn off and I realized I was still holding on tightly to my phone. I pressed it to my ear.

"Chris," I whispered, but there was no response. I looked down at the phone to see that the call had ended.

Immediately I tried calling back, but it just rang.

"Come on, pick up," I whispered, desperate to hear his voice and know he was okay. But he didn't answer the call and it went to voicemail.

"We have to go," Mark insisted.

"I can't leave Chris," I stated, trying to call him again, but like before it just rang and went to voicemail.

Mark studied me for a few moments before he let out a resigned sigh. He knew me well enough to know there was no way I was going to leave Chris behind.

"Where is he?" he asked.

"He's hiding in his art class," I answered.

"I know where that is," he said.

I looked at him, a little surprised. How would he know where that was if he didn't take art classes?

"It's part of the job. I know the school inside and out," he informed me with a shrug. It was still hard to believe that he was a bodyguard. He was so young.

"I'll go and get him, but you have to get out of the school, do you understand me?"

I nodded my head at him. I trusted Mark to get Chris out.

Quietly, I followed Mark out of the classroom as he looked around. I gave him one last look before I hurried down the hallway as fast as I could.

I had mixed feelings when I reached the entrance of the school. One was relief, but the other was fear and worry about my two friends; even though Mark had lied to me about who he was, I still cared about him.

As my eyes fixed on the scene in front of me, I heard someone call out. The sight of cops with guns aimed at the school scared me and I stopped for a moment.

My eyes scanned the cops in uniform and then I spotted Detective Green with his hand resting on Damien's shoulder.

Damien. He was here.

I saw the relief and fear in his eyes.

I took put one foot in front of the other and began to walk quickly to Damien. Nervously, I tightened my hold on my bag and I was still holding my phone in my other hand.

My eyes stayed on Damien. He turned away to look at Detective Green for a moment before his gaze swung back to me.

Then I felt my phone vibrate and I stopped.

I couldn't ignore the call. What if it was Chris? I was at the bottom of the steps leading into the school when I answered the call. Everyone's eyes were on me, but my eyes held Damien's.

"Hello, Haven," the voice on the other side of the phone said. My stomach dropped and I felt the dread creep over me.

I'd know that voice anywhere. It was Grant.

"I have your friend Chris," he told me. It felt like someone had ripped my heart from my chest, but somehow I was still standing there with the phone in my hand, still breathing.

Grant had Chris.

Grant was the shooter.

I closed my eyes for a second. Not once from the time this nightmare had begun had it crossed my mind that it might be Grant. Guilt overwhelmed me. It was my fault that this was happening.

"I'm in classroom 21B. If you're not here in ten minutes, I'll shoot him," he warned in a deadly serious voice, and then the line went dead.

The urge to go to Damien was nearly impossible to fight, but I couldn't do that knowing Grant had Chris. Mark had said he would get him out, but I couldn't run the risk. I had to go back inside and face certain death at the hands of the evil that had plagued my life for so many years.

To me there was no choice. Damien watched me. He began to shake his head when he realized what I was going to do.

I knew this might be something he might never recover from, and it broke my heart that I would be doing this to him.

"Grant has Chris!" I yelled.

I couldn't think about all the moments that I'd miss with him. I felt the sting of tears in my eyes and a single tear slid down my face. I felt my heart break as I took one last look at the boy I loved before I turned around and ran back inside the school.

"No!" Damien screamed, when I reentered the school and started to walk swiftly down the hallway. I heard the heartbreak in his voice and it took everything I had not to turn around and go to him.

I gave myself one more moment to think about him and what I was losing before I pushed it from my mind and brushed the tears from my face.

Scared and fearful of what was going to happen, I began to walk down the hallway to where Grant had Chris.

I felt the phone vibrate in my hand but it stopped when the call went to voicemail. It was heartbreaking ignoring his desperate calls.

I put my phone in my bag and began to walk swiftly to my fate.

A gunshot rang out. My heart froze.

Then another gunshot rang out.

"Haven, you have five minutes," Grant's yell echoed through the hallway.

DAMIEN

That fear that settled inside of me when this whole incident had started began to disappear as my eyes swept over her. She wasn't hurt.

I felt a hand settle on my shoulder and turned to see Detective Green. His eyes weren't on me; his eyes were fixed on Haven. He knew I wanted to go to her and he was reminding me that I had to stay where I was.

I swung my gaze back to Haven. With every step she took closer to safety I held my breath. A dreaded feeling began to grow in my chest. I wouldn't relax until I held her safely in my arms.

Her eyes found me in the crowd. She was scared and it took everything in me not to rush to her. Doing nothing went against every instinct that surfaced in me.

I fisted both my hands and dug my nails into my palms while I watched helplessly from the sidelines.

Keeping walking to me, I willed anxiously, trying to relay the message in my eyes. But she stopped and I felt the air lock in my lungs.

She'd just gotten to the bottom of the steps when she pulled her phone from her bag and answered it. The cops and I watched her silently.

Who the hell would be calling her now?

Her features turned from scared to petrified as she clutched the phone closer to her ear.

The night we'd finally started dating I'd told her about good and bad moments that defined who we were, and I knew, the very moment her eyes met mine, that this was going to be a defining moment.

The second she made the decision, I saw it in her eyes. It happened in slow motion. Still with the phone in her hand, her eyes pleaded with mine. I began to shake my head, trying to convince her not to do what she'd already decided.

"Grant has Chris!" she yelled and I felt the pain in her voice.

I watched her eyes glisten with tears, and from where I stood I saw a tear slide down her face. She looked at me with such sadness and resignation, it nearly broke my heart into two.

Then she did the unthinkable—still clutching the phone in her hand, she turned around and ran back inside the school.

"No!" I screamed as I tried to run after her, but Detective Green and another cop held me back. I thrashed desperately, but they refused to let go.

"Haven!" I screamed. All my fears washed over me at once. The fear of losing someone I couldn't breathe without drowned me from the inside. Memories of my brother dying in my arms flashed through my mind.

I felt like someone had ripped my heart out. The pain was too much to bear and, when the cops released me, I fell to my knees. If I was broken before, I was shattered now.

I'd promised to keep her safe and I'd promised I wouldn't let Grant hurt her again. Now I knew I was breaking both of those promises to her and there was nothing I could do but watch it happen.

She'd gone back inside. She wasn't safe and Grant was going to kill her. I felt so helpless.

"You have to do something," I begged Detective Green, while I was still on my knees.

"We are doing everything we can," he assured me. "But we can't let you go inside."

I knew that whatever they were going to do wasn't going to be enough. The detective helped me back up to my feet.

"Who is Chris?" he asked.

"Her friend."

"She went back inside to save her friend," he said softly. The thickness growing in my throat stopped me from answering him, so instead I nodded my head.

In this type of situation it was impossible to hope that everyone would make it out alive, especially Haven. It angered me. She'd just been getting her life together. We were finally happy.

I couldn't think about a life without her, it just wasn't possible to live and breathe in a world she didn't exist in.

A gunshot rang out. My heart froze.

Then another gunshot rang out.

Before the thought even formed in my mind, I started to

run toward the school. Detective Green had been preoccupied with the gunshots and hadn't been paying attention to me.

I heard shouts from behind me as I reached the entrance to the school, but I didn't care. Nothing was going to stop me.

All I could do was hope I wasn't too late.

CHAPTER THIRTY-THREE

Haven

Fear of the evil I was about to face made me hesitate for a moment. I pushed the fear down as I forced myself to take another step forward, and then another.

Instinct screamed for me to turn around and run to save myself, but I ignored it.

As I turned the corner I saw Mark standing inside the classroom doorway beside the art class peering toward the art classroom that Chris and Grant were in. The classroom door to the art room was slightly ajar. He turned at the sound of my shoes on the floor. His eyes locked with mine, and then widened in surprise.

The last time he'd seen me I was headed out the school and to safety, but that had changed.

I wondered if he knew it was Grant.

He shook his head at me when he realized I was walking to the classroom where the gunman and Chris were, but I kept going. He wasn't going to stop me. If he stepped into the hallway to stop me then Grant might see him—and then no one would be getting out of this alive.

I have to, I mouthed to him when I walked past him to

the door. I pushed the door open as I stepped into the classroom. Grant held Chris with one arm around his neck, the gun in his other hand held against Chris' head.

I felt relief at the sight of Chris being unharmed. The relief was short lived, though, because he was still in danger.

"Close the door," Grant instructed with a triumphant smile. He'd won. After attempting to kill me once before, and stalking me for weeks, he had me firmly in his clutches.

Nervously, I turned and closed the door behind me, and then I turned back to face him.

"I thought a couple of shots would hurry you up," Grant sneered with an evil smile. The fear I'd felt before was nothing to what I felt now, facing evil in human form.

When I looked at him I remembered every beating he'd given me, every time he'd told me I was worthless. He personified every bad memory I'd had in the past seven years.

"I'm here," I said with a calmness I didn't feel. Inside of me was the little girl that wanted to run and hide from the evil I was facing. My heart hammered in my chest.

"Haven," Chris whispered. There was despair in his voice. He knew why I was here. I could see he was torn between his own fear for his life and the fear of what Grant would do to me. There was also helplessness in his eyes because he couldn't stop it from happening.

I dropped my bag to the floor and took a step closer, offering myself to him so he would let Chris go.

"Let him go," I said, feeling my fear and panic begin to rise. I was at his mercy. "You have me now, you can let him go."

Grant's evil smile widened as he looked from me to Chris, and then his gaze returned to me.

"What if I don't want to let him go?" he taunted, tightening his arm around Chris. Although Chris struggled against him, he couldn't ease the grip around his throat. My heart stopped.

I don't know why I thought he would let Chris go. He wasn't going to let either of us live.

My eyes moved to Chris to plead for his forgiveness. I wanted to tell him I was sorry. Sorry that I'd dragged him into this. If it hadn't been for me, none of this would have happened.

At that moment I couldn't help but wish that I'd been able to ignore Chris in the beginning. Even though it meant I wouldn't have had the incredible and happy moments I'd experienced with the people I loved, I would give it all up to save my friend.

I felt the tears sting as the realization set in that my best friend was facing death because of me. The thought that I wasn't going to survive this didn't scare me—all I could think about was Chris.

"I think I'm going to make you watch me kill him, and then I will put you out of your misery," he explained as he pointed the gun at Chris and then pointed it to me.

No!

"Please," I began, begging for my friend's life. I felt the tears begin to slide down my face while I struggled to face the fact that Grant was going to punish me by shooting Chris in front of me. I'd rather die than face that.

"I'll do anything you want if you just let him go," I tried to plead. Grant's smug smile widened as I dropped to my knees in front of him.

"Please," I begged, my eyes fixed on Grant.

Tears began to form in Chris' eyes as he watched me beg for his life.

"No," said Grant calmly as the smug smile slipped from his face. He pointed the gun to me.

I dropped my head into my hands. There was nothing I could do. Grant wasn't going to change his mind.

"It was your fault that the woman I loved died." He said it with such venom that I flinched. It was hard to believe that he was capable of loving anybody. I wasn't surprised he blamed me for my mom's death.

"Every time she looked at you, she remembered what she'd lost," he spat at me. "She remembered the man she'd lost. That's why she drank so much. Then, when drinking wasn't enough, she started taking pills to block the pain. It's your fault!"

In his eyes I'd pretty much held a gun to her head and pulled the trigger. I'd been responsible, and there was no arguing with him. I swallowed hard as I looked at Grant. The grief in his eyes was real, but I didn't care. My mother and him meant nothing to me; and after everything they'd put me through, I hated them. Hate was a strong word to use, but it was the only word to describe how I felt.

They had been supposed to take care of me and love me, but they hadn't. Instead they'd abused me mentally and physically so badly that I would never be the same carefree girl I'd been before.

They'd taken something away from me that I would never get back, no matter how much I tried to push on with my life now. They'd broken me.

And now he was going to take one of the most important people to me from my life.

I'd never felt such hatred.

"If it weren't for you she'd still be with me," he argued and I saw the glistening of tears forming in his eyes. I'd never seen him cry. "Now I'm going to make you watch him die."

He paused for a moment as his gaze flickered from me to Chris, then it settled back on me.

"But I need to make sure you won't try anything."

He pointed the gun to me and before I could even understand what he was about to do I felt the pain explode in my left shoulder. He'd shot me. The force of the gunshot pushed me backward and I landed on my back on the floor. I screamed.

I smelled the metallic smell of my blood pouring from the wound. I had no idea how to deal with a gunshot wound, but I was pretty sure if I didn't stop the flow of blood from it I'd bleed to death.

Closing my eyes, I put my hand to the wound to stop the bleeding. The pain was indescribable and I bit my lip to keep from screaming out again. Tears streamed down the sides of my face as I gasped in pain.

"Haven!" Chris shouted while he tried to break free of Grant, but Grant held him tighter around the neck. In my haze of pain I saw Chris elbow Grant in the stomach and stamp on his foot.

"No," I gasped.

In pain and momentarily stunned, Grant released him.

I wanted to get up and help Chris but the pain was too much and all I could do was lie on the floor, watching it unfold in front of me.

Tears slid down my face and blurred my vision slightly.

They began to struggle. Chris had his hands wrapped around Grant's wrists, trying to stop him from taking another shot. But Grant was bigger and his evil grin widened as he managed to force the gun to point at Chris.

"No!" I managed to scream.

Almost simultaneously I heard two shots and breaking glass as the classroom door crashed open.

My eyes fixed on Chris as he fell to the floor. I watched in horror as a dark red stain began to form on the side of his shirt.

Grant grunted as he fell to his knees, the gun still in his hands. Blood poured from a bullet wound in his right shoulder. I couldn't understand how they'd both taken a bullet.

Grant tried to shift the gun he still held into this other hand but Damien tackled him to the ground and wrestled the gun from him.

Please don't let him get shot, I chanted in my mind.

I glanced to see Chris grimace in pain as he held his hand to the wound to try and stop the bleeding.

The classroom window opened and I glanced to see that Mark had jumped through the window. The window was broken.

The pieces of what had happened began to connect together: Mark had shot Grant through the window just as Grant had shot Chris.

Damien stood up and pointed the gun in his hand at Grant, who was still lying on the floor, holding a hand to his wound. The hatred I felt for Grant was mirrored in Damien's eyes as he glared Grant.

Mark ran over to me and when he reached me he dropped to his knees as he stuffed his gun behind into the waist of his jeans.

"How are you doing?" he asked, with a crease in his forehead as he lifted my hand from my wound. I cried out in pain.

He ripped his shirt off, bunched it together and pressed it to my open wound. The pain was so bad I nearly passed out, but I held on for Chris. I needed to know he was going to be okay.

DAMIEN

Once I got inside the school I knew the cops couldn't stop me, but I had no idea where Grant was with Chris.

For a moment I stopped to listen for any telltale sounds that would indicate to me in which direction Haven had gone. But it was hard to hear anything over the beating of my heart that seemed to echo right through me.

I tried to fight off the panic. I felt I had to stay calm. I had trouble remembering where my own classes were, so there was no way I'd remember which class Chris would have been in when Grant had started his attack.

And for all I knew he could have dragged him into a different class.

The soft sound of my footsteps thudded against the floor as I frantically started walking down the hallway trying to find Haven.

I felt the hopelessness of the situation wash over me. I was running out of time and the only way to try and find them was to look. It was all I could do.

The chance of actually finding them before it was too late was slim, but I couldn't do nothing. I couldn't lose her. It just wasn't a possibility I could comprehend.

I began to jog down the corridor, peering through some of the gaps in the slightly open classroom doors. I leaned against some classroom doors to try and hear something, but all the classrooms I checked were quiet.

I was running out of time. I squeezed my eyes closed and tried to push that feeling of loss I'd felt when Dylan had died out of me. I never wanted to feel that again.

Then I heard a gunshot and a scream. It was a sound I would never forget.

It was Haven!

Fuck! Was I too late already?

"Haven!" I heard Chris scream.

The panic in me made the air lock inside my lungs. I knew where they were. The sound of the gunshot had come from the opposite side of the hallway.

As desperately as I wanted to find her, I couldn't help the fear that I might be too late and she was already gone.

Not knowing was better than knowing she wouldn't spend another night sleeping in my arms, or smile at me and make my heart flutter. If she were gone, my world would be over.

I began to run toward the side of the hallway that the sound had come from.

Even though I was closer, I had no idea in which classroom they were in.

"No!" I heard someone scream. It was Haven.

Fear and relief intertwined filled me. She was alive but she was still in danger.

I sprinted down the hallway. Just as I came up to the classroom I'd heard the noises coming from I hesitated for a moment and then I heard another gunshot.

Although I had no idea what was going on, I crashed through the door and into the classroom.

Adrenaline pumped through my veins as I took the scene in. Time seemed to slow down as I glanced at Haven, lying on the floor in a pool of her own blood. Horror filled me at the sight. I wanted to go to her but I needed to take out Grant first.

I swung my gaze to see Chris lying with a hand to his side, where blood was beginning to seep from. Then my eyes settled on Grant, who was on his knees with a gun wound in his shoulder. He was still holding a gun.

Hate filled me at the sight of the monster that I'd never met. I could see he was trying to change the hand that held the gun. I couldn't let him do that, so I charged for him.

I didn't care about my own safety. Haven and Chris were both lying in pools of their own blood and I needed to make sure that Grant didn't fire off anymore shots.

I tackled him to the ground and grabbed the gun from

his weak grip. At the sight of me with the gun held to him, he lay still and I saw fear in his eyes. *He should be afraid.* It would be so easy for me to point the gun at him and pull the trigger.

Then it would be over, and he would never be able to harm Haven ever again. I was so tempted.

I heard the window open and I turned to see Mark jump through the window. He didn't even glance my way, he went straight to Haven to check her. As much as I wanted to swap places with him, he knew what he was doing and right now, Haven needed him more than me.

It had been one of the perquisites of the job: they had to have medical training. After Grant had left that horrible message for Haven on the garage door my parents and I had been so frantic with worry, and there was only so much protection the cops could offer. My mom had suggested we hire a bodyguard to protect her and I'd agreed.

I gave Grant one more glare before I walked over to Chris, with the gun I was holding still pointed at Grant. I was reluctant to take my eyes off him but I needed to see if I could help Chris while Mark checked Haven out.

"How are you doing?" I heard Mark ask Haven. He sounded so calm. When I heard Haven cry out in pain it sliced right through me, and I looked toward her.

Mark was checking her wound. I took a deep breath to pull myself together. Mark had Haven covered. I needed to be there for Chris, and to make sure that Grant didn't try anything.

Once I reached Chris, I bent down beside him. He was in pain and his bloodied hand covered the bloodied mess to the side of his shirt. He grimaced in pain as he lifted his hand away so I could have a look at his wound. I glanced at it briefly, trying to see where he'd been shot, but I couldn't see anything past the blood.

My gaze swung to Grant, who was still lying on the floor, holding his wound by his shoulder. I couldn't stop the anger that shot through me at the destruction he'd brought to all of us.

CHAPTER THIRTY-FOUR

Haven

"Chris," I mumbled.

"I'm okay," I heard Chris say in a pained voice. Even though he was still alive, I felt my guilt grow. It had been my fault.

"I can't see the wound," Damien said, beside Chris. I glanced over to see Damien, still pointing the gun at Grant, trying to check Chris' wound.

There was so much blood, and it was hard to look at. I closed my eyes for a moment.

"Hold this as hard as you can," Mark said to me as he moved his hand from the shirt and pressed my hand to it. I bit my lip to keep from screaming, but pressed as hard as I could with his shirt against my wound.

Mark stood up and rushed over to Chris.

"He's going to die and it will be your fault," Grant taunted me, from where he lay bleeding.

"Shut the fuck up!" Damien yelled as he stood up, still pointing the gun at Grant. Mark took Damien's place beside Chris and lifted his bloodied shirt to try and get a look at his wound.

"Give me your shirt," Mark instructed Damien while he held his hand.

Damien ripped his shirt off over his head and threw it to Mark. Then he lifted the gun to settle back on Grant as Mark put his gun away, taking the shirt and pressing it to Chris' wound. I heard Chris's pained intake of breath.

"I'll survive this and I'll come for you again," Grant promised. He meant every word he'd said. He would never move on or forget.

"You're going to jail for this," Damien said, angrily. I'd never seen him so angry. For a moment it looked like Damien was going to shoot him, but then he took a step backward and took a deep breath to calm himself down.

"I will get out and when I do, I will hunt her down. She will never be free of me. She will live every day with the fear that I will come back for her," he threatened with a hoarse laugh. He was right. As long as he still lived and breathed, I would never be free of him. Even if he went to jail, he might still get out and I would live every day in fear of him.

I couldn't help the tears that began to slide down my face.

"Go check on her," said Mark when he stood up and took his gun out and pointed it to Grant.

I glanced in time to see a long and silent look pass between Damien and Mark. Their look was so intense that I couldn't help but feel there was more going on than I was seeing.

Damien gave a nod and he handed Mark the gun he'd wrestled from Grant.

"Haven," he said as he dropped beside me and feathered a desperate kiss to my forehead.

I closed my eyes for a moment.

There was a loud bang. My heart skipped a beat and I opened my eyes to see Damien turn to look behind him.

Relief flooded through me when I saw that Damien was fine. Then my eyes went to Mark, who stood above Grant with the gun aimed at him.

"He tried to attack me," Mark said calmly. It was then that my eyes went to Grant, who wasn't moving. Blood poured from a single gunshot wound to the head.

For a moment I was stunned and then the realization of what I was seeing hit me like a ton of bricks. All the emotion that I'd been suppressing for so long bubbled out of me. He was dead, and I was finally free.

Free.

"Shh, Haven," Damien soothed beside me. I felt him remove my hand from Mark's bloodied shirt and replace it with his. He pressed down firmly on my gunshot wound to stop the flow of blood. I cried out.

"I'm sorry," he apologized.

"It's okay," I told him between gasps.

"You stay with them, I'm going to get the paramedics," Mark instructed after checking on Chris once more. He stood up and ran out of the room to get help.

I couldn't comprehend the fact that Grant was dead. The proof was right in front of me but I still couldn't believe it. It was like I still expected him to stand up and keep breathing even with the bullet wounds.

He'd been the evil that had plagued me for so many years; it was unbelievable that he wouldn't be able to hurt me anymore.

Tears slid down my face.

"It's okay," Damien said, trying to soothe me as he brushed my tears away. "He can't ever hurt you again."

The reassurance from Damien helped calm me down and the tears eased.

"You okay, Chris?" I heard Damien ask.

"I'm okay," Chris said. I could hear he was in pain.

"I'm so sorry, Chris," I mumbled. He was hurt because of me and I wasn't sure if it was something I could ever forgive myself for.

"I'm okay," Chris assured me.

"He is going to be fine," Damien said. I looked into his eyes.

"I feel cold," I said to Damien when I began to shiver. It also hurt when I tried to breathe. Shallow breaths seemed to lessen the pain.

"The paramedics will be here soon." He was trying to stay calm, but I could see the fear in his eyes—he couldn't hide that.

It was like we were reliving the first attack all over again.

Moments later Mark rushed back into the classroom with the paramedics and cops behind him.

As two paramedics rushed to me, one on either side, Damien stepped back to allow them access to me.

"Is she going to be okay?" Damien asked the paramedics.

"We need to get her to the hospital, she's lost a lot of blood," the one paramedic answered as they began to work on me.

I held on as long as I could, but as the paramedics worked on me I drifted into the darkness where there was no pain.

DAMIEN

"Chris," Haven mumbled.

"I'm okay," Chris tried to soothe her in a pained voice. I knew Haven well enough to know that she always feel guilty that Chris hurt because of her.

"I can't see the wound," I said to Mark. There was just

too much blood. I made Chris press his hand to the wound as I glanced at Grant, making sure he wasn't going to try anything.

"Hold this as hard as you can," Mark said to Haven while he pressed his shirt to her wound and made her hold it with her hand. I could see her wince in pain. As much as I wanted to rush to her and whisper words of assurance to her, I couldn't. I needed to keep it together until the Mark took over the gun.

Mark stood up and rushed over to Chris.

"He's going to die and it will be your fault," Grant taunted, from where he lay bleeding.

"Shut the fuck up!" I yelled at Grant, making sure the gun was pointed to his head. It took everything in me not to pull the trigger and kill him. Mark took my place beside Chris and lifted his bloodied shirt to try and get a look at his wound.

"Give me your shirt," Mark instructed me as he held his hand open to me.

Still holding the gun in one hand I managed to pull my shirt over my head and I threw it to Mark. I let the gun to settle back on Grant, when Mark put his gun away and took the shirt, pressing it to Chris' wound. I heard the pained intake of breath from Chris.

"I'll survive this and I'll come for you again," Grant promised. I hated the fact that his words were true. He would survive this. He would go to jail for this, but there was always the chance he would escape and he would track her down and try and kill her. She would never be free as long as he lived and breathed.

"You're going to jail for this," I said, trying to remind him that he would have to wait years to have another chance to hurt Haven. Anger at a level I'd never felt before began to overwhelm me, I hated that he'd hurt Haven for so long and he wouldn't give up until he killed her.

I wanted to pull the trigger and watch him die. I knew it was a horrific thought, and I was no murderer, but after everything he'd done to her I wouldn't feel any guilt. But I didn't want Haven to see me as that type of person. I took a step backward and took a deep breath to try and calm myself down.

"I will get out and when I do I will hunt her down. She will never be free of me. She will live everyday with the fear that I will come back for her," he threatened with a hoarse laugh. I tried to ignore him but it was hard.

I glanced to Haven and saw tears slide down her face. She knew she would never really ever be free of him.

"Go check on her," Mark said when he stood up and took his gun out. He pointed it at Grant.

I looked at Mark and he looked back at me. But it wasn't just any look; the words that he spoke with his eyes reached me. I knew what he was going to do and he wanted to make sure I was okay with it.

Even though Mark was assigned to Haven as her bodyguard, it didn't take much to see he cared for her like Chris and I did. It was the main reason I'd been so jealous of him. He, like us, would do whatever he could to keep her safe. And now he was going to do something to make sure she would never have to worry about Grant ever again.

I gave him a slight nod, giving my consent as I handed the gun I'd been holding to him. It was finally going to come to an end.

I turned my back on them and went to Haven. The sight of her lying on the floor of the classroom with her hand pressing down on the shot she'd taken to the shoulder was hard.

"Haven," I said when I dropped down beside her. My lips feathered a kiss to her forehead. I wanted to make sure I kept her occupied so she wouldn't see what Mark was about to do.

She closed her eyes for moment.

Although I was expecting it, when the shot rang out I was still surprised. It was one thing to contemplate something like this, but to actually do it was something else entirely. I would be forever indebted to Mark.

Haven's eyes shot to mine. They were filled with fear. She had no idea she had nothing to fear anymore.

I saw relief in her eyes when she saw I was fine and then her eyes shifted to Mark, who was still standing over Grant with the gun in his hand.

"He tried to attack me," Mark said calmly to Haven without blinking. It took moment for the realization to settle in while she looked at the Grant's still body. His eyes stared out unseeing and blood slid down his forehead from the gunshot that had ended his evil existence.

For a few moments she looked shocked, and then she began to cry. It was emotional sobs, like all the tears she'd refused to cry in the last seven years were pouring out of her all at once.

"Shh, baby," I tried to soothe her but she was too lost in her own emotions to try and calm down. Her hand eased on the shirt she was holding to her wound, so I took over and pressed it down hard with my hand. She cried out in pain.

"I'm sorry," I whispered to her. I didn't want to hurt her, but I had to make sure I stopped the flow of blood out of her body. There was a big pool of blood forming around her and I feared she'd lost too much blood already.

She had to survive this. We'd been through too much for her to die now. Especially when she had a chance to live a life where Grant's shadow wouldn't hover over her. She was free.

"It's okay," she said to me breathlessly, looking up at me with tear-streaked cheeks.

"You stay with them, I'm going to get the paramedics," Mark instructed. He checked on Chris once more before he stood up and ran out of the room to get help.

She glanced at Grant's body again. It was almost like she expected him to get up irrespective of the gunshot to the head, but when he didn't move, she sobbed even more desperately.

"It's okay," I tried to soothe as I brushed the tears from her face. "He can't ever hurt you again."

Wherever he was he would never be able to hurt her ever again. As far as I was concerned, he was burning in hell.

As much as Haven needed me I was also worried about Chris. He'd been quiet through most of it.

"You okay, Chris?" I asked while I kept my eyes on Haven.

"I'm okay," Chris said. He was in pain.

"I'm so sorry, Chris," Haven mumbled through her tears. I could see the guilt already beginning to form in her eyes.

"I'm okay," Chris assured her.

"He is going to be fine," I reassured her. I didn't want to tell her that she looked to be in worse shape than he did. It was as if as long as I didn't say it aloud, she had as much chance as he did of surviving this attack.

But there was no doubt about it: the pool of blood around her was a lot bigger than the one around Chris.

"I feel cold," she said to me as she began to shiver. Every time she tried to breathe she grimaced in pain, so she started to breathe short and shallow breaths, which seemed to ease the pain.

"The paramedics will be here soon."

She needed to hold on. I needed to reassure her that everything would be okay.

Moments later, Mark rushed into the classroom with the paramedics and cops behind him.

As two paramedics rushed to Haven, I got out of their way so they could work on her. It was hard to step back and let them do their job.

"Is she going to be okay?" I asked the paramedics as they began to inspect her wound.

"We need to get her to the hospital, she's lost a lot of blood," the one paramedic answered, their actions becoming more frantic, and I couldn't help my fear of losing her grow.

I ran my hand through my hair while I stood there watching and praying that she was going to be okay.

I glanced to Mark, who was watching over the paramedics seeing to Chris.

When I glanced back to Haven, her eyes were closed. I anxiously watched the paramedics work on her.

While it felt like forever, it was probably only twenty minutes later when the paramedics had her on a gurney and were wheeling her out of the classroom and to the ambulance.

My mom and dad came up to me as I exited the school behind Haven. My mom threw her arms around me and began to sob.

"I'm fine. I need to go with Haven," I told my mom before I pulled out of her hug. She tried to suppress her tears and gave me an understanding nod.

"Go with her, we'll meet you there," my dad said.

I hurried to get to the ambulance, and got there just as they put her inside. I held her hand the entire journey to the hospital, praying she wouldn't leave me.

As soon as we arrived at the hospital they rushed her into surgery and I waited in the waiting room, pacing up and down. Not long after that, my parents arrived and paced with me.

I didn't want to talk about what had happened to anyone —all I was concerned about was Haven.

A couple of hours later the doctor, walked into the

waiting room. The air locked in my lungs as I tried to decipher from his expression whether he was going to be giving us good or bad news.

Moments. This was going to be a deciding moment for me.

"She's stable."

CHAPTER THIRTY-FIVE

Haven

My eyes fluttered open. The pain throbbing in my shoulder was a relief—it meant I was still alive. I recognized the beeping of the heart monitor as I began to take in the scene around me. The white clinical walls and surrounding sterile room told me I was in the hospital.

"You're awake," Damien whispered from beside me. He looked tired and I could see that he hadn't slept much.

I gave him a weak smile, and he squeezed my hand gently.

Everything was a little fuzzy as I tried to piece together my fragmented memories of what had happened. Damien watched me silently while I processed each memory, one memory leading into another. I remembered Grant coming into the school with a gun, and I remembered Mark trying to get me out.

It was still a little unbelievable that he was a bodyguard employed to keep me safe. The memory of Damien's reaction to me going back into the school was one of the hardest memories to relive in my mind. It had nearly broken him.

"I'm sorry," I mumbled to him when I opened my eyes

to see him watching me silently.

"Why are you sorry?" he asked.

"For going back inside the school," I managed to whisper.

"You have nothing to be sorry for. He had Chris, I would have done the same," he assured me, brushing a stray piece of hair from my face gently with his finger.

"Chris?" I asked softly. It was like I was scared of what the answer would be.

"He's fine," he assured me. I let out the deep breath I'd been holding as relief flooded through me. "He is in the hospital room next door."

As much as I was desperate to see my friend and hold him close, I was in no state to get out of bed. Although I could remember everything, it was still hard to process everything that had happened. The pain from my shoulder was a reminder of how close I had come to dying.

I couldn't believe that Grant was dead, and that I was finally free.

"Mark?" I asked.

"He was here earlier to check up on you and Chris," he answered as he reached out and caressed my cheek with his fingers.

"He's a bodyguard," I stated softly while my eyes held his.

"Yes, he is," he confirmed with a nod. "After Grant left that message on the garage door and the cops still couldn't find Grant, we had to do something. We were so worried that the cops wouldn't find Grant before he tried to hurt you again. My mom suggested hiring a bodyguard."

It was still so unbelievable.

"How old is Mark?" I asked. He didn't look old enough to be a bodyguard.

"He is twenty. I knew you wouldn't be happy with the

idea of a bodyguard, so we needed someone who could blend into the school as a student so you wouldn't suspect anything, and we'd know there was someone watching over you if I wasn't there."

Then it dawned on me. Mark had asked me out on date. I couldn't help feeling a little embarrassed to think that I'd seriously thought about dating someone who'd been paid to protect me. I'd been a job to him.

A few moments of silence settled between us.

"Are you angry with me?" he asked softly while he studied me.

How could I be angry with him? He and his family had been so worried about me that they'd taken extreme steps to try and keep me safe. I understood why they had kept Mark's true identity for me. I shook my head. Besides, I was pretty sure that had it not been for Mark, things would have ended very differently. I was okay, and the people I loved were okay, too.

"Are you sure?" he asked, gently rubbing his thumb over the outside of my hand.

"How can I be angry with you? You were trying to keep me...safe." The last word was hard to say. For the first time that I could remember, I finally *felt* safe. "I went out on a date with a guy that was being paid to watch over me."

"It was his job to keep close to you, but I don't think that's why he asked you out."

I chewed on my bottom lip while I processed what he said.

There was still so much for me to wrap my mind around, and I knew it would take a while.

"How long have I been out of it?" I asked.

"It's been about a day," he said. He ran his hand through his hair.

There was a more burning question that I was too scared

to ask. Chris and I hadn't been the only ones that could have been hurt by Grant.

"Did anyone…"

It was hard to form the question. Understanding appeared in his eyes. He knew exactly what I was worried about.

"No one died," he stated. There was a hard edge to his eyes that was fierce with anger. "He won't ever be able to hurt anyone again."

I closed my eyes for a moment and tried to keep the emotion that those words pulled inside of me at bay. I wasn't sure if I believed in heaven and hell, but I knew that if they existed, Grant would be in hell for all the things he'd done.

"It's okay, Haven," Damien assured me as I felt the light brush of his lips against my forehead. The simple action from him made my throat thicken with emotion again.

I opened my eyes to look directly into his. After everything I'd been through, I was so lucky to have him in my life. I didn't know what I would have done without him.

"I love you," I whispered hoarsely, trying to put the overwhelming feelings inside of me into words. There had been moments that I'd been convinced that I would never see him again.

"I love you, too," he whispered back as he pressed his lips to mine.

As his lips left mine, he sat back down beside me and held my hand.

"Haven," I heard Amy say when she entered the hospital room. She put two coffee cups down on the table beside me before she leaned over and pressed a kiss to my cheek.

The relief I saw in her eyes made my throat tighten.

"I'm so glad you're okay," she said gently as she brushed my cheek.

But the emotion that I'd managed to keep bottled up

began to break free as the tears slid down my face.

"It's going to be okay," she assured me in a gentle tone as Damien squeezed my other hand.

At that moment a nurse entered to check on me.

"How are you doing today?" the slightly overweight and smiling nurse asked from the foot of my bed while she scanned my chart.

I brushed the tears from my face as I tried to pull myself together.

"I'll have to ask the two of you to step out for a moment so that the doctor can check on her," the nurse said to Damien and Amy as the doctor walked in.

Amy pressed a kiss to my cheek and Damien gave my hand one last squeeze before they left me in the room with the jolly nurse, and a doctor that looked familiar.

It was Dr. Johnson, the doctor who had looked after me Grant had nearly killed me the first time.

"Hello, Haven," he greeted with a friendly smile.

"Hi," I said.

"How are you feeling?" he asked while he checked my shoulder. I winced in pain as he removed the dressing. He gave me a friendly smile but I could see the concern and sympathy hidden in his eyes.

"Okay."

It was the only response I had. I was feeling a lot of things at the moment, and a lot of them were emotional. I felt raw. Not a lot of people survived what I had; I'd effectively survived death twice, and I was still living and breathing. So, I was okay.

After the doctor and nurse left, Steven entered the room.

"Hi," he greeted when he came to stand beside me. "How are you feeling?"

"I'm fine," I replied.

"Amy and Damien went to get something to eat, they'll

be back soon," he told me, sitting down in the chair beside me.

"Why didn't you go with them?" I asked softly.

"We didn't want you to be on your own, so I'll get something when they get back."

It was sweet that they didn't want to leave me on my own. I was closer to this family than I'd ever been with my own flesh and blood. It showed that family wasn't just people who shared your blood.

"I'll be fine," I assured him.

"You mean a lot to me and my family," he said softly. "I'm so glad that you're going to okay. The doctor says you'll be in for another couple of days and then we can take you home."

It was good to hear that I'd be going home soon. Hospitals weren't happy places, so the sooner I got out of here the better.

Home. In the short time I'd lived with them it had started to feel like home.

"I can't wait to get out of here," I replied as I shifted in the bed. The pain in my shoulder reminded me why I was in here in the first place.

It wasn't long before Amy and Damien returned. Amy fussed over me like a mother for a little while before she left with Steven, promising she'd check in with me later.

A couple of hours later, during late visiting hours, Mark walked in holding a rainbow of flowers. They were beautiful.

He smiled at me. I smiled back. I owed him so much.

"Hey," he greeted Damien when Damien stood up and walked over to him. He extended his hand and Mark shook it.

The incident had changed all of us in some way. For Mark and Damien, it had pulled them closer together; they'd bonded over their hatred for the evil who had abused me for years. Thanks to Mark, Grant would never get another chance.

"I'll give you guys a moment," Damien said before he kissed my forehead and left me alone with Mark standing at the foot of the bed.

"These are for you," he said when he set the flowers down on the table beside me.

"Thank you," I said softly, holding his gaze. He knew I was thanking him for more than just the beautiful flowers. If it hadn't been for him, things might have gone horribly wrong and Grant would still be alive.

No matter how many times I replayed the memories of that day over and over in my head, I couldn't see how Grant had tried to attack Mark. It began to dawn on me that Grant hadn't tried to do anything.

Considering the weird interaction between Damien and Mark just before Mark had pulled the trigger, I'd come to the realization that they'd planned it. They had known as well as I had that as long as Grant had lived and breathed he would have haunted me, until one day he would have succeeded in taking my life or died trying.

"You're welcome," he said softly while he stood by the side of my bed. "I know you've been through a lot. When the Knights employed me to protect you, I needed all the information they had on you to be able to do my job. They sent me the police reports of the attack, as well as all the information the doctors had. It was the hardest thing I'd ever had to read. I'm sorry that happened to you."

He reached for my hand and he gave it a squeeze. I shifted my gaze from him. I felt raw and exposed. Although he didn't know everything, he knew enough to know that my life had been hard. I felt the emotion begin to clog my throat and I squeezed my eyes shut. It wasn't his fault that it had happened to me, and I wanted to say that but I knew if I tried to I would just burst into tears.

"I feel like I failed you," he said, his eyes meeting mine. For the first time he looked unsure of himself, even nervous.

"Why?" I asked, a little confused. If it hadn't been for him, I didn't think all of us would have made it out alive.

"I was supposed to protect you and I failed...you got shot," he said, watching me carefully. It was almost like he expected me to hold him responsible for that.

"You tried to get me out safely...I was the one that turned around and went back into the school. It was my decision," I assured.

"I should have made sure you got out of the school before I went to find Chris," he told me.

"I'm sorry. I couldn't take the chance that Grant would have killed him if I hadn't done what he asked," I said to him.

"I get why you did it. I had to think quick to figure out a way to try and see what was happening in the classroom, so I climbed out of the window as quietly as I could. I can't help thinking that if I'd been quicker I could have stopped him before he shot you," he contemplated.

I reached out and touched his arm as his eyes held mine.

"I don't want you to sit and think about any 'what ifs.' You did the best you could and the most important thing is that we all made it out alive," I explained firmly, leaving no room for any doubt. He needed to realize that if things hadn't gone the way they had, we all might not have made it out alive. I saw his eyes lighten and he smiled.

"You're one of the strongest people I've ever met," he informed me softly. I never thought of myself of as strong. I saw myself as more of a survivor. I hadn't been strong; I'd just survived.

A few moments of silence descended as I struggled with the compliment.

"Thank you for everything you've done for me," I said

softly. He'd been paid to protect me, but he'd killed Grant to free me from a life that would have been shadowed from fear. My eyes conveyed what my words didn't. Grant had taunted me with what he had in store for me and we all knew that he would have spent the rest of his life trying to end mine. I'd never be free.

"As your bodyguard, I was supposed to stay close to you but my asking you out hadn't been a part of it," he began to explain as he released my hand. "I genuinely liked you. When I first met you, despite the fact that I knew so much about your situation, I saw a vulnerability in you that made me want to protect you—but it was the way you picked yourself up and got on with it that got under my skin. Damien better realize how special you are, because if he screws it up I'll be around to make him sorry."

It was hard to imagine that I'd gone from such a sad and lonely existence to where I was now. I had a family that loved me, an amazing boyfriend that understood me, and friends that would do anything they could to keep me safe.

CHAPTER THIRTY-SIX

Haven

"What's on your mind?" Damien asked, pulling me out of my thoughts.

After Mark's visit, Damien had returned. He'd climbed up onto the hospital bed, making sure not to hurt me, and lay on his side beside me. Having him so close make me feel safe.

I chewed my lip for a moment as my eyes met his searching gaze.

"I know everyone's been telling me that Chris is okay, but I can't help but worry about him," I told him, letting him in to the thoughts that had been occupying my mind. "I want to be able to see him and tell him how sorry I am that Grant hurt him."

"He is really going to be fine. Unlike you, he only suffered a surface wound. He is only in the hospital for the night and they are going to release him tomorrow morning," he explained, trying to ease my guilt.

Logic would dictate that his information would make me feel slightly better, but emotions didn't follow a logical route, and none of what he told me make me feel any less guilty.

"I have an idea," Damien said out of the blue, shifting off

the bed slowly so that he didn't jolt my already throbbing shoulder.

He disappeared out of my hospital room. I had no idea what he was up to. A tired sigh escaped me while I lay waiting to see what Damien had gone to do. I didn't wait long. Not even ten minutes later, he came back.

"You happy to see me?" Chris asked, with a cheeky smile from the doorway of my hospital room. He was dressed in a hospital gown like I was and he was sitting in a wheelchair manned by Damien.

"Chris," I whispered. My eyes scanned his features. Happiness and relief flooded through me at the sight of him.

Damien wheeled him to my bed and he gave me a tentative smile.

"Are you sure he's okay to be out of his bed?" I asked Damien, my eyes remaining fixed on Chris.

"I'm fine. Just a little scratch," Chris assured me with his little white lie, reaching for my hand and giving it a squeeze. His scratch wasn't just a little one—I remembered how much he'd bled.

I had a feeling that the memories from that day would haunt me for the rest of my life no matter how much I tried to put it behind me. Damien watched the two of us from behind the wheelchair. I looked to him for a moment.

"I'm just going to get something to drink, do you guys want anything?" he asked, looking at me and then shifting his questioning gaze to Chris.

Both of us shook our heads.

"I won't be long," Damien assured me before he left.

One moment's silence turned into two.

"I'm sorry," I whispered. Guilt strangled me from the inside.

"Haven, you have nothing to be sorry about," he assured me.

"I'm not sure...I'll ever be able to forgive myself for what happened...to you," I told him haltingly.

"It wasn't your fault." His eyes held mine. There was no anger directed at me. "You had no control over the situation. The person who is responsible for what happened is dead, hopefully burning in hell. He won't ever be able to hurt you or anybody else ever again. Now you pick up the pieces and you put yourself back together, and move on."

He was right. I had to pick myself up and move forward, I couldn't spend the rest of my life living in my past.

"What about all the other kids he shot?" I asked the question that had been bothering me.

I wouldn't blame anyone if they hated me for what had happened to them. It didn't matter how many times I was told it wasn't my fault—if I hadn't been at the school, it never would have happened. I couldn't hope that the other students who had been traumatized by the attack would forgive me as easily as Chris had.

"They will heal and they'll move on," he assured me with a determined look on his face. "We are a part of your life and we love you. Your life up to this point has been tough, and from now on you get to live the life you should have had."

That was one thing about Chris: he could be so easygoing and cheeky but when it came down to it he was full of beautiful words that could be strung together to make me feel better about anything.

I studied him for a moment.

Despite his upbeat and "carry on" attitude, even he couldn't dispute how close we'd come to death.

"I couldn't help feeling relieved when Mark shot him," he revealed softly.

"Me too."

For a while a look passed between us.

"We owe him," he said. We both owed him for saving

our lives.

A few moments of silence settled between us.

"Mark killed the man that would have stalked you until he took your life. We all heard him threaten you..." he reminded me as his eyes flickered to mine. "He was never going to give up or just walk away. If he'd made it out of that room alive none of us would have been able to live our lives without that fear hanging over our heads."

As if on cue, Damien walked back into the hospital room.

"Your nurse is running around the hospital trying to find you," Damien informed Chris, with a slight laugh.

Chris rolled his eyes.

"She's a pain," he said. "But at least I'm outta here tomorrow."

"Thank you for coming to see me," I said to my best friend. But "best friend" didn't feel right, considering how important he was to me. He was my family.

"It was good to see you," he said. There was that seriousness that I didn't often see in him.

"Come on, it's time to go," Damien told him as he took hold of the handles on the wheelchair.

"I could always hire Mark to keep me safe from the nurse," he quipped when Damien began to wheel him out of my room. Damien chuckled and I couldn't help but laugh, even though it jerked my wound and shot pain through my shoulder.

"I don't think Mark stands a chance against her," Damien weighed in. I didn't hear Chris' reply.

I must have fallen asleep, because the next thing I felt was lips touching my forehead. I opened my eyes to see Damien lying in the hospital bed next to me.

"I'm sorry, I didn't mean to wake you," he whispered as he shifted a piece of my hair out of my face with his fingers.

"It's okay," I said, giving him a smile. "Have I been sleeping for long?"

"Just a couple of hours," he answered. I was lying on my back and he was lying on his side, facing me. It was dark but the soft lighting from above illuminated his features.

"Thank you for bringing Chris to see me," I told him.

"You're welcome. I just wanted you to see he was fine," he assured me.

"I feel much better now that I've had a chance to see him," I replied. My shoulders felt lighter from all the guilt I'd been carrying since the incident at the school.

Silence descended as I thought about how we'd all survived such a traumatic event, and how it would affect us all going forward.

"The cops are still waiting to get a statement from you," Damien informed me.

My eyes shot to his. I felt a little nervous at the thought.

"It's merely to wrap up all the loose ends," he assured me. "They've already collected statements from countless students and teachers as well as statements from Mark, Chris and me."

I kept quiet while I studied him.

"They know everything about what happened, including how Mark shot Grant when he tried to attack him."

My eyes held his for a few moments and I gave a brief nod.

"Mark shot Grant when he tried to attack him," I confirmed, setting that lie deep into my subconscious.

All four of us would stand by that story for the rest of our lives, even though we all knew it wasn't true. That incident pulled us closer together and the friendship that connected the four of us before had evolved into a deeper connection that went way beyond friendship. What happened that day in the school made us family.

The day before I got released from the hospital, Detective Green and another cop came to get my statement. I was a little nervous, but everything went smoothly, and with a smile Detective Green said goodbye.

I spent a week off school recovering from my injury before I went back to school.

Nervous knots had made me sick with worry as I'd stepped into the hallway for the first time since the incident, with Chris and Damien with me as moral support. The first day had been the hardest. The fear and worry I felt was mirrored in the eyes of the other students.

The school offered counseling to all the students who had been affected by the shooting.

As each day went past it got easier, and everyone seemed to carry on as normal. That was one thing about life: no matter what happened, it carried on, whether you were ready or not.

Damien, Chris and I became inseparable and I missed not having Mark around at school. Although he'd moved on to another assignment, he visited our house every Sunday for lunch. Damien's parents had insisted.

A few weeks after the attack, the cast on my arm was removed and I'd been so excited. I was able to get my license and the day after I passed my driving exam, Amy took me shopping for a new car.

It was hard to believe that my life had changed so dramatically in such a short space of time. I'd gone from having nothing to having everything that I'd ever wanted. I knew how lucky I was, because things could have worked out differently.

I still visited the therapist once a week, and slowly but surely I was working through my issues.

There were days I had to pinch myself to make sure I wasn't dreaming.

And Damien—well, he was just awesome. I didn't experience any nightmares anymore, which I put down to me talking about my past with my therapist. Damien still slept in my bed every night. I would never get tired of waking up in his arms every morning. He was serious about me and I was serious about him.

One morning about six months after the attack I was laying in his arms, kissing him. We'd been making out for a while and my hormones were raging. Not once had he pressured me into anything that I wasn't ready for.

"We need to stop or I won't be able to," he said when he broke the kiss.

I lifted myself up onto one arm as my eyes swept over him. I loved him in every way, and in that moment I was ready to share myself with him in every way that two people who loved each other could.

"I don't want to stop," I said, watching him for his reaction. His eyes held mine.

"Are you sure?" he asked in a whisper. I nodded.

To cement my decision I lowered my lips to his and kissed him. He lifted his hands to my face as he began to kiss me back. He pressed his tongue into my mouth, and I groaned as he explored it. My tongue moved against his and I felt a flutter come to life in my stomach.

In between kisses, we removed our clothes, until we were both just in our underwear. He switched positions and I lay beneath him. My hands reached out and skimmed his hard chest. I loved the feel of his skin beneath my hands.

His lips touched my scar on my shoulder and I closed my eyes for a moment. His lips trailed down my body and he kissed the scar on my stomach.

I hated that I still felt self-conscious about the scars; they reminded me of how close I'd come to dying.

"I love every inch of you," he whispered against my skin.

I opened my eyes and lifted my head to look at him.

"I hate my scars," I said.

He stopped kissing me and lifted his eyes to meet mine.

"I don't. They're beautiful."

I gave him a confused look.

"Really?"

"Yes. I love everything about you, including these," he said as his finger touched the scar on my stomach. "Each one of them brought you closer to me. Every time I see them I remember how close I came to losing you."

"Wouldn't that make it more difficult to love them?" I asked.

He shook his head.

"Nearly losing you reminds me of how lucky I am to have you now. I don't look at them like a negative reminder of what could have happened. When I look at them, I see every day I still have with you."

I swallowed the lump in my throat.

He moved up and I lay down. Our eyes met and I saw in his eyes how he felt about me. The time for words was over as he kissed me.

I thought I'd feel shy when he removed my bra and underwear, but I didn't. Beneath his gaze, I only felt beautiful. He removed his last piece of clothing before his body covered mine and I put my arms around him and held him close.

We gave ourselves to each other with our hearts filled with love.

Afterward, we lay in each other's arms. I don't think I'd ever felt so happy or content.

"I love you," Damien whispered to me.

I raised my eyes to his and smiled at him.

"I love you too," I replied as I pressed my lips to his briefly before I lay my head on his chest again.

"It's more than that," he added and I lifted my head to stare at him. He suddenly looked nervous.

"I want everything with you," he began to explain as he ran his free hand through his hair. "I want the marriage, the kids, and forever with you."

I was speechless for a few moments as he waited for my reaction.

"Okay," I said as I smiled.

Events we'd both experienced had broken us. We could wish those experiences away to make us whole again, but it had made us into the people we were today, and all those cracks made us perfect for each other. With Damien, I'd experienced so many beautiful moments, but this one was the most beautiful, because it was the moment I started to believe in happily ever after again.

ABOUT THE AUTHOR

Regan discovered the joy of writing at the tender age of twelve. Her first two novels were teen fiction romance. She then got sidetracked into the world of computer programming and travelled extensively visiting twenty-seven countries.

A few years ago after her son's birth she stayed home and took another trip into the world of writing. After writing nine stories on a free writing website, winning an award and becoming a featured writer the next step was to publish her stories.

Born in South Africa she now lives in London with her two children and husband, who is currently doing his masters.

If she isn't writing her next novel you will find her reading soppy romance novels, shopping like an adrenaline junkie or watching too much television.

Connect with Regan Ure at www.reganure.com

CPSIA information can be obtained
at www.ICGtesting.com
Printed in the USA
LVOW04s0242130516

488080LV00022B/412/P